Adrenaline Rush

I0636493

Lee Michael Harris

chipmunkapublishing

the mental health publisher

Lee Michael Harris

Published by

Chipmunkapublishing

PO Box 6872

Brentwood

Essex CM13 1ZT

United Kingdom

http://www.chipmunkapublishing.com

Chipmunkapublishing gratefully acknowledge the support of Arts Council England.

Dedication

This book is dedicated to Maddie, without whom I would have never begun writing this book, and to her parents for giving me constant support and advice while I wrote Adrenaline Rush, and to my friends and family, who had to listen to me ramble incessantly about the book.

And lastly, to anyone whom has brought this book, I sincerely hope that if you enjoy it half as much as I enjoyed writing it, then you will be pleased.

Lee Michael Harris

Chapter 1: The Reunion
4:06am Norfolk, United Kingdom

Alexis

She lived in a small coastal town that didn't have a very good economy, its highlight was the summer season where people from all over the country would flood the town for cheap holidays and flock to the town's very average quality beaches and the average amusement arcades. But that was life there, jobs were sparse there and even harder to hold down when you're more than a little crazy.

Even with all this, she still felt attached to the town, even when her father moved away after forcing her to move there in the first place, the thought still bitter in her mouth. *If life was fair, no one would need to dream* she thought to herself. With this thought, she decided she might as well get up, after all this was one of her favourite times of the day. She knew she was borderline nocturnal but she didn't have a problem with that. It just meant there were less people in the way when she wanted to do something.

Shopping was a lot easier at 04:30 than it is during the day, with the crowds of people pushing and shoving everyone out of their way, to the long queues at the checkouts. She considered this as she walked to her bathroom and turned on the light.

Of course the light was fairly dim, she didn't react well to bright lights when she first awoke and generally avoided bright lights full stop and even had colour changing glasses to combat intense light. But even with the light on low, she could still see everything in the room, from the pale pink paint on the walls to the transparent toilet seat.

However by the time she got to the mirror, she forced herself to fight back a laugh, her hair was in such complete disarray that she could almost imagine a nest of sparrows living in it. *Now that's what I call bed hair!* She silently chuckled to herself.

She knew that she could look very pretty when she felt good enough about herself to make the effort, her dark chocolate brown hair, curled ever so slightly so that it had a wavy look and with the right amounts of makeup she knew that she could look breath-taking, however she first had to feel like making the effort.

After she had finished washing and brushing her teeth and had brushed her hair to get all the knots she had managed to create while she slept, she decided she might as well go downstairs and have something to eat.

As she caught sight of herself in the mirror again, she was almost amazed at the transformation that had happened to her, she had gone from a hideous monster fresh out of the sea, to a radiant beauty, whose hazel eyes twinkled, she felt her cheeks flush with colour as she admired herself in the mirror.

When she got into her front room she looked around to make sure everything was in its proper place, that nothing had been moved, she walked around the room repositioning everything that just didn't seem exactly in the right place, she knew she was a bit odd at this time in the morning, but she also knew that unless she got everything just right, it would eat at her until she moved everything. *It's easier to just get it over and done with.*

She hadn't realised which photograph she was holding until she looked down and saw those deep blue eyes, eyes so perfect that you could lose yourself in them for hours at a time, and they held so much lustre that she was often mesmerized.

She reminisced about the day the picture was taken, and how it had been such a perfect day, and that at the time everything in her life had been going well. *I miss him so much* she thought to herself.

I miss everything about him, from his smile to his gorgeous eyes, and the way he could turn anything, regardless of how bad it was, into something to laugh and smile about. Even the thought of this almost brought tears to her eyes.

Adrenaline Rush

What did I do wrong? Why did he leave without at least saying? She couldn't bear to think of his name, as she knew it would have only gotten her down.

She could feel her mood dropping already, which reminded her that she probably should eat and then have her morning anti-depressants, this thought prompted her to remember the reason for needing them and the effect that they would have on her, she thought about how her life would be if she refused to take the medication and how long it would take before she turned into a total fruit loop as she liked to call herself when she was suffering from the extremes of her illness.

Though she didn't like to admit it, but she had been clinically diagnosed with bipolar disorder for many years and had spent most of her adolescent life going from one extreme mood to the next, without much control over it.

It had put a strain on almost every relationship she had ever had, she barely talked to her family anymore as they would get worried about her, and she had trouble with anyone wanting to look after her, and her elder sister was a borderline hypochondriac, who would probably worry herself crazy and get ill herself because of it.

She sighed to herself thinking about how blissfully unaware she would be if she were having a manic episode right now, she could almost forget how much danger she could put herself in while she wandered around in a world almost completely on her own.

She could picture herself walking around feeling so happy and unaware that she would feel like singing, dancing and skipping all the way, the downside however was that she would likely be such a danger to herself that she would end up in hospital, from not paying attention to traffic, to forgetting to wear oven gloves when handling food from the stove.

To how difficult it would be for her to communicate with anyone, between talking too fast and changing subject mid-conversation, not many people had the experience or patience to even try to understand what she meant, and even then they couldn't keep up with her train of thought for long.

No one can be around me for long. Even though everyone enjoys the manic high points, where I'm the life and soul of the party, none of them can stand the bouts of depression for long, the recurring inevitability of it all. She let out a sigh.

Enough of that she said silently pulling herself together, as she continued her survey of her front room. Making sure everything was in its proper place.

Though it was early by most people's standards, barely after four, this was one of the times she most savoured, it was one of the most quietest times of day, most people were fast asleep and there would be very few people in her local 24/7 supermarket, this is something she always preferred as she was not comfortable in crowds and always felt the anxiety putting pressure on her chest, slowing her breathing and making her tense and paranoid.

With this in mind, she decided she would quickly check her kitchen and see what shopping she needed for the coming week, surveying it quickly from the fridge freezer to the table and stove and then finally to the sink and the front door.

Everything seems fine. She thought to herself quickly, before opening the fridge and checking the cupboards.

She decided to quickly check that the door was locked, not that it was ever unlocked, but out of habit and caution, for whenever she saw a door that led outside, she would feel anxious unless she checked that it was locked.

With everything secured and her shopping list at hand, she headed for the front door, careful to turn out all her lights on the way. *And wondering what he was doing. Probably fast asleep she suspected.*

Adrenaline Rush

Xander

It was a dark night outside, the street lights barely illuminating the road and pathways, but that didn't bother him, the skies were clear and the crescent of the moon provided him more than enough light to see everything around him, his vision wasn't much different to how it would have been if it were during the day, and it allowed him to stalk his prey.

Hmm how predictable. He chuckled silently, as he tracked the group of men. And even though it was the dead of night, he could see them as if it were mid day.

They think they are dangerous just because they are in a group and carry a few cowardly weapons. He thought to himself

Of course he wasn't following them due to thirst, he was merely bored and honing his hunting skills while he tried to find her, he had been out of contact with the Covenant for several weeks, the group which he had pledged his loyalty to for millennia, but he knew that even years meant little to them, the moment they had a use they would send out a call and expect him to hurry back to them like an obedient lapdog.

But he knew he had made his bed, he had served them for over two millennia now, they had given him eternal life and all they asked in exchange was obedience. Some would think that was a fair exchange, but not Alexander, or Xander as he preferred to be called these days

All this had changed over the past few years, he no longer considered himself to be part of their community, he was a renegade now, totally alone, and he would stay alone until he found her, and he knew that when he did find her, it would either make him or it would break him.

He spent several minutes following them along the rooftops of the back alleys, watching them and listening to their voices, making mental notes to determine the hierarchy of the group, he didn't need to be psychic to realise that they were criminals; they ran the local drugs cartel.

They had just come out of a local nightclub and were heading back home, taking the roundabout route throughout the shadier dockland parts of town hoping they would find some sport along the way.

This was what they loved doing, he realised very quickly that they actually enjoyed forcing other men to defend themselves and their loved ones in futile gestures.

And people would say I'm a monster. He laughed bitterly.

I don't harm innocent people for no reason. I don't kill unless I must kill to survive! He knew people like them sickened him to the core and decided he might as well have a little fun with them and teach them a valuable lesson.

He put on a quick burst of speed and he knew instantly that he would need to be at the utmost peak of his abilities in order to frighten them and get away without any witnesses, so he placed the glass vial with the transparent liquid in his mouth, and bit down with a single powerful bite of his jaws.

The glass cracked instantly, momentarily cutting his mouth and releasing a liquid that made his mouth feel like it was on fire as the clear liquid infused with his blood sending a rush through him, he lived for this, this was his life, the thought of the hunt began to overpower his senses and he could hear them approaching his position, he could feel the cuts in his mouth healing instantly as they absorbed the liquid and were strengthened by it.

He knew they hadn't spotted him yet or they would have started the game off as they invariably do, by splitting up slightly so that their victims would feel like they might have a fighting chance at winning.

Their footsteps grew louder, he could feel his heartbeat racing, his mind going wild over all the information his senses were sending to him and he could smell not only the alcohol and narcotics in their bloodstream, but the excitement and adrenaline in their blood. He knew that they would have seen him by now, so he turned to face them for a fraction of a second before he continued walking.

"Steve, look what we have here." The tall balding man, whom he already knew to be called Patrick, said to the lean, slightly muscular man to his right. "What you think? Should we just have some fun with him? Or should we see if he's got any cash? He looks loaded to me."

Of course Xander could hear every word they'd said and smiled, deciding he would play their game, and quickly turned and started walking away from them, like he was intimidated.

"Quick! We're going to lose him if we don't go for it now, Terry! You and Rob quickly go right and block him off." His whisper trailed off as he tried to give his instructions quietly.

But Xander could feel the adrenaline building in his system now. It was penetrating all of his muscles and organs now. He could feel his strength increasing, his heart rate picking up to nearly three times the normal rate for a human. He could smell the testosterone and adrenaline building up in the men pursuing him, he could almost taste it, and right now he desired nothing more than to turn around and launch himself at them and bite into one of their carotid arteries, to feel the eruption of blood and adrenaline pumping through their necks into his mouth.

No. He thought to himself. *I will control my thirst and settle for a bit of sport.*

It begins. He thought to himself. At that moment Rob and Terry came around the corner to his right, he could smell and sense them long before he could see them, but that didn't matter anymore.

It started quicker than he had expected, he thought they were going to try and harass him a bit first, but then he realised their intentions as Rob lunged at him with a telescopic metal baton, the type that most of the locals referred to as a 'kosh'.

The blow hit Xander on the collarbone, it would have been enough to drop a normal man to the ground, but he shrugged it off like it was nothing. Using the split second time while they regrouped to make sure he was smiling at them.

He loved to smile during confrontations, he'd found it always unnerved his opponents and usually gave him a lot more information about how they would react as he attempted to read their body language, he had been alive for so long that he could read almost anyone, it was so effective that it seemed as if he could read their very minds.

Rob's body language showed Xander that he was in complete turmoil; he couldn't comprehend what had occurred with their prey any better than his companions could, but he was the closest one of them to the lone man, that they had intended to be their sport for the night, a way for them to let off some steam before going home to sleep.

Xander decided he would play with them a little, rather than frightening them away, so he acted like his shoulder had received some damage and feigned a slight list to the right.

Apparently sensing the vulnerability Steve quickly pulled out one of his knives, it was obviously used frequently by the way he held it, the jagged stainless steel blade that would cut through flesh like butter glinted in the moonlight.

He decided he wasn't going to take any chances and quickly stabbed the Xander in the right kidney, the blade instead of sinking deep into his flesh, and Xander knew that it would have felt like it had struck a solid wall, and as the mans hand slipped and sliced open his own hand on the edge of the blade, his face conveyed that he couldn't believe what had happened as he stared at his hand.

Almost instantly Xander turned around, he could taste the blood now in the air, the pungent odour filled every fibre of his being with a thirst to rip and tear the man in front of him apart.

He tried to resist the aroma of the man's blood and adrenaline, but knew he would have to end this quickly or he would not be able to resist the urge.

Adrenaline Rush

Time seemed to freeze in place for Xander now, none of the men were moving now, their faces were contorted with aggression and rage, and in a way it looked almost artistic the way they were trapped in those positions and expressions. And in the barest fraction of a second that had passed he had decided exactly how to handle these men,

As he jumped high in the air he kicked out hard at the chest of his first two targets in a single fluid motion as he had spiralled in the air, landing lightly on his toes without even dislodging a single hair.

That left two of them remaining, and they had scarcely moved a fraction of a millimetre now, and he knew that they would not even see him moving, he punched the one that he had knew was named Steve hard in the ribs and watched him as his body flew against the wall and crumpled in a ball on the floor.

The only man still standing, fell to the floor abruptly as Xander jabbed him hard in the forehead which he was certain would leave a large bruise there, to go with a very bad headache the next day.

They wouldn't have known what had hit them. To them it was over in under one tenth of a second, it was as if time had frozen, one second they were all fine, and then the next all four men were knocked to the ground either unconscious or incapacitated, but he knew he hadn't fatally wounded them he could hear their heart beats and sense the spark's of their lives, and he also knew that they wouldn't be harming anyone else for a while either.

That was pitiful. He thought to himself, and laughed to himself that some people consider the only real sport to be hunting human prey.

No. He thought. *The only real battle is against another powerful immortal, a killer against a killer. The older and more powerful the better, even more so if they have lived long enough to know how to use their gifts.*

As he hurtled along the rooftops, he laughed to himself. He could feel the heat emanating from his muscles, raising his body temperature to extremes far beyond what any mortal could withstand.

He thought about this often, in most mortal literature all of their blood drinking immortals are ice cold and cannot go out in the sunlight, this made him laugh as he thought of all those vampire legends.

Even with the ones that involve immortals who could travel at great speed, you would think at least one of them would realise that any object moving at a high speed through the air will generate enough friction to raise its temperature substantially, without the friction created by his muscles alone as they propelled him to extreme velocities.

Chapter 2: Full Circle
4:46am Norfolk, United Kingdom

Alexis

She had just left the local supermarket, carrying as much as she could back to her car, of course she knew which one it was immediately as it was the only car in the car park, but that didn't stop her looking around and making sure no one else was around, paranoia was almost like a friend to her, she'd had it so long.

As she set out driving her small but nippy Fiat home, she kept careful watch on the roads and streets around her. This was her favourite time for driving. *Very few people about the town* she thought to herself.

She had hardly noticed the CD playing in the background. It wasn't what most people would expect of her, most people assume you can only like a certain style of music, however Alexis preferred to think of it in a difference sense, she liked good music rather than a certain genre.

Her mind was still following this train of thought when she spotted someone on the sidewalk, someone who couldn't possibly be there, shouldn't have been there; he was slightly less than six foot tall with short brown hair, she wouldn't have noticed at all if he hadn't turned and faced her at the exact moment she came into view, his eyes reflecting the light from her car's headlights, his perfectly smooth face that had such a charming and almost unearthly smile.

She hit the brakes immediately, the force of it sending her forwards so abruptly that her seatbelt cut into her shoulder as it stopped her from going through the windscreen, the shock of seeing him again in this town of all places sent chills through her bones, she had not seen him for almost three years and even then, that was in a different country.

The surprise of this shocked her into replaying the memories she had of him, which had left a permanent indentation into her subconscious, how she had been on a tour of Italy, travelling through the cities and towns, such as Rome, Milan, Florence and Venice. She had met him a few days into the tour, and they spent almost every waking minute together after that, he was more knowledgeable than most of the tour guides, the depths of his knowledge was amazing at times. She had never clicked so well with anyone in her entire life, he really seemed to understand her like no one else ever had.

They spent days visiting every museum and sight they could together, and travelled as much of Venice as they could, travelling by gondola's, dining at some of the best restaurants she had ever been to, the food was mouth-watering, even now the thought of it made her crave it. She had never felt anything like that before, it was the most emotional journey she had ever been on, and when they weren't discussing history and different cultures over dinner, they were going on guided tours of the local landmarks, architecture, churches, cathedrals, monasteries and museums.

Everything about him seemed perfect, from his crystal clear skin, even though he was just a little bit too pale, it suited him, it set off the dark contrast of his hair perfectly, his face carried with it a regal look in his eyes and finally to his Armani suits which he wore when we went out to dinner in the evenings. The only thing about him which hinted that he wasn't perfect was that he was diabetic, but at least that wasn't something he could control having. But he was very discrete about having his injections of insulin anyway so it didn't really matter to her.

When they had to part company to go back to our homes, it was one of the hardest days of her life, she would have done anything to go home with him and not have to worry about anything, he made her feel so safe like nothing could harm her while he was with her.

He had promised to phone her and write to her until they could be together again, but she had a bad feeling about it in the depths of her stomach, and when she hadn't heard back from him, even though she phoned him and left messages for weeks, and sent letters every week for a month.

She resigned herself to believe that he wasn't really that interested in her, and would never get the chance, as she had moved six months later, so he would have no way of ever finding her again, even if he wanted to, which she doubted that he did.

She was shocked out of her memories by the sound of a familiar husky voice. "I've missed you." The tall, pale stranger said.

It took her several moments to recompose herself, *I must be hallucinating* she thought to herself. *How did he know? Why is he here? Has he decided he wanted to be with me after all?* Her mind was running wild, so much so that she barely heard the words he said next.

"I have missed you more than you could possibly imagine." the husky voice said as she stepped out of her car now that she had parked it.

"Then why didn't you come back to me sooner." she murmured, blushing faintly.

"It wasn't safe for you, it still isn't safe, but I had to see you, and it took me a while to track you down." he nodded slyly to her "you don't leave many traces."

"Are you really here? Or am I going crazy?" she whispered silently, noticing the amused expression which spread across his face.

What can I do? I can't bear to have him in my life again and then lose him, but I can't send him away. She tried desperately to hide her frantic thoughts from him.

"Yes I am really here Alexis, as for how long I can stay, I'm not sure, it might not be safe for me to stay, and no I can't explain that yet, not right now." the pain emanating from his voice made her want to run up to him and hug him tightly.

At that moment he began walking up to her. *Of course he would,* she thought, *we'd always been on the same wave length, it was almost like he knew what I was thinking.*

As she looked up at his familiar blue eyes, a blue so deep and luscious that it almost seemed a midnight blue, she almost lost herself, almost forgot to begin questioning him about what he had been doing these past three years and why he had broke off all contact with her so suddenly without explaining why.

"Are you coming home with me?" she asked him sheepishly watching as his eyes lit up with interest.

"Yes, I guess I am." He smiled as they started walking back to the car.

By the time they were at her home in her small two bed roomed house, it was nearly five in the morning, she hadn't realised how much time had passed since she stopped so suddenly in the street, seeing the man she thought that she'd lost forever. She had a hundred questions for him, but she tried desperately to resist the urge to push him into answering every one of them.

The tension was building as they sat down on the wooden chairs facing each other in her kitchen, she decided that she would at least try and break the silence "So how come you came back?"

"I never left you, it just took me longer than I expected for me to tie up my loose ends and come after you." he smiled as he said it, his face looked stunning under the lights, she had almost forgotten just how beautiful he was when she was staring at him face to face, he would have outshone any masterpiece by Da Vinci.

"Why couldn't you have at least called me? Or written a letter? Anything would have been better than nothing!" she continued on. "I thought you weren't interested, I thought I was just some holiday fling to you and that everything you said was a lie."

"I had to, it wasn't safe for me to contact you in any way that could lead others to you, but I swear to you that I have thought about you every single day and I have missed you more than you could possibly believe." His voice was quiet yet firm, she could tell that he honestly believed what he said.

"Why wouldn't it have been safe?" she let him see how puzzled she was.

"You wouldn't believe me if I told you." he looked directly into her eyes as he said it, as if he was trying to make her see just how serious he was.

"I don't understand why would anyone to want to harm me? I haven't done anything wrong." she tried not to get emotional, but she knew she was fighting an uphill battle.

"It's not what you've done, it's what you might do, and..." he trailed off putting as much emphasis as he could on his next words.

"I want you." He caressed the nape of her neck, the barest touch of his fingers as he spoke, and then moved his hand upwards to run his fingers through her hair.

"I need you." He pulled her towards him gently, and then softly kissed her gently on her forehead; his lips were oddly cool, yet still sent a shudder of joy through her body.

"And I love you." As he looked into her eyes, she could tell that he meant it, every word, but that didn't stop her feeling like the story was only half explained and that he was missing out a lot of details.

"I love you too, and now you can tell me what the hell is going on."

"It's a long story, and even if I tell you, you won't believe it." he replied, looking faintly disheartened.

"Try me; if I don't believe you, then that'll be my problem."

"Fine then, I am immortal." He looked very serious, she thought, but she knew he had to be messing with her.

"Yeah me to, I'm a lot of things when I'm having a manic episode." she laughed as she said it, trying to break the tension in the room.

"I am serious, I'll show you." as he said this, he walked over to the knife rack almost impossible fast and pulled out a serrated kitchen knife.

"STOP!!" she screamed rushing to stop him as was about to cut his arm open with the knife.

"What the hell do you think you are doing?" she raged at him furiously "Do you honestly think I want to see you do that?" she pulled the knife out of his hand, and slammed it down hard on the worktop.

"I merely wanted to demonstrate for you, my love." he murmured to her apologetically.

"I'm sorry, that was tactless." he said, regaining his composure "There is something we need to discuss." He continued "I cannot stay for long this time, but I will be back, but first I need to make sure you are safe and that you take precautions."

"What do you mean? How long will you be gone? And why the hell would I be in danger?" she struggled to remain calm.

"I have told you but you will not believe me, I am immortal, and others might try to harm you to stop me from leaving." He looked deadly serious as he said this

"Fine, if you're going to make up excuses to leave, then I can't stop you, but why couldn't you have just told me you have someone else to go home to." A tear glistened in her eye but she fought it back, determined not to show how upset she was beginning to feel.

"You do not understand." he said as he gracefully walked towards the door "But you will." He opened the door, and whispered "Until we meet again my love, stay safe." As he said this he simple vanished, she could see him one moment, but he was gone in the next, leaving nothing but the wind blowing through her open doorway.

This set her mind on fire, she could not comprehend what happened, she ran to the door and looked around, he was nowhere to be seen and he left no trace that he had ever been there.

He's gone again. She thought to herself. *How the hell can I be sure that he was ever really here?*

She sat there in silence for a while, staring into the empty space before she had settled on her next plan of action. She walked over to her computer and turned it on, after the screen had finished loading, she opened up a search engine and typed in 'immortal' as she scanned the different search results, laughing to herself that she even considered for a moment that he might have been telling her the truth. The only things even remotely related to immortality were the occasional links on vampires, the philosopher's stone and the Holy Grail.

Yeah right. She thought to herself. *I'm in love with someone who's immortal.* She had to hand it to him though, he'd done his homework, after all she remembered the way he had spoke about ancient history in the museums and sights around Italy, as if he had been trying to show her then that he had actually lived in those times.

There is another option. She thought to herself. *He's crazier than I am.* She laughed as she thought that.

After a few minutes reading through everything she could find on immortality and still not finding anything relevant, she decided she would email one of her online friends who was very knowledgeable and had always been able to find out information quicker than she ever could.

'*Hey Ronnie, how've you been I haven't heard from you in a while and I need to ask a favour if you have some free time? I need you to do some research into immortality in ancient history and see what you can find out. I know it's very random and I'll try and explain it when I have time. Hope to hear from you soon.*

Alexis'

She knew it wouldn't be long before she got a reply, he had always enjoyed a puzzles, even more so when it was a chance to show off his 'skills'.

7:25am London, United Kingdom

Xander

As he drove back down on the long trip back to London, he knew that he would be forced to interact and work with some of the shadier aspects of the city. He would need counterfeit passports for both himself and Alexis, and they would need to be good enough that they would get them through customs anywhere in the world.

And fake identities like that, cost a lot of money, as it would require a skilled counterfeiter to be able to manage it, and it would take several days, he could only hope he had that long before Luccia's people realised what he was planning and sent someone after Alexis.

He had arranged a meeting with a man named Dominic; he was a tall man with a weasel like face, who had short ash blond hair, with twitchy nervous eyes that Xander found extremely untrustworthy, but experience had taught Xander that people with those eyes, were some of the most cunning and clever people around.

To make the point perfectly clear, Xander demonstrated his speed and agility by moving from across the room, to standing right next to the man so fast that he was a blur of light, almost appearing to be in several places at once, he could tell by the nervous look in his eyes, that Dominic had planned on cheating him, but that he had had second thoughts now.

He knew that this man would cause him no problems in the future; fear was such a useful tool to those sorts of criminals, especially when they were smart enough to know that their client is very dangerous, even more so when he knew full well that no one would believe him even if he did try to expose Xander.

As he left the building, he was tempted to drive back to Alexis, but he knew that if he stayed in London it would not lead others to her, and it also meant that he would be able to pick up the documents from Dominic as soon as he had completed work on them.

He had told Dominic to choose any names for them, it really didn't matter what they were going to have to pretend to be called.

That was mainly because he had sufficient money to throw around that the majority of mortals wouldn't care who he was or what he was doing, the main reason for the false identities was to make it harder for Luccia to trace them.

He had guessed it would only take a few days at most before she would find Alexis' home in Norfolk once Luccia decided to, and he wanted to return to her before then, it all hung upon how fast Dominic would act.

As he drove back to his hotel, he knew that he couldn't rush things or it would leave too much of a trail behind him, he was a patient man, but when the woman he loved was in danger, it would be enough to make even the most quiet person go into a rampage.

Chapter 3: The Prophecy
9:25am Vienna

Luccia

The room was large and open yet still managed the remarkable feat of feeling very confined, the walls were a plain white colour that had faded slightly, so that it looked closer to a grey now than white, there were desks placed around the edges of the room, so that there was an empty space in the centre. One by one they entered the chamber and took their seats at their desks, one desk was empty though and she wondered where he was and why he was late.

It had been a long time since she'd felt the need to convene this council, after all when you have all of eternity, why waste it in meetings over trivial details. She preferred to let humanity take its own course and leave the details to someone who cared, not that she wouldn't intervene if something catastrophic was on the horizon for humanity. But that would be another matter all together. She could count the number of times she had involved the Covenant in human affairs on one hand, after all there wasn't much that could really affect the immortals or their way of life.

She had seen so many prophesies over the millennia, some of them good but many of them horrific, most of it on a massive scale, wars and times of great unrest, she had been enjoying a pleasant respite in recent years.

Mainly because the collapse of the *Union of Soviet Socialist Republics had lifted a heavy burden off of her, she no longer had to concern herself with yet another global nuclear war.* She had considered eliminating the threat totally, but that always prompted catastrophic repercussions in her visions, and that was something she generally avoided unless there were no other alternatives.

The latest prophecy she had had, shook her to her very core, it was rare that she would ever see a direct vision concerning someone she knew, but even more disconcerting when she considered the vision itself. As she looked at her fellow council members, recognising their familiar faces she considered most of these family, even the ones who were not blood relatives of her. But they had been loyal to her for countless millennia and she trusted them implicitly.

"Where is Alexander?" she asked, looking around the room at the two females and two males each lounging at their desks as if they were sitting in their thrones.

"He has been absent for a long time, I haven't spoken to him much since we last convened, the last time I saw him was several months ago." His voice was strong, masculine and confident and belonged to the larger of the males in attendance, his hair so blond as to be almost white, and his skin was a pale olive yet so smooth as to be almost like solid marble.

"I know Xavier my love, but we are about to face a disaster, we need him and his abilities." her voice soothing and compelling her audience. This was of course the time when everyone worried most; she was usually much more aggressive than this. But she found using this approach to be much more intimidating.

"What have you seen sister? Who faces a disaster? Is there anything we can do to avert it, can we stop whoever is involved?" The quiet and calm voice belonged to one of the females, she had short dark brown hair, it looked almost black in the lights of this room, but Luccia knew that her hair was not black, and she had silky smooth skin, of course anyone who saw them together would notice almost immediately that they were identical twins and that only by strict vocal control did they sound quite so distinct and that they could whenever they wished sound identical.

"The mortals are not the problem this time Narcissia, it is something else entirely, and I cannot make out exactly, I merely see a fragment of a vision, the remains of it are shrouded in darkness, you will see what I mean shortly." as she said this she pulled a dagger out of her jacket's pocket, it glistened and sparkled as the light shone on it.

"Before I show you, you must promise to keep yourselves under control; we will find a way to avert this." Her voice was low and ominous, the threat was clear to all of them and they knew it.

She walked over to the table on the far side of the room and picked up four goblets and then walked back to the six desks. And then she cut a deep wound across her wrist, and let several drops pour out into each goblet. The wound had healed by the time her companions had picked up their goblets, and she wiped away the excess blood with her tongue.

Then the room went dark; everyone was temporarily blinded by the sheer force of the projected memory.

As the vision unfolded; there was a thick layer of snow on the ground and on the leaves of the trees, there were no buildings in sight. Her pulse was beginning to quicken, she could feel the adrenaline building, her body priming itself for battle. She breathed deeply, not out of necessity but because she found it calming.

As she looked across the field, she saw several people, and she knew they were immortals because of the way they carried themselves without even looking at their eyes, three of them she recognised instantly, for they had been a thorn in the side of many of her plans for over the past three millennia now.

Paul, Anthony and Michael, *The leaders of the Illuminati all in one place, primed for their final defeat.* She thought to herself silently, while the three men did not look quite as white as the members of the Covenant did, they had a pale chalky look about them, a more alive and vital look than the council members, as they had an almost polished look. And their eyes, the eyes of the Illuminati were the biggest difference between the two factions.

As she thought this, she remembered the history of the Illuminati, the group of scholars and alchemists who had been desperately seeking the philosopher's stone in a bid to learn the secrets of immortality. *That was a long time ago.* She thought to herself.

They had been cunning then, even as mortals, they had some of the finest minds and abilities she had ever seen, what made them work together and not make a vie for individual power, she never knew.

All she knew was that she had somehow captured one of her subordinates and drained him of his blood and then set to work experimenting on it; they eventually found out that they could use his blood as a catalyst to transform them from ordinary mortals into immortals with powers and abilities they had no comprehension of.

One mistake and over three millennia of conflict She thought. *They had kept the Covenant at bay for all that time, never able to take their rightful place as the rulers of the immortal dynasty. But they do not know our secrets, they know nothing of Lantis and even less of the things we immortals are capable of, as it takes millennia for the serum to penetrate every cell and even longer to master those cellular functions.* She speculated silently.

The scene suddenly became foggy; a black mist was spreading over the area, blocking everything from view, it was now impossible to know what was happening.

The vision appeared to jump forward in time judging by the change of light and the new position of the sun, to reveal bodies broken and scattered about the battleground, there were no survivors in the vicinity anymore, the only thing that Luccia could focus on were the ravaged corpses of Xavier and Narcissia, their bodies bled dry, their blood had poured from the gaping wounds covering their bodies onto the snow, melting large portions of it and had left a thick congealed mass on the floor. And then the vision faded.

"Hmm fascinating, have you seen any other paths?" Xavier said coolly his eyes avoiding Narcissia who seemed to be trying to get his attention, a worried gleam in her deep blue eyes.

"No, that is the only path I see, and most of it is covered by the void you all witnessed." her jaw was clenched tight and her body rigid.

"Anna? Morgan? Do you have any contributions to make? You have both been strangely silent on about this." she saw them stiffen as she said their names, knowing that they would have to share their thoughts now.

Morgan had blond coloured hair that had the faint tint of red in his hair, he had a small cherub like face, and Anna looked very much like herself, except she had vibrant purple streaks through her hair, as she was fond of experimenting with hair products.

"The solution is simple; either we wipe out the Illuminati or Narcissia and Xavier refrain from going anywhere that matches the location in your vision." the answer was what she had expected from her daughter, she would always pick the easy route, that was her biggest flaw.

"And you think it would be best if they never ventured anywhere cold? That they take the cowards route?" she snapped back glaring at Anna briefly.

"We need Alexander; his experience might aid us in finding a solution." as Morgan said this Luccia looked directly at him and snapped "And that is what I asked at the start of this meeting, as you would have known had you been paying attention." her voice was edged with venom.

"Two things are blatantly obvious." she continued now that she had their full attention again "The Illuminati are involved and there might be an unfavourable conflict with them."

"What is the latest intelligence on them?" she asked, looking around apprehensively.

"Not much is known and nothing in recent years, in the past they had been experimenting with humans to make a stronger immortal, they still don't understand the cause though, that at least is to our advantage, however they have been attempting to tip the balance of power in their favour." Xavier said disdainfully.

"They were already a match for us before with their insidious elixir of life. Something we have never been able to duplicate." he continued but Luccia didn't pay much attention to him.

Nothing new She thought to herself. *I suppose we could always try and open up that line of study again, we haven't tried for a few hundred years.*

"There is an alternative to that my sister." Narcissia said, cutting above Morgan's intelligence report. "We could try and capture one of them, and then reverse engineer from a sample of their blood."

"Ah, dear sister, don't think I haven't considered doing just that. But think about it that could be the path that leads to the vision. We must be sure and we require Alexander with us, he has the most potential for victory, his abilities notwithstanding." As she got up out of her chair again, it scraped across the floor with a screech, and then she walked around the room impatiently.

"I am not afraid to die, I have lived far too long to fear death." she looked around the room with an expression that meant she didn't mind being martyred.

"However, I am not willing to risk your life for something which can be avoided." she smiled as she said it; trying to make sure her sister understood that her intentions were noble.

"Okay, we have established that no one knows where Alexander is, does anyone know where he was? Or what he was doing?" she asked the open ended question and waited for a response.

"I suspect he is somewhere in England searching for that girl he was enthralled with, perhaps it was foolish to deny her entry." Anna glanced at her mother to see a slight grimace appear and then disappear as soon as she regained control.

"It would not have been safe for any of us, I saw that quite clearly. We have already debated this matter thoroughly and I don't plan on rehashing the same arguments."

"Our rules are clear; we do not give our secrets to those who might become too powerful, Alexander already suspected that she was extraordinarily gifted for a human, we will not risk creating a superhuman. Alexander himself is dangerously close to the mark himself, and we might have to eliminate him in the future if his gifts become much stronger." *let them think on that,* she thought to herself, they would be wondering if they were safe.

"That could be the meaning of the vision though." Narcissia continued as the expressions of her companions changed into that of shock. "It could be that the Illuminati decide to turn her in order to secure Alexander's loyalty and you know full well what would happen if she was given the elixir of life and then shares blood with an immortal such as Alexander afterwards..." her voice trailed off.

"No!" Xavier called out "that cannot be allowed!"

"Yet that might be the key to solving this puzzle." Luccia responded, "If she is the danger, then perhaps she must be eliminated before she can constitute a threat to us." it was a statement of fact they all knew, rather than a question.

"All in favour of eliminating the mortal say Aye."

The resulting chorus of "Aye's." confirmed what she expected. "Its settled then, she will have to die."

"The question now is, do we send a mortal assassin to execute her, or one of our own." she continued "However, I think it would be best to send a mortal, a mortal would stand a far greater chance of getting close to her if Alexander was present, and would give off no early warning like one of us would."

They all knew that the meeting was adjourned, and that they could get back to their usual leisure or business pursuits.

2:25pm Vienna

Narcissia

She knew that she couldn't let the vision she had witnessed earlier occur as soon as she had seen it, but she knew she couldn't avert it alone, she would need help.

Adrenaline Rush

As she approached his private suite on the top floor of the building the covenant had used as their home for decades. She knew he would have sensed her coming already, she could already feel his presence and she knew that the feeling would be mutual. And even though she had not given him notice that she would be visiting him, he had known her for so long that he would expect her to visit him.

As she got closer, she could pinpoint his location easily, through the rhythm of his heartbeat to the electromagnetic field that all living beings displayed. The closer she got to him, the more stimuli she could detect, she could smell all the humans in the vicinity, and she could smell Xavier's distinct odour. *He is worried too.* She thought *of course he would be, he saw himself dead too.*

She knocked on the door, a mere formality at this point, he would have sensed her presence long before she used the mortal gesture of 'knocking' he would have felt her spark as she approached in much the same way that sharks can detect their prey's heartbeat from the electromagnetic field.

She could hear his footsteps as he approached the door and opened it, *damn* she thought, *reading his expression and looking into the reasons behind it. He's not going to make this easy.*

"What can I do for you today Narcissia?" his tone was amicable, but she knew the thoughts behind it were not.

Most people would have considered Xavier to be built like the quintessential thug, and he often seemed to act like it, but really even though he was well built and muscular, the perfect warrior, he was also highly intelligent.

"For a start you can drop the act, I know you're worried too, now we need to figure out what is going to happen and stop it." She couldn't understand why he was so relaxed, he should be as incensed as she was, after all he had seen himself as a corpse in that vision.

"It is not an act, I don't think the Illuminati are as much a threat as you think, they're too passive to orchestrate a confrontation with our forces, they know that we are their superior." he continued on with his voice displaying the confidence he always seemed to radiate "And they do not have our abilities, they have only had three millennia to hone their own gifts, we have over four times that experience, and yes the Elixir amplifies their abilities substantially, but we are still at an impasse."

"But what of this human Alexander is infatuated with?" *does he not see her as a threat?* She thought

"What of her? She is inconsequential." he laughed bitterly as he said it

What a surprise she thought, *he is too arrogant to see anyone as a threat to him,* not really all that surprising considering he possessed combat skills that few immortals could come even close to rivalling.

"Nothing that could turn one of our own against us is trivial!" she replied, her voice was quiet and menacing. "You know if Alexander leaves us, we would be a lot more vulnerable to the Illuminati, we recruited him in order to combat one of them, losing him now is not something we can afford to risk."

"I can handle Alexander myself easily when he doesn't cheat; he isn't a match for any of us." He laughed casually and tensed his body to show his rippling muscular figure off for good measure.

Trust him to think using your abilities is cheating, just because he hasn't got any abilities other than brute strength. What is he really thinking? She thought about this for a moment, and then decided she might as well find out.

She sent out her mental probes, focusing purely on Xavier, trying to break through his mental defences, it was much like trying to look into the centre of a sponge, you find an entry point and then try and navigate through the tunnels to get to the chamber you seek.

As she started to penetrate his mind, she came across random images and conversations which had little relevance; she saw his perspective on the flaws in the Covenant, how he felt that we should take a more active position in human affairs. And then she saw his memories of his mortal life, how he had been the son of army general and had been expected to follow in his father's footsteps, however their civilization was being ravaged by an incurable pandemic, but then the discovery of the Regenus Virus had changed that forever, over seventy five percent of the people who undertook the trials of the virus died painful deaths, and the ones that survived had mutated away from their human origins so that they could survive the onslaught of the virus.

How his father had put his name down for the second stage of trials, knowing that his only son might die from it, and how he had been too ashamed to refuse. The virus decimated his already weakened immune system and his body produced the massive amounts of white blood cells needed to counteract it and hold it at bay, his muscular strength had mutated to run on massive amounts of pure adrenaline, his internal organs had fortified and strengthened during the ravages of the virus until they were running at phenomenal rates, far greater than any mortal could attain.

And his shame when the side effects were discovered, far too late to be factored into the equation, over half the population had been inoculated, infected would have been a better term. The side effects started showing up when dozens of civilians started appearing with broken bones and blood stains around half healed puncture wounds on their bodies, the cause of death was almost always a heart-attack.

It took several weeks before the perpetrators were discovered, and it took them several weeks to determine the cause. The virus fed off adrenaline, fuelling the host body with enormous amounts of supercharged adrenaline that their scientists were astounded at how much stronger it made the recipients.

Eventually the virus mutated yet further so that the canine's extended slightly whenever they were running too low or too high on adrenaline, so that they were more affective at puncturing veins and arteries. And they secreted a form of venom which forced the victim to produce massive quantities of adrenaline right up until the point where they suffered a fatal heart attack even before loss of blood was an issue.

The venom also had another side effect, it was regenerative, it helped keep the victim from having a fatal heart attack instantly, and allowed them to survive until their heart gave up, it also left a residue on the tissue around the wound, repairing it even though the mortal had died, the body's cells had not fully decomposed.

They could produce the adrenaline artificially, but the damage had been done, several of their citizens had attacked and killed mortals belonging to another civilization of humans and their empire soon realised that their rivals had a cure for the plague, and they demanded access to the drug, but Xavier's superiors were unwilling to give in to their demands, and in response to the refusal their opponents declared war on them.

A very *Interesting perspective, I'll have to remember this route for another time, when my attention isn't needed elsewhere so direly.* She thought as she navigated his mind, trying to get to the area of his consciousness that focused on what he was thinking here and now.

He coughed as she got closer to his conscious thoughts. "I know what you are doing, you know that right? I can feel you triggering the memories."

And then she felt it, it was like someone had turned on the street lights on a road that was pitch black, the route was open and easy to follow.

His conscious mind was an explosion of trains of thought, she had expected him to run two or three separate trains of thought, but how many she picked up was startling, he could handle dozens of separate thought processes. *How had he kept this hidden from me?*

I have to have some secrets Narcissia. He thought to himself knowing she could hear him as if he were speaking aloud. *Here let me show you why I'm not afraid.*

And then the vision enveloped her yet again, as if she were drinking his blood, it was deep and rich, she could even detect the pungent odours of the grass underneath the snow and on that grass just above the snow were our lifeless corpses, and then she heard it, the faint rhythmic beating of two hearts, they had slowed to extraordinarily slow rates and only his acute senses had detected it. *Yes you see it now don't you. In this vision Luccia shared held the key all along. We are not dead in this future place, we are mortally injured yes, but it's nothing time won't heal.*

"I think you've done enough poking around now don't you?" he said with a tight smile over his lips. "You've seen all that's relevant anyway, we are not going to die, and I plan on preparing a few counter-measures, just in case."

"What counter-measures?" she asked puzzled. *What can he possibly do other than have his loyal attendee's revive us after the battle?*

"I'm going to make sure that if we are injured then we are found by the right people." he smiled, so sure of himself as he said it, she could tell he honestly believed what he said.

But even so she couldn't get this foreboding feeling out of her chest, she was deeply anxious as to the cause of the violence, and she was beginning to wish she had voted against having Alexander's mortal plaything assassinated. After all she thought, that was certain to provoke him into conflict with them.

As she left Xavier's apartment she began formulating her own plans, she would go after this woman herself and find out what sort of a threat she was. And perhaps if there was some way she could avert this conflict so that neither she nor Xavier will get harmed. *After all she thought, even though I now know that I won't be killed, it's certainly not going to be pleasant and will take considerable time for me to regenerate.*

Chapter 4: Mythological or Mental?
9:26pm Norfolk, United Kingdom

Alexis

    I am not going crazy. She thought. *Not tonight at any rate, I know he was here, I can still smell his cologne.* She was still puzzled after the events that had happened earlier that day, how the man she had fallen in love with over three years ago had finally caught up with her, only to tell her he was immortal and then to literally disappear in front of her very eyes without a trace.

    She knew that if anyone else had told her, she would have laughed and then ignored it, but Xander had told her, she couldn't forgot that or ignore that fact.

    She decided to check her email to see if Ronnie had gotten back to her yet or not, she turned on her computer and logged in. The familiar sound alerted her casually saying "You've got mail!" she clicked on it frantically, sorting through the spam to find the one from Ronnie.

    'Hey Alexis

    Right, I've done some preliminary research that I figured you'd want to hear about, so far the only things which I've found that hint at immortality are ancient cults such as the illuminati, they were group of scholars and alchemists who were searching for the philosophers stone as a means for immortality. Other than that, there are of course the usual vampire, zombie and werewolf legends; there aren't a whole lot of real facts out there. I'm going to keep looking, but don't hold your hopes up. Do you have any other leads that I can start digging for?

    Take care. Ron.'

    "Well that's that theory ruined then!" she said impatiently as she typed out a reply saying thank you for trying and that the only other name she had was Alexander, and how she knew that wasn't very helpful without a last name, but she didn't know his last name so she couldn't give it out.

She tried to think over the things Ronnie had said in the email, about secret cults and mythical creatures, she considered them, well he didn't appear to drink blood, and had a good appetite for Italian foods, he wasn't hairy and she didn't think he howled at the moon, and if he was a zombie, he was remarkably good looking for a corpse, she laughed as she thought this.

That really doesn't leave a whole lot of other alternatives. She thought *unless of course I don't know anything about the real myths and legends.* She considered this for a few minutes. All she knew about vampires was that, they didn't come out in the sun, which doesn't fit well with Xander as he often went out in the sunlight without spontaneously combusting.

He loved Italian food which meant that he consumed substantial amounts of garlic, something which vampires supposedly couldn't stand and he had no aversion to crucifixes as he had been subjected to countless crosses that they had come across while they toured Italy. And well she hadn't had any bite marks on her neck during her time with him so she really doubted he was a vampire. Again she thought *but what do I really know about mythical creatures?*

She finally decided to email Ronnie again before she went to bed; to ask him what he thought was real about the myths and legends. How much of it was fiction and how much was fact?

She woke up the next day at just after four in the morning; she had had a horrible nightmare, she was surrounded by two groups of vampires the first group consisted of two pale faced females fighting each other, they both had deep chocolate brown hair, their faces would have looked almost angelic had they not been facing each other with menacing stares and when they moved, they moved so fast it was like she was watching a blurry movie that was out of synch, it wasn't until it was over that she noticed that the two women were twins, why they were fighting she did not know, she only saw the end result, one woman defeated in a pool of her own blood and then the victorious woman, her eyes were totally blue, a blue so dark it was almost black. As she looked at her mouth, she saw the fangs protruding, she saw the faintly dark tip on each of them almost as if they had a hallow point. And then as the woman faced her and moved her mouth to speak, she woke up.

She had been sweating badly, beads of it stood on her forehead and she was feeling very feint, she decided to just sit there for a few minutes and relax, to try and get her breathing back under control. *It was only a dream.* She thought *only a dream.*

By the time she had finished bathing and had sorted her hair, she had begun to forget the dream already, she couldn't remember the other group of people in the dream, they were just shapeless figures to her now, and she could only just remember the face of the fanged woman, whose eyes would have looked shockingly similar to Xander's if they had the usual white parts outside the centre of the eye.

As she recovered she started thinking how far out of the normal vampires these people had seemed, they seemed so lifelike to her, so lifelike and yet so strange, as even though they had the usual fangs and pale skin, they seemed too human, too alive to be monsters.

This thought prompted her to check her email again, as she knew she was only dreaming about monsters because of her exchange with Ronnie the previous night, how he had suggested that the only immortals he had found in myths and legends were primarily monsters.

"You have email!" blurted out of the speakers as she checked her inbox, she saw she had 3 new messages, two of them from Ronnie and one of them was generic spam. She opened the first one.

'Alexander? The only Alexander I have found is Alexander the Great, he was born in 356 BC, so I seriously doubt it's the same person, not unless he's been keeping the secret of immortality for over twenty three centuries. Oh and he died in 323 BC, so that would eliminate him.

Talk soon Ronnie.'

She considered this for a few minutes, thinking about his knowledge of history, and then chuckled to herself, she could hardly believe that the one man she would fall in love with, just happens to be one of the most famous people of all time. And that's not even taking into account that he died over two thousand three hundred years ago. She sighed knowing that she may never know the truth about it.

And then she opened the second email, this she hoped would answer her questions on mythical creatures.

'Well the whole myth about vampires is mainly misconception, it's hard to tell what's real and what's not, you see as a lot of bits of information have been added to the legend as time had passed, there have been vampire legends for thousands of years, but the name vampire has only been commonplace for these legends for the past few hundred years, before that they were merely demons who drank blood to survive. The curious thing I have found is that the only thing that is the same in all cultures throughout the world is that they are pale, and they drink blood.

The European legends are the ones that plant the whole aversion to sunlight, garlic and crucifixes, which make me, suspect their authenticity.

As for werewolves and zombies, well werewolves are supposedly the result of either a curse, or a result of cannibalism and only in modern literature and beliefs was it transmitted via a bite and only occurs during a full moon.

As for zombies, from what I have dug up, if you'd met one, you probably wouldn't have survived it, as that's some seriously dark stuff, I mean pitch black magic, mainly voodoo as that's where the tales began, but also of necromancy, where someone can by using magic, control reanimated corpses, while this is technically not immortality, as they are mindless machines rather than conscious beings.

Hope that helps you, if you learn anything interesting you know where I am. Take care.

The Purple Ronnie'

Well that settles it then, he must have been messing with me. She thought to herself, unable to face the fact that he might not have really been there at all, that the whole thing could have been just a strong hallucination, her body giving her what she craved.

She decided it was early enough to open her curtains, and walked over to the front of the room, as she opened it, what caught sight of a woman wearing black staring at her house, when the woman realised she was staring back out at her, she turned and walked away at a fast pace.

The thought of this set Alexis off on a paranoid train of thought. *He warned me that I could be in danger.* She thought *what did that woman want? Why was she staring at my house? Did she only leave because she saw me staring at her?*

She began to get more and more worried, worried that she was going to be attacked, worried that she would be in danger if she left her house.

What can I do? She thought frantically, she was beginning to see shapes outside the doors and hearing footsteps around her house. She knew she was going in a downward spiral; she could barely focus on remembering Xander's face now as she huddled in her chair, staring at the front door in front of her. She walked up to it and checked it was fully bolted again.

She was beginning to feel truly terrified now; she could swear that she had seen the woman walk past several more times that day, each time wearing different clothing and each time observing her house until she noticed that she was being looked at from inside the house.

It was almost ten in the morning when the telephone rang, she could feel her heartbeat skip several times, as she reached for it, she felt like screaming for help, telling whoever it was on the phone that someone was after her, someone wanted her dead. Her thoughts were frantic, she couldn't figure out what to do. The telephone continued to ring, she knew she would have to answer it, but she couldn't control her thoughts enough to focus.

She held her breath for several seconds now, trying to force herself into a sense of calm. She answered the phone and a familiar voice was on the other end. It was her support worker.

"Alexis?" The feminine voice asked

"Hello Jen." she replied as calmly as she could.

"How are you today? I thought I better remind you that you have an appointment with your psychiatrist today." Her voice was friendly and passive.

"Today? Can't we change it for another time? I really don't want to go out today." she whispered frantically.

"Why not? Is something wrong?" Jen asked thoughtfully.

"I don't feel very well; maybe I'm being extremely paranoid, but I think someone is after me." It was hard for her to control the hysteria in her voice as she spoke.

"Maybe I should come round? Or I could arrange a home visit, but if you feel so bad you don't want to go out, then I really think you need to see someone." her voice was beginning to show her concern.

"I'm not sure that's such a good idea. I'm really not in a good place right now, and I don't think I would be able to stay out of hospital if I was seen by a doctor." she replied

"But what if that's the best thing? Maybe that's what it would take to make you better? If you're really feeling this bad, are you sure you should be alone?" Alexis knew she was right, but she couldn't quite face the fact that she could get sectioned, even if it was voluntary.

She had always had a deep fear of mental healthcare wards in hospitals; the stigma attached to them terrified her more than almost anything she had ever feared in her life.

"You can't honestly believe that, you know how much I hate the very idea of it, you know how afraid I am of those hospitals, I can barely stomach going there just going there for checkups." she replied, her voice getting frantic again, she knew she was digging a hole for herself but she didn't know what else to do.

"Maybe I should come round? I might be able to make you feel better, or at least discuss it face to face, I know you prefer that than over telephones."

"Okay..." she replied, knowing that she would only be fighting a losing battle if she tried to divert her coming round to check.

"Okay, I'll be round in fifteen minutes; I'll phone you when I get to your street so you know it's me at your door. See you soon Alexis."

The time past sooner that she could have possibly believed, it almost felt like she was unconscious the whole time she waited, fear was beginning to grip her.

Even though it seemed like only seconds had past, her phone rang and she answered it nervously, knowing that she would not be able to hide the crazed thoughts going on in her mind.

Knock.

Knock.

She opened the door slowly; the chain was still on, so she had to shut the door again in order to open it once she confirmed that it was Jen at the door.

"How have you been?" she asked with a slight hint of hesitation in her voice

"I *was* doing fine but..." she hesitated, prompting Jen to ask her "What's happened to set off your paranoia?"

"The man I've been in love with for three years returned to me and told me I was in danger because of him, he says it's because he is immortal, and yes I know how insane that sounds, but that's what he said." *God it sounds even worse aloud than it does in my head* she thought.

"How long was he with you for? You hadn't told me he'd returned." she asked suggestively

"He was only here for a few hours; he said he had to leave for my protection."

"And you're certain that he was here?" her voice was mild and polite, trying not to sound like she was accusing her of anything.

"I'm... I'm not sure" She hesitated as her face flushed red with embarrassment

"Don't worry, why don't you talk it through with me, try to remember everything, every detail you can , every thought, smell and emotion you can remember and we'll try and work out if it really happened."

It didn't take her very long to talk her through it all, and she knew she hadn't convinced her; Jen seemed convinced she was at the start of a manic episode, and was convinced she was suffering from psychosis brought on by the mania.

Psychosis being hallucinations and delusions not anything psychopathic, she thought bitterly, many people seemed to group them together, when they have absolutely no common ground. It was a stigma she had had to fight for most of her adult life and she resented it irritably.

"I still think you should go and see Dr Thames today and explain all this to her." she said calmly.

"But she might want to keep me in for observation." her voice subtly hinted at the panic she was feeling behind it.

"She will only do what she feels is best, you know that she will only keep you in for observation if you are a danger to yourself or others." she said maternally yet forcefully, she knew Alexis well enough to know when and where she needed to be forceful.

"If you think its best..." *she gave in knowing when she had already lost the battle.*

Forty five minutes later they were sitting in the waiting room at the local Hospital, in the mental health care section. She was moving her knees up and down anxiously, the wait was always unbearable for her, the sense of foreboding was almost too much for her to handle, she would often replay in her head every conceivable conversation that could arise while she was in here, trying to make sure she didn't say too much, or give away too much information.

As always they were running late, the delay always made her uncomfortable, she liked to have things running precisely to plan and when they didn't go as smoothly as she wanted them to go it always unsettled her.

"Miss Drake?" the woman called out, she was in her late thirties and had short brown curly hair. And she was a little bit taller than her own height of 5'6", and Alexis had previously guessed that she must have been about 5'9" on one of her earlier visits there. She had however had her hair cut shorter since her last visit here.

And then they walked to her office, Dr Thames using her security key to unlock the doors as they went deeper and deeper into the hospital, the sense of foreboding growing steadily worse, Alexis could sense that this was going to end badly for her, no matter what she said or did.

By the time they all sat down in Dr Thames' office she was struggling to breath, her anxiety was reaching its peak and she knew she must control it now, or suffer the consequences afterwards.

Jen was staring at her, her expression was concern about her wellbeing mixed with concern that she would not be as honest as she needed to be for her own safety.

And then Alexis began to tell Dr Thames everything, from her surprise meeting with Xander, to his departure and then that woman who was surveying her house earlier this morning, to how she had been so frightened and anxious because of it.

She could see concern in Dr Thames' eyes, but knew she had to be honest or Jen would take her aside and explain the situation anyway. *I know she has to, for my own safety.* She thought to herself silently.

And then she said it, almost exactly as I suspected she would, she asked if one of her colleagues could come and give her a second opinion. *I know what that means.* She thought to herself. She knew that it meant that she wanted Alexis to agree to stay in the ward for several days voluntarily and if Alexis refused she would end up considering a section two, under the mental health act; this would give her the authority to put her in a mental health care ward for up to 28 days.

Chapter 5: The Assassin Uncovered
6:30pm Norfolk, United Kingdom

Xander

It had been almost a week since he had last seen her, he was worried now as he began his journey back to her, he was sure he could leave her alone for six or seven days without any problems arising, but even so, he didn't like to leave her now that his absence would have drawn unwanted attention from his superiors.

They would likely reprimand him for his actions, but he didn't care anymore, he had spent too much time alone to care much about their feelings anymore. He wouldn't have left her alone at all if he didn't have to go to London to arrange the false passports and documents so that they could both escape to another country with their true identities hidden from view.

He knew that wouldn't keep them hidden for long, but he had to try and flee with Alexis, it was the only way he could be with her, he remembered the council meeting three years ago where they had ruled against his request to infect her with the virus which would have had a twenty-five percent chance at best, of her becoming an immortal like the rest of them, but they were incredibly selective about whom they offered membership to. And they had refused her because of the visions she had when she was at the extremes of her mood, they suspected this was some latent talent and were dangerously wary about offering anyone membership to the Covenant if they might evolve to have gifts which could surpass the other members of the council, they wanted equality and they were very afraid of anyone becoming an unstoppable super human.

Why they allow me to live, I don't know. Surely my gifts are a concern to them. He sighed. *They're probably too afraid to try facing me in combat; they knew none of them can match my gift when it comes to one on one combat.*

As he thought this, he considered how his gift had evolved over the millennia, how when he was a mortal man, he was an expert strategic planner and could slow down the pace of battle in his own mind, so that he knew when and where to send his troops. He was rarely ever defeated as a mortal, and he had never been defeated since his induction to the Covenant. And how his abilities had turned the tide of the war alongside the Illuminati, how they had both been defeated on every battlefield they had been engaged at before he had joined them.

He knew gifts that his had grown substantially since then, feeling time beginning to slow around him as he used his gift, he looked at his watch and saw the second hand hold still, slowing until whole minutes for him became seconds of real time. And then he relaxed, choosing to return to normal time again and his watch returned to normal.

As he approached her house it didn't take him long to realise that something was wrong, he couldn't detect any heart's beating inside the house, and he couldn't hear anything from the house either. When he got closer he could detect several strange odours, one of them was only ever found on firearms, as he examined the lock, he could see that it had been forced recently but he assumed that whoever it was had not found anything as he couldn't detect any gunpowder residue.

That's a good thing at least she isn't dead. He thought *but that doesn't mean she isn't in danger, where could she be?*

As he opened the door and walked into her house, he quickly checked her calendar to see if there was anything on there, which might explain where she was. *Ah* he thought *she had an appointment with her psychiatrist.* He spent what seemed like several minutes checking everything else in the house; he could tell that nothing had been cooked in the house in days, so he knew that she had not been home for some time.

He then checked her email inbox and browsed the emails which weren't spam, he knew he was being a bit tactless but he couldn't afford to leave her house without knowing what had gone on since he left her the previous week. He found emails from someone called 'Ronnie' within a few seconds and opened those suspecting they were important from their subject headings. As he perused each of the emails he chuckled to himself at how close and yet how far they had come to truth, and how even with this they would never be able to find out the real truth, *not without assistance anyway*. He thought to himself.

He left the house moving back towards his car as fast as he could, as he looked at the time on his car's dashboard he realised how little time he had been in the house. *Four minutes* he thought, *and I still don't know where she is*.

He suspected that she was being detained in the local hospital, and he knew that would be a distinct possibility after what he had told her the previous week. That alone would have been enough to get her sectioned, but he suspected the real reason was the same as the reason he came to believe she was extraordinarily gifted for a mortal.

As he considered this, he thought about the effect immortals have on those mortals who do have latent abilities, sometimes the mortals latent abilities would be triggered and would cause them distress for several weeks afterwards while they were sensitised. Why this happened he had never understood, but he had suspected it was how the Illuminati chose their membership for many years, but had never been able to prove it.

Alexis had shown such gifts during their time together in Italy, she had mild prescience and psychometric faculties, and so that she sometimes saw images from items she touched and sometimes had dreams which were premonitions. And that was the reason they had denied his request for her to become immortal, they didn't want to risk creating a superhuman. *Ridiculous,* he thought *it's more likely that Luccia just doesn't want competition*.

Damn them, I'm going to change her anyway, he thought bitterly.

And then he set off driving towards the hospital to try and get to her before whoever that is after her. He suspected that whoever it was that had the gun was someone hired by Luccia, but he couldn't be certain and he would do his best to interrogate whoever the assassin is before he rescued Alexis and left the country with her.

6:47pm Norfolk, United Kingdom

Alexis

As she sat there feeling sleepy and sedated, she knew that she had brought this on herself, she knew that it probably was for the best and she had seemed to be getting better slowly, even though the anti-psychotics, she had been put on were very strong and left her feeling lethargic. At least the nightmares she had been having had begun to stop, she had to relive the same one every night for the first four days after seeing Xander again, but now it had begun to fade and she couldn't quite remember all the details of it anymore.

She had been in the secured ward in the hospital for five days now she knew she still had several weeks left in there, but at least she felt a sense of safety she knew it would be a lot harder for anyone to break into the ward she was on in order to get to her. And while she was not quite so terrified now, she still felt faintly anxious. *But it is improving* she thought, as much to reassure her as it was the truth.

There were only five other people in the ward with her, everyone there hadn't even filled up one third of the beds in the ward, she didn't mind this though, she hated large groups of people, she didn't talk with most of them though, as several just wanted to keep themselves to themselves, she didn't have a problem with this however, as she had never been a big talker anyway, she had had a few discussions with the only other person there who was her age, her name was Sonia and she had been diagnosed with schizophrenia, this was her first time in a sectioned ward and she seemed to like it as much as Alexis did.

This was the third time Alexis had been in this ward in the past seven years and she had always hated it, she hated the feeling of being trapped in here, and the way the nurse's watched her when she had to take her medication, checking to make sure that she had actually swallowed it.

She hated the smell of the place, how it all smelled so sterile, the smell of the bleach made her nose twinge and eventually her sense of smell faded to block out the attack on her senses. She had hardly spoken since she came here, trying desperately not to make her stay in here longer, she had to think carefully about everything she said and did, to show that she was in control. She had to force herself to make sure she didn't mutter to herself and she had to control the external signs of how anxious she felt, such as not flinching when people entered the ward or if anyone moved suddenly. It was a very taxing experience for her and she was beginning to feel mentally tired.

That afternoon she had almost believed she saw the woman from outside her house again, though this time she was wearing a hospital uniform with a name tag, this made her wonder why she had been outside her house before. *I suppose it's possible she lives near me.* She thought to herself, trying to keep her mind at peace but not doing a very good job at it. *It's also possible that she's not a member of staff at all and she's just wearing the uniform to be able to walk about the hospital freely!* And at that moment, her peace of mind was shattered once again; she knew it would be better if she could move to a different ward.

But she also knew that whichever ward she moved to, it would be on the hospital records so that woman would be able to find her wherever she went. She was beginning to panic again, not knowing what to do or how to keep herself safe, she was flinching every time the doors opened, and every time someone's shadow moved past the doors.

And then the worst happened, the woman had seen her, as she walked through the door, she saw her properly for the first time, she could see the tight lipped smile on her face, which made a thin scar on her left cheek tighten ominously. She had seen her target and knew that she had won, she walked up to her slowly, trying to seem as natural as possible, she realised her mistake in smiling so malevolently and tried unsuccessfully to change her facial expression into a benevolent smile.

Alexis did her best to remain as still as possible as the woman walked across the ward, she tried not to stare at the scar faced woman, and had to use her peripheral vision to her advantage, the woman had crossed half the ward now, checking on the few patients in the ward as she worked her way towards Alexis.

What can I do she thought frantically, the woman was less than ten meters away now, and was only seconds away from her. Her mind raced as she tried to think how to handle this, she looked around the ward desperately looking for something to use as a weapon but couldn't see anything small and sharp, or anything she could use to hit the woman with, and then it hit her, she had been sitting on the answer all along. This thought came to her just in time; the woman was at her, still smiling, whether that smile was a fake smile she was using to try and make Alexis feel safe, or whether she was smiling because she knew she would be getting paid soon, she couldn't tell.

As soon as the woman got within two meters Alexis jumped up out of her chair and as quickly as she could, she grabbed it by its hind legs and swung it as hard as her physically weakened body could at the woman, the woman barely had time to raise her arms in defence as the chair slammed into her arms which buckled under the force of the chair and then smashed into her chest and face. The woman's legs gave way and she collapsed to the floor.

Alexis hesitated then, she didn't know what she should do, she had several options, the first one was to keep hitting the woman with the chair that was in her hands, but the woman hadn't got up again and Alexis didn't think she would do any time soon, the other option was that she could take the woman's pass key and then break out of the secured ward.

However within thirty seconds, several burley orderlies had burst into the room and charged over to Alexis, she knew she couldn't fight them off, so she surrendered and allowed them to inject her with a powerful tranquilizer, she started to feel sleepy very shortly after that, the whole time she tried to tell them that the woman was not a doctor, that she was merely impersonating one, but no one listened and no one seemed to care. The last thing she saw were two nurses and a doctor leaving the room with the scar faced woman on a gurney, the woman appeared to be protesting but she couldn't be sure.

And then she passed out under the weight of the sedative, she didn't have time to think about the consequences of being trapped in a secured wing of the hospital, while there was a trained killer also in the hospital, who knew exactly where she was, and now even worse, knew that she was incapacitated.

7:09pm Norfolk, United Kingdom

Xander

His mind raced as his car entered the hospital's car park, he had already had the time to decide on a course of action, but he had to be able to put it into effect, and he suspected that the assassin was also in the building, so he had to be on his guard. As they had likely been shown an image of him and warned to keep out of his way.

As he entered the building he could smell the odour of the firearm again, but the trails appeared to be criss-crossed as if whoever had the weapon had walked back and forth between the different areas. *That makes this somewhat more challenging* he thought, and then his expression changed to that of a thin smile. He considered this like a game of chess, his opponent might have sent in a pawn, but he had just brought a Queen into play, and they would be no match for him, as long as he could get to Alexis first that is.

Only seconds had passed since he entered the building, but he could already sense the rhythmic beating of over two hundred different hearts, this made it slightly harder for him to narrow his search down, so he decided to ask the receptionist and hope for the best.

"Hello, I'm here to see a friend of mine." he asked the receptionist, knowing that his smile would melt the receptionist and make this a lot easier. She blushed and his heart skipped a beat knowing that he was one step closer to finding her again. *Safe I hope* he thought.

"What's the name?" the receptionist smiled and tilted her head seductively and flicked her hair as she looked at him.

"Alexis Drake." He looked at the receptionist's crestfallen expression when she realised that he was here to see a woman, he supposed that she had hoped he would be here to see a male friend.

But he couldn't let this woman's feelings dampen his need to save Alexis.

"Ah, she is in isolation at the moment, so you can't see her." The receptionist's voice and expression brightened again, thinking that her luck had returned.

"Okay thank you, when will I be able to see her?" he asked quickly, he controlled his voice superbly to make sure that not a hint of how urgent he needed to see her.

"I'm not sure sorry; they haven't updated the records to say when she will be back into the normal ward." He barely had time to look at the woman's expression as he increased his heart rate so that the blood was pumping at his maximum ability, so he could sense her location, he knew the beat of her heart intimately now even thought it was considerable weaker than normal, so he knew he would be able to find her, it was just a matter of time, and time wasn't a problem for him as he could speed up his reactions so that time flowed incredibly slow to him. Only milliseconds had passed since the receptionist spoke and he was already over one hundred meters from where he had been when she spoke, he stormed through the hospital careful to avoid colliding with anyone as that would have been fatal to anyone he encountered, he saw the reactions on people's faces as he passed and they all looked around at the doors as his path through the hospital had just created a strong draft.

It took him a few seconds to get to the room Alexis was currently residing, he could tell by the beating of her heart that she was unconscious and he returned to normal time just before he looked though the security glass in the door, and saw that she was strapped onto the bed, he knew he would have to be careful now as he couldn't risk injuring her. And then he realised that she was not alone, he sensed the odour of the gunpowder residue again, the assassin walked into view now holding a hypodermic needle, as he saw her, his body tensed, automatically released a burst of the concentrated adrenaline and she appeared to hang still in front of him. He knew he would have time to get in and save her, but he had to do it as inconspicuous as he possibly could.

Adrenaline Rush

As he kicked open the door, the wood spraying out of the frame where the lock had been milliseconds before, it moved in slow motion to him, the woman had not even noticed the door had been opened now, as he moved into the room, she had just begun to turn, at this rate it would take her about three minutes just for her to finish turning around to face whatever had broken open the door.

And then he forced himself back into normal time even though the adrenaline was desperately trying to pull him back into overdrive and the woman turned around, her face had a long scar down it, which was scarcely covered by her hair. And now her face had contorted in a grimace of shock and terror. The woman appeared to be reaching for her gun which was in the white hospital coat's pocket.

"Wait!" he said quietly yet with the overtones of a command, few people who were militarily trained would have been able to resist the urge to follow such a command, and to his good fortune she stopped, an amazed look was beginning to spread across her face.

"Who sent you?" he asked, his voice now edged with loathing

The scar faced woman smiled back at him now.

"Do you know who I am?" as he said this he forced himself into overdrive again and moved, so he was face to face with her and barely millimetres away from touching her. He knew that to her, he would appear to have moved before his voice had reached her. As he slowed his body down into normal time again, he saw the smile change into one of genuine fear again.

"Yes." She said meekly now, her expression looked faintly pessimistic now, almost as if she knew she would only be able to stay alive as long as she kept talking, she knew she would not survive this, because if he didn't kill her, then her masters would kill her for failing when she had had the chance to do a clean job.

"*Who* sent you?" he asked again, and he saw the torn expression on her face, knowing that she faced a lose-lose situation and that no matter what she did, she would not survive.

"Luccia." She didn't have time to say anymore even if she wanted to, he let the adrenaline flow through him again, he felt his fangs extend out, he could feel the ache building in his stomach, like there was a fire in the pit of it, he was running on fumes now and he had no choice but to feed, he grabbed the woman and bit down on the side of her neck, he felt the flow of blood begin to pour and knew that it wouldn't take long now, his venom would force her heart to pump faster and force her adrenal gland to produce massive amounts of adrenaline.

And then it happened, the burst of adrenaline reached him and he felt it seep into his tongue and he swallowed it, knowing that it would only be moments before he began to receive the blood visions from her.

He saw how Alexis had attacked her viciously with the chair, how she had tracked Alexis from her last known location, to her home and then to the hospital. How Luccia had told her that this was an important mission and that she would receive £300'000 for it if she could eliminate Alexis Drake without leaving a trace of evidence that would lead back to them. How before that she had killed twenty seven people, almost all of them had been contract targets, and how one of them had been out of revenge, she had tracked down the man who murdered her parents, and tortured him until he told her why, and then she had killed him quietly and cleanly, that was what sent her down the path which led her to become a contract killer. And then he saw memories of her childhood, how she was born into a small yet loving family, her name had been Eleanor Harthon, but she had not used that name in over ten years.

Then he felt her heart start to convulse violently as she began to have the fatal heart attack, she would never have time to return home and feed her fish. And then her heart ceased beating, and he released her. His thirst was quenched, the fire in the pit of his stomach died down and he knew he would have time. He knew the wound at her throat would heal itself within minutes so he merely made sure that he left as little traces of blood as possible.

He knew he did not need to feed on her, but he knew he needed to kill her anyway; he couldn't leave witnesses to return back to the Covenant and tell them what had happened. And then he pulled out the small Epi-Pen and jammed it into his wrist and injected the remaining dose there, he didn't want to get low anytime soon, and he knew he had a case of epi pens in his car anyway, all immortals kept a supply of them.

They had done for many years now ever since they had started producing them and selling the concept to mortals to add substantial sums of money to their already bloated bank accounts.

He gently unstrapped Alexis and picked her up, he knew she would be unconscious for several more hours, but he couldn't leave her here. As he cradled her, he wrapped her up in the sheet so that she would not receive friction burns on her exposed skin because of the speed that he knew they would be moving at when he left the building. He had clothes for her in his car, but he didn't think to bring any with him or he would have dressed her. *And anyway* he thought *my immediate concern is to get you out of here.*

As they reached his car he noticed that her foot had slipped out of the cover and it looked very red, almost as if she had received a bad sun burn, *damn* he thought, blaming himself for not being more careful with her. *But at least she is safe* he thought to himself silently before placing her in the seat, strapping her in the seatbelt and then kissing her gently on her forehead.

"I Love you." He whispered in her ear just before he shut the car door.

Chapter 6: Alexander's Story
10:30pm London, United Kingdom

Alexis

It was dark when she woke up; at first she thought she was dreaming as the last thing she remembered was losing consciousness at the hospital. *If this is a dream, it's incredibly vivid* she thought, as she looked up to see the lights flashing past her, then she realised she was in a car travelling along a motorway and then she looked across to see who was driving and then her heart felt like it was going to burst out of her chest as she caught sight of Xander, *of course* she thought, *if I'm going to dream, at least it's a good dream and has him in it.*

Then she began to wonder whether this really was a dream, the sensation in her body seemed too real to be a dream and she felt sleepy still, the after effects of the tranquilizer hadn't yet left her system.

And then he turned his head towards her and as if he had noticed that she was awake and then he whispered to her "How do you feel, my love?" the sound of his voice making her heart beat even faster, it was now beating so fast it felt like it was a single continuous beat.

"I'm okay, I would be better if this was really happening though, but as far as dreams go, any dream that has you in it, is fine by me." she smiled at him then stretched her arms and legs in a cat like manner, and saw the expression on his face shift to one of amusement.

"You are awake, babes, trust me on that." He turned and concentrated on driving again, and then she realised that if she was awake and this wasn't a dream, then how did she get out of the hospital and worse than that, someone was still trying to kill her, her expression changed to one of fear again and she couldn't shake it off.

"You have no need to fear me beloved, I would never hurt you." he said looking at the scared look on her face.

"I'm not afraid of you, it's that I think someone was trying to kill me in the hospital, and I have no idea where we are, or why we're going anywhere." As she said it, his expression brightened again, and she realised just how much her being frightened of him had affected him.

"You are in no danger, I took care of that, and no one will find us. As to where we are going, we're almost at Heathrow Airport and then we'll be taking a flight to Alaska and then another one to a remote region of Alaska where we will go into hiding for a while." He sounded so confident that she began to believe him; she could believe almost anything as long as he was near her, even though the idea of going anywhere quite so cold was not exactly welcoming to Alexis.

"Are you going to tell me what is going on? I really need to know what's going on and why people were after me and you still owe me an explanation for the whole 'Immortal' thing." She knew she had hit a nerve with that as he flinched slightly.

"Soon" He paused and then said "This isn't the time or the place for my story, as it will take a while to explain everything properly." They were just about to arrive at Heathrow Airport and she knew they couldn't discuss it while there were strangers around so she let the matter drop, she would ask him again once they were comfortably safe in the remote spot he was so ellusive.

7:50pm Ketchikan, USA

Alexis

Xander had woken her shortly before their plane began the decent to land, so that she would have time to wake up, she felt a lot better now that she had had a good long sleep, even though she had the same dream again, and it had given her an ominous feeling, she decided she would talk with Xander about it once they got to the hotel they would be staying at, as she knew they wouldn't be flying again straight away due to the seventeen hour delay till the next flight.

They caught a taxi which transported them to a local hotel where they booked a room for the night, it was expensive, but Xander laughed when she said she didn't mind going to a cheaper one instead, he merely said "When you've lived as long as I have, you'd want to enjoy the finer things." he said slyly. Again she considered asking him about him being immortal, but decided she would settle for discussing her dreams with him in the hope that he would have some insight into what they meant, and also whether it was anything to do with them going to Alaska, which for all she knew could be the location of her dream.

The hotel suite was decorated and furnished with surprisingly good taste; the colours were warm caramels and creams, and had a usual calming quality about them, so she finally managed to really relax in the first time in over a week.

They had not talked that much since he had rescued her, he was giving her time to digest what little information he had given her, and to let her rest. But she had decided that she'd had revived enough now, she no longer felt sedated and her mind was once again filled with questions, questions which she needed answers for.

"Can we talk now?" she asked him, her voice displayed the anxiety she felt asking this.

"Yes of course, but first I think we should get you some food, you haven't eaten for a while." As he said it, she realised she had been hungry, the thought of food hadn't occurred to her until he mentioned it.

Food arrived shortly afterwards along with a bottle of Champagne, she was surprised at this, as she hadn't heard Xander ask for this, so she read the note that came along with it, "compliments of the New York Hotel." Again it made her wonder just how much he was paying them but she decided not to ask him about it.

The food that Xander had picked out for her was a shrimp dish she had never tried before, the sauce that accompanied it was delicious even though she couldn't make out the individual flavours in the sauce, but the spicy taste that ever so gently continued burning after she had swallowed invigorated her, she could almost feel the energy returning to her as she ate the meal, she had never tasted anything like this and especially nothing that tasted as fresh as this.

Xander guessing the look on her face merely said "They were caught less than 6 hours ago, that's why they taste so fresh, and judging by the look on your face, the dish was satisfactory?"

"Yes it is delicious." she replied, wiping her mouth gently with the napkin, something about him made her want to be more refined than she had ever managed to be before.

"Now my love, we can talk." He said while he poured her another glass of champagne.

"Firstly" she said, trying to think how best to phrase her questions. "Why was that *woman* after me?" she said the word woman with as much contempt as she could force into her voice, the way Xander's eyebrows raised told her that it had worked and that he understood what she meant.

"I believe she was sent after you in order to force me to return, you see my superiors must have realised that I was preparing to leave them so that I could live out my life with you." He added thoughtfully.

"But who are your superiors?" she asked, desperately trying to understand. And his hesitation made her worry even more.

"They are known as The Covenant, they are an ancient council of immortals, and they see themselves as the ruling council even though they are balanced fairly evenly with the forces that oppose them."

"I don't understand." She said quietly.

"It will take time for me to explain it all, I promise you I will explain it all properly when we are safe and when I have time to tell you everything I know."

"There is another thing, since you came back; I have been having a strange nightmare that keeps repeating." She said with mild embarrassment, trying to justify it to herself that she wasn't being childish to be worried about something as small as a nightmare.

"I suspected something like that might happen." He said with a knowing look on his face. "What did you see?"

As she explained the dream to him his face began to show concern, and she couldn't tell whether he was worried that he was upset because of it or if it was distressing him for another reason.

"What do you think it means?" she asked after she had finished going over the details of the dream to him.

"I'm, I'm not sure." He hesitated slightly. "It might be a premonition." He added regaining his composure. "I wish I had known before I had chosen this place to escape to..." but before she had time to apologise for not telling him sooner he said "No my love, it's not your fault, you couldn't have known."

"Right we need to go over this dream piece by piece." He said after a few seconds of silence.

"But I've already told you everything I know about the dream." she tried to resist

"I know you have angel, but I need you to describe the two women again, you said they were twins." he added with a sense of urgency in his voice.

"Well I've already told you, they were identical twins, they both had chocolate brown hair. One of them, the one who survived, had long hair that flowed down her neck and shoulders and the one who ended up on the floor in a pool of blood. That one had shorter hair that curved along her jaw line."

"Why does it matter?" she asked puzzled, he seemed to be getting to a conclusion but she didn't have the faintest idea about what.

"It matters because two of the six council members of the Covenant are twins, and you described them almost perfectly, I am however astounded that they would be fighting in this dream of yours, it doesn't make any sense." He remained silent for several minutes afterwards and Alexis didn't want to risk breaking his concentration.

"I'm still worried though, as we don't know what happens after the first battle, so I can't make concrete plans to protect you." He paused and then continued, apparently deciding how he would proceed "I will however try and make some contingency plans."

"Now my love, it is time for you to rest again, you haven't had a good night's sleep in days, and you can now relax in peace knowing that I will be laying here with you, remember that as you sleep, I will protect you." He kissed her on her forehead as he pulled her effortlessly towards the bed and then he lifted up the quilt for her.

He laid their perfectly still while she slept, her thoughts unusually peaceful, and she was falling into a deep relaxing sleep again, feeling safe in his arms.

She woke up the next morning and once again she was in a car travelling, she marvelled at how he had managed to move her without waking her yet again, it touched her at how gentle it must have meant he had moved her, as she was usually a very light sleeper and often woke up very easily.

She had had the same dream again, however this time it did not frighten her as much, as she could feel Xander's hand on hers in the dream, it did however stop at exactly the same place again, so she didn't get anything more useful out of it, she still didn't know why they were fighting when they were apparently sisters but she didn't care, all she cared about was being with Xander. Nothing else mattered to her anymore.

As they approached yet another airport he realised that she was awake again and he asked her "How did you sleep my angel?" as he said it a smile crept across her face and she replied "I dreamt of you, nothing could be better than that."

"Where are we going now?" she asked him curiously as they were about to get out of the taxi.

"We're going to a town called Paxson; it's a remote town that only has a few dozen inhabitants so we should be safe, especially this time of year."

As they entered the airport terminal she realised that they were not taking one of the bigger commercial airlines this time, that they were going to be flying on a small cargo plan, this thought made her feel slightly more confident she thought, as it meant that if anyone was coming after them, they would have to travel in small groups as the airstrip at Paxson probably couldn't handle anything larger.

The trip didn't seem to take long considering the distance, and when they landed she noticed that there were no taxi's there, and she expected to have to walk to the hotel, she hadn't anticipated this and she suspected that even with the heavy coat and clothing which Xander had made her put on, that they would end up frozen right through to her bones. She had not given Xander enough credit, she realised as she noticed the short man with a broad smile across his face next to a big jeep. He appeared to be waiting for them.

10:30pm Paxson, USA

Xander

As they approached their hotel he began to relax again knowing that they would have some peace at last without having to worry about fleeing again. He'd had one of the most stressful weeks of his life not knowing whether he would be able to save Alexis in time.

And he knew that soon he would have to tell her his story, he would have to bear listening to the gasps he knew would come from her, and then he would hope that she could still love him when she finally knew the truth.

When they arrived in their hotel suite, they were hit by a wall of heat as they entered the room, the difference in temperatures was so much that they both hurried to get out of their heavy winter coats, not that temperatures of any type really bothered him that much, his skin could handle bitter colds and sweltering heat with so little difficulty that he could walk out in the snow and not really feel very uncomfortable, he would even feel quite warm if he moved his muscles fast enough.

Once they were both comfortable they relaxed on the couch finally taking their thick heavy boots off and he helped Alexis remove the multiple layers of socks she had to wear so that she wouldn't get frostbite.

"How long can we stay here?" she asked inquisitively

"A few weeks, no more than that and then we'll need to move again." He saw her face light up as he said it, almost as if she had been worried that he would not be staying with her

"Now it's time to tell you my story, it will not be easy for me to tell it, so please bear with me while I explain everything." And then he added "but I do love you, remember that please."

Alexander's story:

I was born in northern Greece in a kingdom that was known as Macedonia, I was the son of the ruling King, Phillip II and his consort Olympias. At the time I did not know what year I was born, we didn't measure time in the same way back then, but I now know that I was born in July in 356 BC.

I spent much of my early life training in the ways of leadership, I was taught by my father's greatest military commanders, and one of my first tutors was a member of my mother's entourage, my uncle Leonidas, he was a strict man who had a very strong sense of discipline and from him I learned that sometimes in order to lead, that I must abstain from things I would otherwise want. This was a substantial aid in my later life as I will explain later.

When I was nine years old my father replaced Leonidas with a man named Lysimachus whom was in my father's good graces at that time, he taught me everything he knew of art, poetry and drama, I had a special appreciation for dramatics and I enjoyed his tuition thoroughly during the time I studied with him.

At the age of thirteen, my parents sensing that I was exceptionally gifted and knowing that they wanted only the best for their only son, hired the Philosopher Aristotle, and paid him well so that he would leave Athens and spend time in Macedonia to train the heir of the kingdom. With him I learnt all about philosophy, we spent time in a temple north of the capital city Pella with just the two of us, where he taught me as much as he could about ethics, healing and politics, all these things helped bring me to greatness later on in my life.

However things did not end well between Aristotle and me, he believed that all foreigners were nothing more than barbarians and didn't deserve attention. Whereas I saw them as potential converts I wanted to bring them into the civilised culture we had founded, I saw them as the future, and this in the end caused the estrangement between us.

At the age of sixteen, my father King Phillip II went off to war to fight a rebellious army in the city of Byzantium. And I was left at home in charge, I was the Regent, this alone showed how much my father believed in me, as at such a young age it was unheard of. He trusted in my ability to command our armies while he was absent, at the time I didn't fully appreciate how extraordinary this was.

During my time as Regent there was an uprising in one of our northern cities, I personally oversaw our army as we put down the revolt and then marched the survivors north and founded a new colony after my own name.

However things were not going well in my home life, my father was growing increasing distant from my mother, because she was not born in Greece and he felt little for her and eventually he remarried a Macedonian woman named Cleopatra. I had a very bad argument with Cleopatra's father who made a comment about my Father, fathering a legitimate heir, I was mildly intoxicated at the time and I went into a rage such as the likes of which none of them had ever seen before, I eventually killed the man, this caused a rift between my father and I, that was never fully resolved.

And that was how I came from adolescence to adulthood.

When I was twenty, catastrophe struck again which changed my life in a massive way, my father was assassinated and I ascended to the throne, In my first year as king I was forced to consolidate my kingdom once again, and put down a rebellion in Thebes, I made an example of them which brought all the other cities which were considering breaking off from my kingdom, back into line as none of them wanted to suffer Thebes' fate.

While I was in Athens I consulted the Oracle, the priestess even though it was forbidden to give out prophecies on the day in question gave me my prophecy, and she told me that I was invincible, at the time I hadn't realised she was talking as much about my future as she was about the present. With that I was incensed and I marshalled my troops and began my military campaign into the continent of Asia.

I won't go into details of my life after that; you no doubt already know much of it from your history lessons. Needless to say, my continuous victories attracted the attention of a group of people who had need of a brilliant military mind, they approached me twice over the course of my adult life offering me riches and immortality, but twice I refused them.

But they were ever ready and always waiting, and then when I was thirty-three years old, I contracted a nearly fatal disease and I sent out my scouts to bring forth their messengers and tell them that I would accept their offer.

I nearly died before they reached me, I had been suffering from a severe fever for nine days and I knew that I was dying, it took them longer than usual to reach me as I was in Babylon at the time of my illness, but they reached me and then offered me the chance to join their congregation. They called it The Covenant, they showed me some of their abilities and then explained their rules, most important of these rules was that no one was to be brought into immortality unless the entire council had agreed and also that no mortals may know about the Covenant unless they had been approved to join them.

I accepted readily, and then they began the process, one of them held me down so that I would not convulse and injure myself, while the other, bit down hard on my wrist, and then she bit down on her own wrist and then put her wrist to my mouth, and then the blood poured into my mouth.

It took three agonising days before the fever had run its course, I cannot explain how painful it was but when the pain ended I was more than just cured, I was immortal, and then we had to fake my death, they gave me instructions on how to do this as I recovered from the fever, towards the end, I was not sure which was the original fever and which was caused by the virus which they infected me with, it wasn't until much later that they explained to me that the virus spreads and then repairs any damage the body has and then restores it to its prime state.

And there I was, immortal, youthful and immensely strong, I helped secure the freedom of the world in those days, as there had been a rebellious group of immortals known then as the Illuminati who had approached the Covenant and warned them of the danger imminent.

A man known as Kane had left the Illuminati because they would not allow him to spread the virus indiscriminately, he wanted to form an army of immortals and then rule the world using them as his powerbase. At the time I did not know how dangerous that could have been, most mortals could not survive the virus and would die of it, the mortality rate was incredibly high and I was amazed that I had defied the odds. This man would kill hundreds, maybe even thousands of innocent people needlessly just to form his army, and by the time we had caught up with him.

He had created a strong core of almost seventy immortal warriors, however they were not trained in how to fight and kill other immortals and even though the Covenant and Illuminati forces were an even twenty immortals, they were twenty of the finest minds and bodies that have ever lived, the Covenants elders were over ten thousand years old at the time, and their powers were incredibly strong, and the Illuminati were strengthened by their own creation, the elixir of life, the substance which amplified the virus exponentially, this was a secret that Kane had never known how to recreate, and so the only immortal in his army that was a match for the combined Covenant and Illuminati force was himself, something which he did not wish to put to the test.

It was then that both I and my superiors learnt about my talent, during the field of battle, I managed to move far faster than my opponents and my allies could see, I could speed up my reactions when threatened so that no one could see my movements or move in time to stop my assaults. In the end we were victorious, and though we lost several of our best, we had saved the world from the domination of Kane.

And as that war ended, the uneasy truce between the Covenant and Illuminati ended as well and we went back to the centuries long stalemate which I had no concept of, and it took centuries before the scope of was fully explained to me. It was a war of ideology rather than a war of dislike. The Illuminati wanted to increase their numbers by recruiting the finest and brightest minds and bodies they encountered, and of those, most did not survive the virus, though their chances were substantially increased by their elixir of life, it was still a shockingly high mortality rate.

While the Covenant did not recruit anyone who could potentially become superhuman, they did not allow gifted mortals or immortals to live, this was their biggest problem with the Illuminati, for they were all supremely gifted Immortals, which were only just balanced with the gifts that the council members of the Covenant possessed. At the time I did not realise how much danger that I myself was in, because of my abilities, they considered terminating my life, but I think my nature softened them substantially, they knew I would follow their laws and obey them. And I had shown them remarkable loyalty during the Kane Wars.

What I have done since that time does not matter anymore, some day I will explain it to you fully, but it would take me weeks to tell you everything I have ever done and everything I have ever seen.

Lee Michael Harris

"But know this, I love you, I need you and I will always want and protect you."

Chapter 7: To Walk With a Monster
2:50am Paxson, USA

Alexis

Her mind was reeling under the amount of information she had to absorb; she could barely comprehend the scope of what he was telling her. *I am in love with Alexander the Great!* She thought, scarcely able to contain her emotions and thoughts.

She had read about him and people like him all my life, and she had always wondered what would have happened if he hadn't died so suddenly, and now she knew.

"Thank you for trusting me." she smiled as she said it, "It's a lot for me to take in all at once."

"I know babes, trust me I know." His voice was calm and his expression was expectant, like he expected her to explode at him or call him a liar.

I do have a lot of questions though She thought, but not daring to put those questions into words yet.

"I'm surprised at you my love; I had expected you to bombard me with a stream of questions." His face was an expression of mock bemusement and she couldn't resist chuckling aloud.

"Okay then." she had decided not to fight it anymore and she asked the first question on her mind right now. "You said that the mortality rate for the virus was high, just how high is it? I really want to know." she added seeing his expression change back to one of concern.

"The mortality rate is between seventy and eighty percent." he said, watching her face drop as he said it, he knew she would not have expected such a high death rate.

"Why is it so high?" she asked quickly, not giving him the chance to change the subject.

"The biggest factor involved is whether the venom causes the subject to have a fatal heart attack before the virus has had a chance to re-engineer and mutate their organs and strengthen them. I don't know the exact details, but the first thirty minutes are generally said to be the deciding factor, depending on the entry vector and how fast the virus reaches the subjects heart."

"Is there no way to inject someone with the virus without using the venom?" she asked inquisitively, the intelligence of her question appeared to have taken him by surprise.

"That is difficult for me to answer, to tell you the truth, the virus has mutated substantially since its initial conception. Originally I believe it was merely injected into the subjects system and then it gradually spread the virus throughout the body."

He continued "But that was a long time ago, and by the time I was infected the method most widely used was to bite the victim and thus putting in the venom into their system and then give them some of the virus in the form of blood, the two entry vectors work together much better than one entry point. Originally the mortality rate was nearly ninety-five percent, but the two pronged approach made it much more effective." He added thoughtfully

"But what of the Illuminati, you said that they had a method for increasing the chance that people can survive it." she knew she was clasping at straws now, but she needed to know as much as possible.

"Yes they created a substance that most thought to be a myth, it is known widely as the Elixir of Life, and we believe that it strengthens your organs and immune system so that you can accommodate the virus much more easily, we cannot know for sure, but we suspect that it reduces the mortality rate to an even fifty-fifty chance." He saw that she was still paying him her full attention so he carried on. "We have never been able to get hold of the formula unfortunately though, so that isn't an option for you my love."

"And I understand if you don't want to take the chance, at any rate we have time, I don't want to risk it yet anyway, in case we need to leave in an emergency."

"How long does it take? How painful is it?" she looked into his eyes and tried not to show any fear.

"It takes anything from two to five days usually and how painful it is varies widely depending on the person, to be honest it hasn't been tested on enough people for us to really know. It could be bad though. I was already dying when I was infected, so I'm probably not a good basis for knowledge." he caressed her left cheek as he said it, trying his best to comfort her.

I'm not afraid of dying she thought *but I couldn't bear causing him pain because of it, after all he had done and risked for me.*

She decided it was time to change the subject, and she reached for his hand as is caressed her cheek, and pulled herself closer to him so that they were entwined in a tight embrace.

Even though they were no longer discussing it, she couldn't help but think about being turned into an immortal and what that would mean to her, after all she really didn't know much about it. She gave in and decided that she really wanted to know more.

"How do you survive? I've seen you eat food, but how do you live forever?" she asked trying to sound as passive as possible.

"it's a lot easier now than it used to be, in the past century it has become far easier for immortals as a whole, with the development of artificial adrenaline and blood donations." he continued on "while I can and do eat mortal food, I do it for the sensory experience." he stopped as he saw the confused expression on her face.

"You mean you don't need nourishment?" she asked, though she knew he would be able to see how confused she was.

"I survive off of adrenaline mainly; it is my main nourishment, but normal blood counts as well." He continued seeing the shocked expression on her face.

They're vampires she thought frantically *how did I not see that sooner.*

"It's not what you think, I don't turn into a bat, and I very rarely ever attack humans, we don't need to these days, and it's only when I really exert myself that I have to feed often." He added trying to show that he wasn't the monster that she suspected.

"So you don't drain people of blood and leave them dead?" she asked trying to keep how frightened she was beginning to feel out of her voice.

"No my love, we have never drained people of blood, however most people die from the venom in our fangs, it's a toxin that stimulates adrenaline production and they produce so much that they end up having a heart attack from it." He continued when she didn't say anything else "Some people do however survive it, not many but some, and they continue to live relatively normal lives afterwards, though they are often traumatised."

She finally found her voice again, and decided to ask the question still on her mind. "So when you say your immortal, you mean you're a *Vampire*?" as she said this, an amused smile spread across his face.

"If you mean am I a fictional vampire? No I am not, while technically I suppose all of those immortals infected by the virus are vampires, they share almost no similarities with those in mortal fiction." His amusement carried out into his face as he said it, and his mouth twisted as if he was disdainful over the term vampire.

"What do you mean, 'all of those who had been infected by the virus' you mean there are immortals that weren't infected?" she asked "Yes I mentioned it earlier; the illuminati discovered the secret of immortality centuries before they became what you would call vampires." He replied, the expression on his face made Alexis deeply curious.

"But why would they want to be a vampire if they were already immortal?" she asked wondering what could possibly make them want that sort of life if they were already going to live forever.

"They wanted the virus, because it brings out and enhances certain human extrasensory faculties which they are very curious about. You for instance would of great interest to them, and no doubt when they hear of you that will approach you." And his voice showed his hesitation.

"But you said that they had a way of making it safer for me to become an immortal"

"If they gave you the elixir of life, they would expect loyalty from you, and to be honest, I don't know much about them, for all I know they are as bad as the Covenant, not to mention that it could ignite the fuse to an all out war between the Covenant and the Illuminati." She understood that this was what really worried him.

She knew she wasn't getting anywhere, but her mind was reeling with questions and puzzles, she was having difficulty believing everything she had heard, but she couldn't deny he seemed to honestly believe everything he had told her. *But what if it's all in my head, and that I'm not really here and neither is he?* She thought to herself silently

She was beginning to feel tired again, all the travelling they had done had left her feeling very drained, and she walked back over to the bed, and crawled under the covers, at first he did not join her, but then he walked over quietly, and lay down beside her, rubbing her head gently and stroking her hair.

5:50am Paxson, USA

Xander

Alexis had been asleep for several hours before he heard his phone ringing in his coat pocket, he had been expecting this for a while now, he was very shocked that he hadn't heard sooner, but he knew he would have to talk to them sooner or later.

As he pulled the phone out of his coat he looked at the display and saw the familiar number with the name he was dreading, he had mentally played this out in his head hundreds of times in anticipation, but he was still incredibly nervous about what was going to happen.

"Hello Luccia." He said, trying to sound as friendly as possible.

"What do you think you are doing Alexander?" she asked him, he knew she would get straight to the point, she didn't like to leave her intentions open to interpretation.

"I told you I wanted to be with her, and you had the audacity to send someone after her." his voice was in quiet control, but menace was emanating from him in every word. He heard her breath in deeply though it was not quite a gasp.

"I did what was necessary, as you knew I would!" she snapped back at him, her high pitched voice oozing of pure fury.

"How would you have felt if I had tried to murder someone you loved!"

She seemed taken aback at first, she didn't respond for several seconds, he knew this was a long time for her, she must be thinking deeply he suspected.

"I did it because I saw a vision of the future which left Xavier and Narcissia dead, I cannot allow that to happen, and that woman is at the heart of it."

"I know." He replied knowing that this would catch her off guard.

"What do you mean you know? How could you possibly know that, you're not prescient, I know that well enough." She snapped at him, obviously incensed.

"You are not the only one who has abilities." He added knowing that she would fill in the details herself. He knew how she would react to this; she would see it as a threat to herself, she would think that he was planning to replace her.

"You are signing her death warrant Alexander, you know that!" her voice had reached an even higher pitched note now that she was beginning to get really frightened, for the first time in many millennia she was frightened and she didn't know how to deal with it.

"You already did that, so what do we have to lose!" He hung up on her now, he didn't have anything further to say to her, and he knew it would infuriate her even more and make it harder for her to use her abilities to track them.

He knew her implicitly, he knew her better than he suspected anyone else did, he watched with the eyes of a warrior, he knew that even with their Acolytes at most they would only be able to field a dozen immortals at most, they had always been too afraid to create more.

He had to plan this out, he had already committed phase one of his plan to save Alexis, he had infuriated Luccia, and he had always found that when she was overly emotional her prescient faculty ceased to work reliably, as she couldn't focus properly. He had observed this twice over the millennia he had been alive, so he knew that if he could force the conversation onto the right note, that he would have been successful.

He knew he would eventually have to go after them in person, he couldn't hope to kill them, but it would delay them longer and it might just keep Alexis alive longer, long enough he hoped to save her. Or at the very least give him time to plead with the council to allow her to become an immortal, he knew that the leverage Luccia was using against Alexis' life was very strong, so he would have to be extremely persuasive.

He guessed that he would have about two weeks to make his move before they could track them here.

11:20am Paxson, USA

Alexis

She had enjoyed a nice long sleep; she was beginning to feel rested and recovered after all the travelling that they had done recently, she hadn't realised the time until Xander came back in with a tray so she could have breakfast in bed, he brought in freshly made pancakes with maple syrup, One of her favourites.

"Don't you ever sleep?" she asked him inquisitively as she realised he was always awake before her and always awake when she went to sleep.

His reply shocked her deeply, she had heard of insomniacs but his reply really surprised her "I need very little sleep, I sleep on average five to six hours every month, and even that isn't really what you'd class as sleep, think of it more as meditation."

"What do you mean meditation? Like a Buddha?" she laughed slightly trying to make light of it.

"Surprisingly similar actually my love, my body doesn't produce enough melatonin to make me tired anymore, and the virus repairs any damage to my cells caused by sleep deprivation, so we meditate to give our minds time to relax, especially if we exert ourselves or we end up putting too much strain on our minds."

When she had finished eating, he announced to her "We're going on an alpine hike today once you're ready." He smiled at the bewildered expression on her face. He knew she didn't often get exposed to very much nature; *and it wasn't for lack of opportunity* she thought to herself silently.

As she got dressed she decided to ask him about it, when she asked if there were bears in the local forests, he laughed so much that he fell off the bed. "That serves you right." She said in mock indignation.

"I'm sorry my love, but you really are one of a kind, only you would be worried about a few furry beasts while there are almost a dozen highly dangerous immortals intent on killing you." He trailed off for several moments and then she heard him mutter something about. "afraid of a few bears..." The mirth in his voice was readily apparent to her and she understood the irony of it all.

It didn't take her long to get ready and he had prepared some food and plenty of water for their hike along the trail. He promised her that she had never done anything like this, and she was hoping that he was right. She generally didn't do nature, she didn't like getting muddy.

When she told him she was ready to go, he chuckled silently and pulled out a heavy arctic coat he had purchased for her from one of the local residents, it was very heavy but she felt by the thickness of it that she could be out in a blizzard and she wouldn't feel that cold.

As they left the building she was surprised at just how warm it was, she was expecting it to be so cold as it was when they arrived, it had been so cold then that it felt like tiny needles were attacking all of her exposed skin, but now it was so warm that she felt she would have been okay with her other coat.

He looked at her suspecting what she was thinking and winked at her saying "You will thank me later, trust me."

She was amazed when they went outside, she had expected to see enormous amounts of snow, but she was pleasantly surprised to see a wide range of different greens, reds and oranges colours, she could hear the birds singing.

They walked for hours without realising it, she totally lost track of time, she had seen so many animals, and the lands they had travelled were luscious and teaming with wildlife, when she asked them how far they had travelled, he replied telling her "About fifteen kilometres at a guess." He leaned towards her and kissed her cheek playfully.

And then he pulled her towards the next group of trees along the ridge and told her that he was going to lay the blanket down so they could have a picnic, she was amazed that he had thought of something so sweet. And she pounced on him shouting her love for him in their isolation, confident that no one could hear or see them, and he playfully fought her off of him.

They spent quite a long time laying there under the tree, she didn't have a clue what type it was and she didn't really care anyway, all that mattered to her was that she was there with him, *my Alexander* she thought to herself, she chuckled quietly to herself, thinking about how the man of her life, was Alexander the Great.

Xander eyed her suspiciously when she chuckled, she was impressed at just how sensitive his hearing was, and she wondered just what else was so sensitive and she for the first time decided she really wanted to feel his skin.

He laid there perfectly still while she ran her forefinger along his lips and along his cheek bones, she was surprised at how supple and soft his skin felt, she hadn't really noticed before, but his skin felt perfect, like there wasn't a single flaw in it. She thought about how the vampire legends say they have cold skin, but his skin was warm to the touch.

She decided she would ask him about it and he looked at her and said "I'm warm because I am alive, my body temperature is lower than most mortals by several degrees, but I'm not stone cold dead like the myths say I should be." He continued sensing that she didn't understand "We have walked quite far today, the more I move the more the friction heats up my body just like a mortal, except however when I move at superhuman speeds, I can reach temperatures which would burn you if I touched you"

She looked at him surprised and then asked him "Is that why my foot got sunburnt?" he looked deeply into her eyes and said "You didn't get sunburn my love, you got a bad friction burn because I was careless as I moved you through the air." he kissed her eyes when she closed them, one after the other.

He was ever so gentle with her as he kissed her, she would never expect someone who could be so strong could be so gentle, there were depths to him that she hadn't even began to fathom.

She relaxed as he caressed and kissed her, she felt so peaceful and relaxed, so much so that she didn't realise she had fallen asleep, she could hear the faint sound of someone saying "I love you." But it sounded so far out in the distance, like it was a faint echo.

She didn't wake up for several hours and when she did she realised that she was wrapped up in the blanket they had been laying on. As she looked around she realised that she was moving, again she marvelled at how he could move her ever so gently that she hardly moved at all.

"Thank you." She said to let him know that she was awake. "How long have I been asleep?" she asked curiously.

"Only a couple of hours, it started to get a bit darker and the temperature was dropping so I figured that I had better get you back." He smiled at her warmly and it felt like she was drinking a warm drink, the heat spread throughout her body. If she had been standing she felt like she would have gotten weak at the knees.

"What did I do to deserve someone as wonderful as you?" She asked sincerely

"You fell in love with a monster, that's what you did." He smiled and then he chuckled at the look of mock horror on Alexis' face. She looked at him expecting a real answer to the question and then he stopped walking, looked her directly in her eyes and said "Boo!" they both burst out into fits of laughter and he had to sit down to steady himself, with her still in his arms.

Then they embraced again and she kissed him ever so softly before he got to his feet and helped her get onto hers.

When she was on her feet again she realised that he had been right, it was getting cold, and the wind was beginning to get really chilly she thought.

After they had walked for what felt like hours she decided to ask him the question most on her mind. "How long till we're home babes?" she tried to keep the sense of urgency out of her voice, but she was beginning to feel an achy stiffness in her muscles and she longed to get back to the hotel and get in a nice hot bath.

"We won't be long now, are you tired angel? I can carry you again if you need me to, you have absolutely no need to overly exert yourself." He didn't wait for her to give an answer as he swept her off her feet and carried her in his arms again.

"I can get you home in a few minutes if you want to get wrapped up in the blanket again" he smiled at her playfully.

"How long will we be if we walk normally?" she asked, not daring to tempt him to show her how fast he can move.

"My best guess would be about an hour." He answered, and sensing that she didn't want to wait that long, pulled out the blanket from the pack he was carrying on his back and wrapped it around her in one fluid movement

"Close your eyes and cover your ears angel, I don't want you to get disorientated and travel sick and your ears might sting a bit if you don't."

She did as he asked, she cupped her hands around her ears and squeezed her eyes shut, she could hear a whistling sound that she assumed was what he had meant that her ears might hurt, it was loud even with her ears covered, she would have hated to hear what it would have been like if her ears were exposed to it. Other than the whistling sound, she couldn't really detect all that much that showed they were moving, she was amazed at how fluidic his movements were.

She tried to talk to tell him she loved him, but her voice felt and sounded like it was caught in the wind, she was amazed, she knew this meant they were approaching dangerously high speeds, and she clenched her eyes shut tighter and put even more pressure on her ears.

It didn't take long before he placed her vertically on the ground and held her upright until she had regained her balance; this took several seconds as their trek had left her with very little balance. Her ears were ringing ever so faintly and he kissed her tenderly and whispered in her ear "Thank you for trusting me my love, now let's get you inside and I'll run you a nice warm bath."

As he kissed her she noted how hot he felt, his lips felt like they were radiating massive amounts of heat, she laughed as she imagined him getting in a bath and all the water fizzling away. He looked at her with a puzzled expression and then she explained what she had been thinking.

He laughed and then said to her "I haven't moved enough today my love, but yes it would be possible if I ran for a sustained period of time."

They both laughed as they walked back to the hotel, hand in hand, and she decided to ask him if he would get into the bath with her, he laughed and told her that he would love to. *My own private hot water bottle* she thought to herself.

As they climbed into the bath tub together she felt faintly curious, she wondered to herself why he was so pale if he could stand such high heats, surely he could tan himself, as he wasn't afraid of sunlight like most vampire tales. When she asked him he laughed to himself and said "If only I could, you see the virus doesn't allow my body to produce melanin, that's the hormone in your skin that allows you to tan as a reaction to sunlight." She considered this as she lowered into the water which felt so good to her aching muscles.

Chapter 8: Paul's Story
4:20pm Utah, USA

Paul

As he was driven from his mansion in the town of Daniel, Utah in one of his limousines towards the local airport in Salt Lake City he knew he would have to act fast in order to avert the danger he felt brewing, he had always had a curious sense of knowing when something was going to effect the Illuminati. He wasn't prescient by any means, but all of the Illuminati were sensitive when it came to their survival, it was something that they had developed over the three millennia they had been working together.

Three thousand years now he thought, he really felt ancient today, he hated feeling that old, but he knew it was just a mental thing, and while physically his body was around thirty-five years old, it was in perfect condition and most people would have suspected he was in his late twenties.

He was feeling unusually apprehensive today, he had spent over an hour on the phone to the man who was like a brother to him, he had known Anthony from his mortal lifetime and even though they were not blood kin, they were so alike that most people would not have guessed that they weren't related. They had been discussing the call they were both feeling, the feeling that they were drawn towards Alaska, they did not know why, but they suspected, this was one of the ways they recruited members of the Illuminati, it was the by-product of spending thousands of years searching for gifted mortals.

In their mortal lives they had spent decades searching for the secret of immortality and the mysteries of the human mind and body, they were very sensitive and now whenever someone who was gifted as they were gifted began to use their abilities, then they felt it and it drew them to the location of that person.

The feeling had been growing stronger and stronger for the past week, and it had traversed continents so that they could feel the urge drawing them closer, they had several hypotheses as to why this was, one of them was that the person was fleeing something, and the other was that they were drawn there themselves, why this would be he did not know, but he was determined to find out.

Neither Paul nor Anthony had experienced the call this strong for nearly two thousand years. It was a very rare occurrence at the best of times; most humans even when they had gifts were not strong enough to send out the unconscious call for help. And they had never felt a distress signal this strong before.

That had settled it to both of them; Paul was the closest of them, so he would fly from his home in Utah, while Anthony who was spending time with his mortal descendants who were located in southern England would catch the next available flight. They had alerted the other members of the Illuminati and they had all confirmed that they would travel to Alaska at the earliest possible time.

He arrived at Ketchikan four hours later and as he disembarked from the airliner he felt a stab of pain in his chest, it was the pain he felt whenever he smelt an unfamiliar Immortal, it was a massive shock to his awareness, and caused all his senses to flare, but he knew that whoever it was had been gone for at least several days if not longer.

This left a sense of foreboding in him as he arranged to charter a small cargo plane to the town of Paxson, he was paying an extortionate amount of money for the pilot to take him there a day early, the man knew he was ripping Paul off, but money mattered very little to Paul right now, he knew that another Immortal had been here recently and he suspected that the Immortal had something to do with the distress call he could feel emanating from Paxson.

He knew he would not have very much time, he suspected the involvement of the Covenant, they had beaten him to several mortals before, executing them before he had a chance to communicate with them and offer them membership in the Illuminati. They claimed that they did not want to risk creating a superhuman, yet they themselves were super humans, *hypocrites* he thought bitterly.

The flight to Paxson did not take long, it was far quicker than he expected and he could feel the presence of an immortal long before he arrived, he saw that the man awaiting him was not the mortal whom he had spoken to on the phone earlier that day to arrange transport from the airport to the local hotel. His senses flared and he saw the imminent danger.

The man was quite tall with short brown hair, he was eerily pale and he was emanating hostility with his body language. Even if he had not met this man several times before, he would have known him immediately anyway. He was Alexander, a legend in his own lifetime and more than that in his immortal life. He had been the key to the Covenant, thwarting the Illuminati time and time again.

Paul began to fear the worst as he disembarked from the plane, he knew that if Alexander was here, then the mortal was in grave danger, though he still felt the distress coming from the gifted mortal so he assumed that Alexander had not killed the mortal yet, but he knew he would not have long.

"Hello Alexander." He boomed. His voice was deep and very loud. He watched Alexander's expression and then continued. "I will not let you harm the mortal; it is under my protection now!"

What happened next astounded Paul, for Alexander's face brightened and turned into a warm smile "You have nothing to fear from me old friend, we are once again on the same side."

Paul was almost in shock, he had expected a lot of words to come out of Alexander's mouth, but never anything like that. He walked up to Paul and embraced him in much the way one old army veteran would embrace another. "It has been too long." He said, and Paul could hear the pure elation and relief in his voice.

Paul was still reeling when they got in the car and Alexander began to drive them towards the town, towards the pull he felt from there, he was amazed at how this was turning out, not only was the mortal safe, but he had somehow miraculously escaped doing battle with one of the most dangerous immortals of all time.

7:00pm Paxson, USA

Xander

As they drove away from the airport a sense of relief spread through him, he knew that he would be able to keep her safe now, especially now that he knew the Illuminati would help him protect her, he looked across at the burly man sitting next to him, his hair was thinning slightly on top and he remembered everything he knew about him, about how close they had been during the Kane Wars millennia ago when they had planned and discussed the strategies that they would use, he was an honourable man whom he respected greatly.

When he had first felt the presence of another immortal his first reaction had been one of panic, he knew he would have to intercept them at the airport or risk them getting close enough to Alexis to harm her, and that he could not allow. It wasn't until the plane had landed that he knew he hadn't underestimated the Covenant and that they weren't arriving to eliminate the threat they both now posed.

"How did you know where to find us?" Xander asked the man sitting beside him

"We always know when someone is gifted and uses their powers, but it is unusual for them to specifically call out to us, both Anthony and I heard a call emanating from this place and I was closer so I arrived first, but Anthony should be here within a day." He replied, his deep violet eyes looking deeply into Xander's midnight blue eyes.

"Good, we will need them, The Covenant will be coming, and they have sentenced her to death." He knew that his voice would convey his worry, and his love.

"Ah so that explains why the great, the loyal Alexander, has turned his back on his home, and has gone into self imposed exile." And his voice was displaying a surprising amount of compassion as he said this.

"You love her." his voice was compassionate still and he knew it was not a question, it was a fact.

"Yes, more than I have loved anyone in my life, I begged, I pleaded with them to let me turn her, but they refused." He added bitterly

"Luccia still trying enforce her draconian rule, I see? She has never been tolerant of anyone who could compete with her." A very feint echo of bitterness escaped his voice as he spoke.

"Indeed, the hypocrisy of it reeks" Xander replied scornfully.

As they arrived at the hotel, Xander waited for him in the lobby so that Paul could sign himself in and put his suitcases in his room. As he waited there he could not quite believe his luck, but he knew he would have to handle this very carefully, or this could escalate into a full scale war between the Covenant and the Illuminati, and what that could mean he did not fully comprehend. They had always been fairly evenly balanced in the past. *Until now* He thought to himself in silence

Paul came back down the stairs and saw him waiting there and asked "Shall we?" he nodded casually.

"Yes it is time but please, try to talk her through it slowly, it's a lot for her to take in all at once." Xander added thinking of Alexis.

"As you wish." He said and tilted his head slightly to show that he was agreeing to Xander's request

They entered the hotel suite one after the other and the surprise on Alexis' face was apparent the moment she set her eyes on Paul, for his eyes unlike Xander's were not a deep midnight blue but rather a vivid violet that was piercing and made it difficult for her to notice anything else.

"Greetings, I'm told your name is Alexis, I am Paul." His voice boomed out in his basso voice, at first it startled her. But as he continued talking she began to sense that he was a very paternal figure and that he did care deeply. "I am here to help you." He said looking at her confused expression.

But before she could ask him how he found them, he said "I felt you calling to us." He carried on sensing that she was getting more and more confused "You have been sending out a telepathic call to us for several days, one of deep distress. I and my family are very sensitive to gifted mortals such as you are."

"Your family?" she asked, Xander could tell that she was wondering whether or not he was a member of the Illuminati, but that she was avoiding being rude and asking him.

"We are known as the Illuminati, I assume you have heard of us." He said, he was trying to control the volume of his voice now, but he was still very loud.

"Yes Alexander has told me a bit about you, but he couldn't give me many details as he said he did not know very much." She replied ever so politely, she looked like she felt intimidated by the bear of a man.

"That does not surprise me; Alexander's former associates did not want its members knowing that they had an alternative." He smiled warmly now and let out a loud laugh, she jumped and he apologised and explained "I am not often around mortals my dear; I sometimes forget that not everyone knows me."

He noticed that she was still staring at his eyes mesmerised by them and he answered her unasked question. "My eyes are violet rather than blue, because I have an additional catalyst in my body that Alexander doesn't have."

"We call it the Elixir of Life, it is a bi-product of the Philosophers Stone, and we discovered it when we were mortals." He explained trying to make Alexis feel comfortable.

"If you are interested, I will tell you part of my story, I think you will find it interesting." And he continued. "And I think you will find it easier to trust me once you know more about me."

Lee Michael Harris

7:25pm Paxson, USA

Paul

Paul's Story

I was born around 1200 BC in what is now southern Norway, it was an area which much later grew to fame because of the Vikings, but even then we were still of the same Norse culture and they stayed pretty much the same for over two millennia, but that's another story altogether.

I was born into a small fishing village, my birth name was Páll, bear in mind that most of our original names are not used anymore so we modify them so we don't arouse the suspicion of mortals, and for the first seven or eight years of my life, I lived a happy life with my parents, but they both died of an influenza like illness and I went to live with my uncle who was not overly close to my father, but nevertheless agreed to take me with him.

He travelled far and wide as a Merchant, I cannot remember exactly what he traded, but he traded as far away as Egypt and I went along with him, learning as much as I could from him and everyone that we met.

But yet again disaster struck when I was in my early teens, my uncle was murdered while we were in Egypt, he was stabbed by someone, I never knew who did it. And I was forced to beg for food. Eventually I found work as an assistant to an Egyptian Alchemist and he fed and clothed me for many years.

He eventually tutored me and trained me as his protégé; I learnt everything I possibly could from him, including his language. He treated me like a son and I respected him as a grandfatherly figure I had never known. I stayed with him for over a decade, but he was already old when I came to live with him, when he died I was distraught and spent many years travelling what is now Europe and Greece.

During my journey I met some of the finest alchemists of the age and I first heard of the Philosophers Stone, a magical

90

substance that they said could turn any metal into pure gold, and could be distilled into an Elixir which would grant everlasting life.

While I was in Athens, I met Anthony when I was around twenty seven years old, we discovered very early on that we both shared the same dream, we became obsessed with discovering the secret of immortality, and we spent months discussing it and we were planning to travel back to Egypt where I already had a fairly well established residence and a well stocked laboratory.

One evening we discovered another mutual fascination, something I had never been able to confide in with anyone else in my life, I could make objects move with my mind, it is known now as telekinesis, but at the time it had no name and Anthony could also make people do almost anything he asked, we were enchanted with our new found confidante's and we began to test just how strong our abilities were.

Eventually we decided to travel back to Egypt and using Anthony's ability to control people by his voice, we managed to get ourselves appointed to the Pharaoh's court, as the official court alchemists. From there we had almost limitless resources to continue into discovering the secret of the Philosopher's Stone. And we spent over six years experimenting without any leads until one night, when we were both very sleep deprived we had a breakthrough, at first we both suspected we were asleep and dreaming.

But we continued testing throughout the night and realised we had done it, we had the secret to limitless wealth and everlasting life. It took us a further two years before we could produce the Elixir of Life, but we managed it. We had been relying on Anthony's powers in order to keep the Pharaoh's advisers off of our backs as we experimented and developed our secrets and then when we had discovered exactly how to recreate it, we left. We burnt the laboratory to the ground as well as all the documentation which showed our tests.

We settled again in southern Europe and started to build up a new powerbase. Once again we used Anthony's powers to secure ourselves and we had an added advantage this time, we could turn any metal even common metals into pure gold, and we used the wealth this gave us to build ourselves a fortress that could survive for a thousand years.

At first we were content, we lived a life of luxury but that can only give you so much, we both chose partners and we produced children, we were amazed at first as we suspected that due to the elixir we would not be able to reproduce, but no we were successful, Anthony fathered a daughter and I fathered two sons.

When they were old enough we gave them the elixir as well so that they could spend eternity with us, but even with our new and ever-growing families we were not content, we needed a new project, and we had settled on developing our mental faculties even further. And we searched for ways to increase our extrasensory abilities. I found myself a wife who also had an unusual and powerful ability, she had not had it during her mortal life, but my wife Deborah had a fiery temper at the best of times, and once she had partaken in the Elixir of Life, it manifested as what is now known as pyrokinesis. When angered or upset she would cause objects to burst into flames.

We experimented further for centuries and we eventually discovered we were not the only immortals living in Europe, we found a colony of pale skinned immortals that seemed to feed on the mortals around them. We saw them as monsters, but we observed them for decades learning everything we could from them.

In around 700 BC, Anthony's daughter, Charlotte was attacked by one of them while she observed them, and she suffered agony as the venom the man pumped into her body eventually left her catatonic, we found her and nursed her back to health, and then we learned the cause of her ailment and we devised a plan to even the score.

We captured one of the weaker immortals and we brought him back to our fortress where we demanded answers from him, he was incredibly strong and we only managed to hold him at bay by a combination of my telekinesis and Anthony's power of voice. He eventually succumbed and told us all he knew about the Covenant, an organisation of immortals that fed off the mortal population, they were ruled by a council and were forbidden to infect anyone else, their leadership wanted to keep the immortal virus within their control.

Anthony still burned with a desire for revenge, a desire than my own son Kane agreed with, and even though our experiments with the immortal's blood had not fielded viable results Anthony decided to experiment on himself, he drank the pure blood of the immortal, and he then fell sick, with a high fever and painful white lesions, he suffered agonisingly for four whole days, we had almost believed him lost when he eventually pulled through it.

And to our surprise he was pale skinned and had their strength, his powers of persuasion had been increased tenfold and over the course of the following months, almost all of us had submitted and agreed to be converted into the new breed of immortal. Unlike the original monster, we had violet eyes rather than blue, this made us stand out significantly, but we discovered something else. We could last for far longer without feeding. This helped our consciences greatly and we began practicing with our new powers, confident that we would never again be at risk from the Covenants members.

It wasn't until much later that we found out how lucky we were that none of us died when we infected ourselves with the virus, but regardless on the whole, our anger against the Covenant had faded somewhat, we decided in the grand scheme of things that they did not matter.

Naming ourselves what was essentially an old form of the word Illuminati we decided we would form our own council to oppose that of the Covenant, and we would set our own mandates, that we would find the best and brightest minds and those who had extrasensory abilities and we would bring them into our community, at first they would have an internship with us where we would help them with their gifts and then eventually if they were suitable, then they would be offered the chance to join us.

Kane however was still seething over the attack on Charlotte, for he had always felt an unrequited love for her, even though she had no love for him other than that of an extended family member. He plotted revenge and tried to subvert several members of the Illuminati, we eventually found out about this and we banished him, forbidding him from ever returning to us until he would renounce his militaristic ways and agreed to rejoin us peacefully.

It took several decades before we heard back from him, he had been using the gold we gave him to form an army of raiders, and they pillaged mercilessly throughout Europe and Asia, they were incredibly successful, for Kane had always had a keen mind and had a superb sense for strategy. Eventually we discovered that he had decided that he wanted to form an Immortal army so that he could conquer the known world, and that was when we heard word from our informants that an unstoppable army had begun annexing large parts of Asia and Eastern Europe and was working its way towards us.

"Now my dear, I suspect that you might need some time to refresh yourself, we can continue tomorrow, I will be in the room next door should you need me, but I must convene with my fellows over the telephone, Anthony will be here soon and I need to bring him up to speed." He departed the room briskly, knowing that he had given them both much to think about.

Chapter 9: The Illuminati Illuminated
10:55am Paxson, USA

Paul

He had a lot on his mind as he awaited Anthony at the small air strip; he was due to arrive anytime now. As he stood there he replayed the conversation they had the previous night in his mind, Remembering Anthony's warnings about telling the girl their history in front of Alexander. Anthony knew that he had a soft spot for Alexander from when they worked together during the wars against his own son.

But he had felt it was far too risky to give Alexander too much information in case he returned to the Covenant and informed them on everything he had heard. That was something they dared not risk, for there was much that they did not know or suspect, things which could shift the balance of power dramatically and cause the re-ignition of the fuse that was already very short and might well start off the war once more.

Anthony's plane arrived several hours after he had arrived, Paul was still deep in thought, considering everything Anthony had argued against and decided that it was worth the risk, as he disembarked from the small two engine cargo plane, his face was a mask of stern consternation, Paul knew that it was an act, Anthony had never been able to stay angry with him for long, they were too close for that.

"Greetings Tony." He boomed, using the name Anthony preferred to be called by his close friends and family.

"Paul." his greeting was in the form of a nod, it was something he had always done, he knew that Anthony liked to show his feelings without words; it was something that always surprised people about them. One of them loved to talk while the other loved to listen, and Anthony spoke more with his body than he did with his voice.

He was a short man by modern standards, some three inches shorter than Paul was, with short sun kissed brown hair, his natural blond highlights making his hair appear lighter than it was, he was well built and muscular, of a similar build to Paul, this was one of the things that led most people to believe they were brothers. His face had jovial rolls and when he smiled people couldn't help but smile back at him. He was however on guard now, as he was deep in thought and concerned for the future of their family.

"Shall we?" he asked, trusting that Paul would know what he meant, that he really meant 'shall we go and see this strange young mortal.'

It didn't take long for the two of them to get back to the hotel and for Anthony to arrange a room for himself, Paul waited patiently while Anthony stored his luggage in his room and they walked down to the suite Alexis was staying in, his body stiffened and Paul could see the tension in the muscles in his neck and shoulders.

Alexander opened the door before they had time to knock, his face tensed as he saw that Anthony was not his usual jovial self, this appeared to worry him. Almost as if he thought that Anthony was a threat to Alexis.

Anthony almost as if he were sensing what Alexander was thinking smiled and nodded to him and then said "I mean no harm old friend." It was the common greeting that they both used when greeting an equal. Alexander relaxed after that and he allowed them into the room, and they sat down at the table.

Alexis was already there, her face looked bright and eager and she was staring at Anthony curiously, like she was interested in finding out what strange secrets this new violet eyed man would tell her that would make her question everything she had ever known and heard.

"Shall I continue?" Paul asked curiously, seeing Alexis's eyes light up as he said it, and Anthony tensed a little but then relaxed again.

"As I told you last night, when we banished Kane he began to form his own army and began to raid and conquer lands in Europe and Asia, I will carry on from there"

Paul's story continued

Kane's lust for power grew as he won battle after battle, he was always at the forefront of his troops and this inspired them, the mercenaries were not used to fighting side by side with their leaders and they grew fanatically loyal to him because of this.

Eventually he began to infect his most loyal warriors with the virus, and while most of them did not survive, he managed to create and elite group of immortal warriors, he stopped once he had sixty of them and he then taught them everything he could about how to fight other immortals, but as they practiced against each other, rather than against himself they were greatly weakened by their inability to fight against immortals stronger than themselves.

He also told them a great many lies about the Covenant and the Illuminati, forcing them to hate and fear both of our organisations, his core of warriors were even more loyal to him now than when they were mortal, and he told them several more lies, such as that they would not be able to create other immortals themselves and that they would kill anyone that they tried to infect.

This lie held true, for one of his warriors tried to infect his dying wife and she died in excruciating pain, the man was executed personally by Kane as an example to the others, and none of them dared step a foot out of line after that.

With his mortal and immortal army now reaching an estimated three thousand mortal mercenaries and some sixty immortals, he carved out an empire for himself, we did not hear about it until it was almost too late. Our spies informed us of the pale skinned warriors that tore their enemies apart as if they were indestructible.

We tried to resolve this peacefully and I personally went to communicate with him, we talked for several days but he refused to stop his campaign, he mentioned that he still had a score to settle with the Covenant and that he would not stop until they had been destroyed. He knew that he would need an overwhelming army in order to defeat them, and he was gradually increasing the power of his army month after month.

When I returned and explained the situation to our family, we were deeply concerned, for we knew that if they defeated the Covenant then there only remaining competition would have been us, and we suspected that Kane's family loyalty would not have stopped him or his guard from attempting to wipe out their only remaining threat.

As a result we decided that we would finally show ourselves to the Covenant and we amassed our entire family and marched towards the Covenants home, in what is now Vienna, Austria. They were appalled at first that we had managed to steal their secrets, it would have come to open combat there and then had it not been for the telepathic ability of the twin known as Narcissia, and she forced the Covenant to stop and to listen.

As we explained everything that was happening because of Kane, they grew more and more concerned, they said that they had never had to fight any other immortals in the whole time they had existed and they had not even suspected that there were other immortals out there. And then they found out that there was not one group who was a match for them but two groups, one of them highly militaristic.

They suspected there was something different about us though, mainly due to our eye colour, and Narcissia tried repeatedly to breach our minds and learn the secret, finally Anthony used his ability on her and forbade her from entering the mind of a member of the family of the Illuminati again. This was the first time they had heard that name and they began to suspect then that we had delved into the abilities brought on by the virus.

Again we almost ended up in open combat, but we appealed to them, that it wasn't the time for hostility between us, they saw the truth in this because even with the combined forces of the Covenant and the Illuminati we were outnumbered two to one, and that was not something either of our groups took lightly.

We worked together closely to build up an army of mercenaries of our own, over the course of a year we amassed an army of nearly four thousand mortals, none of them suspecting the real reason why we hired them. And then we set off and we went out to fight a war we knew we would struggle to survive.

Our first confrontation with the forces of Kane was a resounding defeat, we did not know how to lead the mortals properly and we lost a full half of our mortal army, Kane used his elite troops so well that they decimated our forces. And while we had not lost any of our own Immortals, we felt the sting of defeat incredibly strongly.

It was then that we decided jointly that we would search far and wide for a mortal leader to aid us in our war with Kane, we left the field of battle with our tail between our legs, and we did not dare to face him again for over a decade and he left us alone, content to build an empire for himself.

It was during this time of quiet that we found Michael, well more accurately, he found us, his family had been butchered by Kane's armies and he burned with a furious desire for revenge and joined the ranks of our mortal armies, where he came to our attention almost immediately, we could feel the power radiating from him, even the Covenant could feel it, but we managed to turn him before they could do much about it.

We regained hope when the Covenant managed to recruit the most talented military mind of the age, they had managed to successfully infect Alexander of Macedonia, he was a legend in his own lifetime, and he had never lost a battle.

With him on our side, we set about rebuilding an army to face Kane once again, and we built up an army of some five thousand mortals this time, determined that we would not stop until we had defeated Kane, we knew that this time, we could not leave the fight up to the mortals, we would join the fray ourselves this time.

I won't even try to explain everything that happened in that war, it is a story for another time, but I will summarise it, we fought the war with as much skill, intensity and boldness as Kane did and our Immortals were strengthened by not only time as the Covenant had been, but by the Elixir of Life as the Illuminati had been, combined we proved far too strong an enemy to defeat.

Over the course of the next four years we defeated Kane's armies and destroyed his powerbase, we lost many of our oldest friends and loved ones including Anthony's wife and my other son, Jason, even the Covenant suffered heavy losses, but we won in the end. We tracked down and eliminated the entire core of Kane's Immortal army, and every mortal that suspected the involvement of the Immortals. We cleaned up after ourselves so that history would never suspect that there had been a war between two factions of Immortals. And as the victors, we wrote the history.

Even though survived and has not been seen for millennia, he gave up his plans for conquest and disappeared after I defeated him in single combat, but I could not force myself to kill him, I allowed him the chance to escape. The Covenant however believe him to be dead, they had not forgotten the losses they suffered at his hands.

At the end of the war, the alliance between the Covenant and the Illuminati dissolved, we were fairly evenly matched in terms of abilities, even though they were vastly more powerful due to their age, we had on our side, mental faculties which tipped the balance.

Even though the Covenant would have destroyed us if they could have, we eventually agreed on the terms of a treaty to ensure peace between us. There were heavy stipulations against creating new immortals; we were not allowed to increase our number above twenty heads and neither were they.

Another stipulation was that neither of our forces should engage in hostility towards each other, and that we were not allowed to risk the mortal populations every finding out about our immortal communities, any mortal that found out was to be silenced permanently.

The final stipulation, which was the hardest agreement forced on the Illuminati was that we were not allowed to create Immortals out of humans that already had powerful psychic abilities. This was something which stuck in our throat heavily, but at the time we were unwilling to risk a war over this matter and so we agreed, not wanting to lose even more of our family.

Peace lasted for nine centuries until a massive plague spread among the mortal population, decimating them, however one man survived the plague and was gifted with the ability to heal others, we eventually found him he came to spend time with us where we helped him develop his abilities, the Covenant found out and considered this a breach of the treaty, as a result they assassinated him whilst he was travelling the lands ravaged by the plague, hoping to save other's from the illness.

With the treaty no longer in effect, we were no longer willing to follow their rules and as such we began recruiting as many gifted mortals as possible in an attempt to fight off the attack we expected the Covenant to launch at any moment. The Covenant however did not attack us themselves, they used mortals as pawns to attack our family and when they attacked us, we mobilised our forces and they were massacred with no losses to the Illuminati.

After thirteen years of bloodshed the war cooled down, the Covenant were unwilling to risk fighting the Illuminati in direct confrontations and as such they set about killing every gifted mortal they could, determined that they would starve the Illuminati of members to stop them growing too powerful to stop. This uneasy cold war has lasted until the present day, there is more to it, but that is a story for another time.

2:20pm Paxson, USA

Alexis

"And that was our history." The immortals in front of her said, her mind was still reeling from all she had learned in such a short time, it was a lot for her to take in and she was thankful that he had split it into two parts so that it would be easier for her to comprehend.

"Do either of you have any questions?" Anthony asked. He was a fairly short fair haired man, who unlike his companion did not have any facial hair, whereas Paul had a brownish-red beard which covered most of his full cheeks.

She was shocked by this question as much as Xander appeared to be, she was amazed at how deeply human they appeared to be, they just didn't seem like mythical creatures to her anymore and if it wasn't for the violet eyes and pale skin she didn't think she would have been able to tell the difference between them and mortals.

Xander broke the silence first by asking "Has Kane been seen since then?" he kept his voice calm and even, almost as if he was worried about asking this question.

Paul answered first, "I have not seen my son in over two thousand three hundred years, I don't even know if he is still alive, but I am not shocked by this, something about the war broke him, and I honestly don't think it was losing that did it, towards the end it was almost as if he wanted to be beaten."

She let this sink in a bit in case Xander wanted to ask another question, but when he quietly nodded and did not speak up again, Alexis asked the question most on her mind "How does this affect me? Now that you have found me what are your intentions?"

Anthony smiled at this while Paul let out a deep chuckle, this laugh thundered across the room and he slammed his hand down on his leg which sent vibrations across the floor.

"We will protect you, of course." Paul said and Anthony nodded his approval as Paul spoke.

"But wont that mean war?" she asked curiously, her fear was edging her voice subtly

"We are already at war, and we are not afraid of fighting; besides the rest of my family will be here within seventy-two hours. The main thing I want to know is do either of you know how long we have until Luccia and her lackeys find us here?" this was the most she had heard Anthony say, as he generally let Paul do the talking. His voice had a warm calming effect and she noticed that it didn't just effect her.

"Just over a week at my best guess, but it might be sooner I do not know for sure." Xander replied, the confidence in his voice made her heart skip a beat, it made her worry knowing that he could be injured trying to protect her from those savage immortals that wanted to kill her for being alive and not fitting into their plans.

"But what if I don't want you fighting and dying for me?" she asked, panic escaped her and he voice was unsteady.

"My dear, we would help to protect you even if you did not want us to. We cannot stand by and allow the Covenant to oppress and murder people for being born how they are." It was Paul again his deep voice in more control than he usually managed.

"But you cannot stand against them, they are too strong." She said frantically.

"No my dear, they used to be evenly matched with us, neither of us would risk full out war as the losses would have been great on both sides, but we have Alexander now, and believe me, you have no comprehension of what he can do. Without him the Covenant no longer has such a strong advantage." It was Anthony again; the wisdom in his voice settled her and helped her remain calm.

Could he really be that big a factor? She thought as she considered Xander and what he had told her in his story.

"But he is young compared to them, and you aren't much older than he is, how can you face them?" she asked, the previous conversation had not fully sunk in yet and she didn't understand what they meant.

"The Illuminati were strengthened by the Elixir of Life my dear girl, which has amplified our abilities exponentially and bridges the gap between our power and that of the Covenant. The other deciding factor is that almost all of us have extra abilities." As Paul said this, he made the coffee table in front of them move up in the air and spin around as if to demonstrate his ability.

She gasped, even though she had believed him before, seeing it was a completely different matter altogether.

"What other gifts do you have?" she asked curiously, she looked beside her to Xander and his eyes held the same curiosity that she felt.

"Well other than Anthony and myself, as you already know our gifts, my wife Deborah is a pyrokinetic, she can light fires with her mind, this can be devastating when used offensively, Anthony's daughter Charlotte can send an opponent into a kind of unbreakable trance by the power of her voice. And that is just the tip of the iceberg. That does not include the rest of our family."

He continued sensing that she did not believe him that they would be safe "I told you about Michael, he was powerful as a human, but since his immortality he has grown vastly more powerful, he can control the elements in your body and force it to tear apart if he focus' enough power on you, think what that could do to an Immortal that carries more far more iron and other minerals in their body than a mortal does. Or even Michael's wife Celeste who has a very unique ability, she can wipe out memories of her opponents, or even their entire identity if she tried hard enough."

"Trust in us my dear, we will keep you safe, but first of all we need to decide how to handle it. Whether we attack them the moment they arrive or try to handle it peacefully." Anthony said calmly, his voice was brimming with affection, as if he found it heart warming that she was worried about their safety.

"I will go and try and sort out a solution peacefully." Xander said boldly, Alexis glared at him as if he had poured boiling water over her. But she melted as soon as he looked at her, she could sense the love in his eyes and she fell silent and didn't voice her opinion on the matter.

"They will not harm me, my love I promise you that." She sensed the truth in his voice and she leaned forward and kissed him tenderly. Paul and Anthony looked at each other and sighed; she could have sworn that she heard Paul chuckle and whisper "young love..." to Anthony.

"I do have one question, it's totally unrelated of course but I'm really curious about it." The look she received from Anthony and Paul made her laugh quietly; they seemed amused at her ability to change the subject away from matters which made her uncomfortable.

"Feel free." Paul said jovially

"It's just that I wanted to know how you pass as mortals with eyes like yours." As she said it, Paul roared with laughter and it took several seconds for him to regain his composure.

Anthony replied with the answer as Paul was still laughing quietly. "We wear tinted sunglasses whenever we are outside; when we are indoors our eyes are less noticeable unless you look at them close up. Which most people do not really do, they just assume that we are wearing contact lenses and on the odd occasion people ask us, that is what we say. People are generally willing to believe anything if it will stop them from feeling confused or worried."

She was beginning to feel more and more comfortable now, as both Paul and Anthony were beginning to feel human to her, she had passed the stage where she was intimidated by Paul's loudness and Anthony had begun to be more talkative which set her mind at ease. At first she had suspected that he was not committed to her defence, but now she was convinced that even though she did not want them to get hurt, that they would ignore her anyway.

Everything she had learnt since she arrived in Alaska was beginning to fall into place ever so slightly, but she still felt very anxious and she knew that the anxiety would only get worse she knew. Especially if and when Xander decides to travel to Europe to intercept the Covenant and try and talk some sense into them, before it was too late.

Chapter 10: Even Old Friends Can Surprise You
9:58pm Paxson, USA

Alexis

She knew she wouldn't have long alone with him and now that Anthony and Paul had left to go and meet some more members of the Illuminati, she wanted to spend as much time with him as possible.

She really didn't like the idea of him leaving to travel back to Europe but she couldn't seem to persuade him not to, they all seemed convinced that the only way they could avert a war would be for him to talk the Covenant around, she didn't think it would work, but they were determined to try. *Even if it might cost Xander his life in an attempt to save her own.* She thought painfully.

As she left the bathroom he looked up at her, his eyes showed that he was deep in thought, and judging by the expression on his face he was worried, not for his own safety but for hers. He got up from the chair he had been sitting on and walked over to her, and pulled her into a tight hug, she could feel his breath on her neck and she could feel the hairs on the back on her neck raise as she held onto him as tight as she could.

She hadn't been able to be this close to him all day and she had missed it terribly, but she knew it would have been disrespectful of them to openly display how much they loved each other while they had company, especially while that company were here to try and keep her alive.

He had not told her when he would be leaving and this worried her, it made her think that he would be going away sooner than he wanted to, and far sooner than she would want him to, because if it was up to her, he would not be going at all, it was a risk he should not have to take, especially for her.

The door bell chimed so they knew someone was at the door, as he released her and walked over to it, he did not seem worried, she supposed it would be Paul and Anthony again, but to her surprise when he opened it, it was a member of staff from the hotel, he brought up a tray of strawberries, rich black cherries and champagne.

This was not something she had expected, and she hadn't heard him ask for it, so she thought he must have ordered it while she was in the bathroom getting refreshed.

As he fed her each tiny piece of fruit one by one, and kissed her gently along her cheek and eyes, she knew he was buttering her up for something, she suspected he planned to leave tomorrow, but she couldn't bear to face it, so she kept silent, trying desperately to forget her worries and enjoy the moment.

He looked into her eyes and she lost herself, she had never seen anyone with eyes like his, in some lights they were deep and dark, whilst in others, especially candle light they sparkled with so much intensity that she was amazed, she could lose herself forever in his eyes.

As she thought this, she wished she would have forever to lose, but unless things turned out miraculously well then she would not have that chance.

She decided that she would not waste tonight with sleep, that she would spend as long with him as she possibly could, she imagined spending a candle lit night, under the stars with him, of having another tour of Italy, but she knew that was not something they could do until the death sentence hanging over her head had been withdrawn.

"I love you." She said as she regained herself from her day dream, and he eyed her with a playful suspicion that made her laugh, he replied "I love you more."

She laughed again after this. *No you don't* she thought but she couldn't think of a way to say that to him without wasting time debating the amount each other loved the other.

"Surrender, my love." he said as he ran his fingers down from the nape of her neck to the base of her spine, a shudder passed through her as she felt her body giving in to him long before she consciously decided she would.

"Forever." She said in between the soft, passionate kisses he was covering her with. *Life cannot get better than this* she thought, wondering what it would be like to see life as an immortal.

"What do you see when you look at me like that?" she asked him

His response shocked her. "I see everything my love." Because it wasn't what she had expected him to say.

She thought about this for several seconds before deciding that he hadn't answered her question, she was about to ask him what he saw in her when he put his index finger to her lips and said "I have lived for twenty three centuries, and in all that time I have never seen anyone that I have found as beautiful as you are to me."

He carried on "You are more precious to me than any gem, jewel or metal, I grew to love you more in the three weeks we shared together in Italy than I have ever loved anyone."

She wasn't sure how to handle this, as from her old history lessons in school, she knew he had had lovers of both sexes during his reign as king, and she decided to ask him about it. He replied saying "Yes, I loved them, but in comparison with how deeply I feel for you, my love for you is like an eclipse, once you have tasted such light you cannot see anything else."

She blushed as he said this and he kissed her warm cheeks, and as he pulled away, for the first time she saw his extended fangs, this shocked her deeply, for even though she did not fear him, it was a deep shock to actually see the vampire side of him face to face.

He immediately covered his mouth, and before she had a chance to say anything, he dissapeared out of the room, so fast she didn't see him move, she heard the bathroom door slam and she ran over to it, desperate for him to trust her and let her in. She didn't fear him, she could never fear him, but she couldn't bear for him to feel like he had to hide a part of himself.

"Let me in." She said as she banged her hand on the door.

His response came several seconds later, and she heard the door unlock with a click. And as she opened the door, she saw his face, his expression was one of deep distress, and he was covering his mouth with his hand.

She reached out and pulled his hand away, he was biting down hard on his bottom lip, and she could see a small trickle of a very deep red blood flowing from his mouth, she could see that he was causing himself pain by doing it, and she reached out again to touch his cheek, he flinched at her touch, but he released his jaw and the blood flow stopped almost instantly.

She walked into the toilet and picked up the roll of toilet paper that was there, and she began to gently wipe away the blood that was on his chin, his expression was heartbreaking to her, he looked so upset, so ashamed that she wanted nothing more than to hug and kiss him and tell him that it was all alright.

But she knew that she couldn't kiss him without risking infection, so she needed to clean him up first, she noticed that the marks on his lip had healed already so once she had finished washing the blood away he was back to being pristine, even if he was not feeling it.

She asked him "Did I do something wrong?" *everything had been going fine* she thought, and she hadn't done anything to annoy him, well she didn't think she had.

"No my love, I didn't realise how hungry I was, I forget myself around you, I am so sorry, but at least now you know." His voice held so much sadness she nearly cried, she couldn't bear to see him upset. But she didn't know what to do.

"Now I know what?" she asked trying to change the subject. His response was what she had expected and yet dreaded most "Now you know I'm a monster!"

"You could never be a monster, no one who acts and talks like you could ever be a monster. But I do need to know what I did wrong, and what we can do to fix it." She said her voice was full of compassion and sorrow.

She continued before he had a chance to say anything, and she pulled her thick top aside, so that her neck was exposed and asked him "Do you need to bite me?" she said playfully and winked at him, she smiled afterwards as she saw his eyes lighten

His expression broke into a grin and they laughed together, and he reminded her "I rarely drink blood, but I will need an Epi-Pen, from my suitcase."

As he walked over to his suitcase and unzipped it, he pulled out a small silver tin and opened it, inside it was black foam and several thin, long cylinders that she suspected were the pens, full of adrenaline.

He looked at her and said "You might want to look away if you're squeamish." He laughed at this and even his eyes looked like they were laughing as he tried to break the tension they both felt in the air.

"I'll watch, after all I will need to get used to it myself, for when I have to do it." She said absent minded, not really thinking of the deep implications on relying on adrenaline for sustenance.

"That won't be anytime soon my love, and possibly never if things don't work out with the illuminati, it's too risky." His voice was firm yet she could sense the truth in his words, he was deeply worried about it, she could tell.

"But what if the Illuminati give me the Elixir? You know they might do that now." This was what she was hoping, she knew it might be the only way she could live forever, and it worried her deeply that they might refuse her.

"That is a hope; we shall have to see what happens, as well as what they would ask of you in return." He sounded suspicious as he said it,

And they both thought about that unanswered question, what the requirements for membership would be in their exclusive club, something they do not give out lightly and almost never to someone who hadn't shown their gifts, and she wondered then what it was they saw in her.

She decided to ask him what he thought they saw in her and his response was not what she would have expected. "They most likely sense that you have a strong psychic ability buried deep down, as for how it will manifest itself, I am sorry but I do not know. And we won't know until it happens."

"Okay." She replied, giving up, and he leaned forwards and kissed her on her forehead before he went into the other room and got changed out of his bloodstained shirt, once again giving her a display of the his perfection of his body.

4:23pm Paxson, USA

Xander

As he lay there, holding Alexis in his arms, he knew she was deep asleep, she had tried to fight it, but it had eventually got the better of her, he hadn't exactly helped her though, as he had done everything he could in order to relax her and make her comfortable, not the best thing to do to someone who was determined to stay awake, but he knew that she needed her rest.

She'd had a very strenuous week, and he was worried that it would affect her even more if she added sleep deprivation to the list. He knew that he would have to leave soon; if he left it much longer then there would be no chance for a peaceful resolution.

He knew that he would have to try and persuade Luccia that she would not be a threat, that she would be content to live forever in his company, but he knew that she would not care even if she did by some miracle believe him, she would be after his blood now as well anyway.

But he also knew that if he could convince the rest of the council, then he might stand a chance, her sister Narcissia he counted as a potential ally, as she had suffered greatly in the past due to Luccia's inflexibility when the rules were in question.

He knew that the majority of the council were loyal to Luccia, that was how she had managed to hold onto power for so long, they all trusted in her abilities, and she had convinced them that no one else's gifts could be trusted. But he knew he would have a slight chance at convincing at least some of them.

He gently moved Alexis onto the bed properly and surrounded her with pillows so that she would be able to hug onto them without worrying that he had left, he knew he would have to go now, or she would try and make him stay. And he couldn't delay it any longer; he decided he would leave her a note explaining why he had left.

'Alexis

I could not stay longer, I have a very bad feeling about this, even now that the Illuminati are involved, I have to go and stop this before it begins, it is the only way that I can stop this from becoming a disaster.

Do not feel sad, I will return to you, I promise you that, there isn't a force in the universe greater than my love for you, and nothing could keep me away.

If things go badly, I will do my best to get out of there and return here to you, and if things go well, then we won't need to hide anymore.

Take care my love, you mean the world to me, and I plan on giving the world to you.'

He knew that she would panic when she woke up and found that note, but he could not delay any longer, instead of waiting for a flight back to Ketchikan, he decided that he would be able to get there faster if he ran. Before he left, he used up both charges in two Epi-Pens and put another two in his pocket; he would have to be at his maximum abilities to be able to survive this storm.

It didn't take him long before he arrived at Ketchikan but when he did arrive, he had to go and buy some new clothes, as his were frayed and burnt from the trip, he figured that Alexis would not even be awake yet, but he would try and board the next outbound plan to Europe he could find, which turned out to be Paris, he was lucky as it would only be a short trip from Paris to Vienna.

By the time he arrived in Vienna he guessed that Alexis would be awake now, and that she would have found a few of his surprises, and he decided he would send her a text message from a new mobile phone he had purchased from an electrical store and then disposed of once he had sent the message.

"I love you my angel, I wish I was there with you xxx."

He knew it would make her smile even though she was worried, but that was the only thing he had left to hope for. He knew the first of his gifts would have arrived several hours before, he had arranged for all of her meals to be delivered at set times, as he knew that she probably wouldn't be in the right frame of mind to remember her needs.

8:03am Vienna, Austria

Narcissia

She was deep in thought as she sat in the lounge of the airport, she was planning to catch the next plane to America, and she had made a guess that the location of the vision her sister had was somewhere in north America, she doubted it would be Russia or Antarctica. So she had guessed that it would be America or Canada, they would not have been foolish enough to have gone to a country in northern Europe.

She had been there for two hours now and she was beginning to feel impatient, she didn't like having this feeling. She felt like Damocles, with the proverbial sword hanging over her head. She was determined to solve this peacefully but she didn't know how, and her biggest problem was that Luccia had been so blinded with rage that she couldn't use her ability to track them.

They all knew they only had a small window of opportunity, because if Alexander and the woman had long enough, they would come across the Illuminati, and if that happened then it would strain the already dubious relationship between both factions to breaking point, and then that would mean war. And that wasn't something that she felt would end well, especially now that Alexander was no longer loyal to the Covenant.

It was then that she felt him, he was still several miles away but she could still detect his presence, she couldn't believe her luck, as she checked all inbound flights and she made a rough guess as to which one he was on, so she waited near the terminal she suspected he would land at and waited patiently for him to disembark.

As soon as he had passed through customs, she knew that he had sensed her presence, but he didn't seem to be antagonised by it, she saw this as a good sign, and she walked over to greet him.

"Hello Narcissia." He called out casually "We need to talk, privately." He said afterwards.

She knew what he meant, so she allowed her mind to reach out and touch his, and for a few moments their minds were linked. She was surprised that he would risk this, but she was glad that he trusted her enough to try.

What is going on? She asked him

His reply shocked her because of its honest simplicity. *I could not allow your sister to kill Alexis, I love her and I will not allow anyone to harm her.*

But why have you come back, you've left her alone, won't she be in danger? As she said this she caught sight of Paul and Anthony in his mind, and she knew that they were involved, that they were protecting her. She knew what this would mean if Luccia carried out her plans it would cause a war between them.

She decided to do a bit of poking around while he was giving her the chance, she knew that if he didn't want her to, he would never have allowed her to get close, so she began exploring his mind, trying to pick out all relevant information, and he came across the previous night he had spent with Alexis, and the wave of pure love that poured out of him into her mind, made her ache to be with Alexis, It had been a long time since she had ever felt such adoration and she then realised that he would do anything to protect her, that what they had was special, and that he would risk his life for her willingly.

At that moment, they looked into each other's eyes, and they both knew that even she could not allow anything to happen to Alexis. Not just because she herself had lost loved ones, but because of how strongly he felt, and she had touched his mind and it had left a taint on her own soul. Part of her felt love for this woman now, and had she known that such a thing could have happened, she probably wouldn't have risked it.

"How can I help?" she asked him, knowing full well what he would ask of her, and she began to suspect what the outcome for her would be now, she had already seen it.

"You already know, I cannot ask you to risk your life for her, but I have to save her, there has to be some way to stop your sister!" he said, the anger and dread emanating from his voice when he said it made her recoil.

"I saw in your mind what you've been told about the dream she had, I know the outcome to it, and I'll take my chances." She said resigned to her fate.

She left him there, he was shocked by her decision and he obviously didn't know how to respond, and he didn't follow her as she went to catch the next plane to Alaska.

Chapter 11: The Impasse

9:00am Paxson, USA

Alexis

She awoke to the sound of someone ringing the buzzer on the hotel door; her first thoughts were *who is it and what do they want?* she hadn't even realised that she was alone in the bed.

She got up and walked to the door, she felt drained, and as she got to the door, she caught the waft of scent that she had always associated with pancakes and maple syrup, but she knew she had not ordered any so she assumed that they were for someone else.

As she opened the door, she was shocked to see a waiter at the door with a tray of freshly made pancakes with a small pitcher of maple syrup, there was also a plain white envelop in the corner of the tray, only one word was on the envelop and it was written in an elegant calligraphic script that said 'Alexis' it was written almost in the exact centre of the envelop. As she saw this, she suspected the worst, for the first time since she got out of bed; she noticed that she was the only person in the room. She thanked and tipped the waiter before frantically hurrying the tray over to the coffee table so she could open the letter.

As she read it, her heart felt like it was going to burst out of her chest, she was so filled with dread that she couldn't think straight, everything that mattered to her, everything she loved was in grave danger, and the one person who believed in her, was risking his life for her, she could not bear losing him again, she had already been through that once, and the pain of it had almost killed her, it had sent her into a depression so deep that she ended up hospitalised before she eventually crawled out of the deep dark hole she ended up in.

The past week had been like a dream to her, she hadn't imagined that she would ever be so happy again, and now it was gone, snatched away and quite possibly wouldn't be returning, she knew deep down that they would want to kill him for his choice. *Why did he have to go, I would rather die than allow them to harm him* she thought frantically.

The more she tried to rationalise what was happening the worse she felt, the more she tried to convince herself that he would be okay, the deeper her mood began to fall, when her dinner arrived three hours later, the fact that he had pre-arranged all her meals along with letters telling her how much he loved her, left her in tears. She had been desperately trying to hold herself together, but she knew she was fighting an uphill battle, and that she could not be truly happy again until he had returned to her and she knew he was safe.

Later that day, Paul decided to come around to check on her, he came with a woman whom she didn't know, but he introduced her quickly as Deborah, and the look of anger that spread across her face as the woman flinched when he said her name, made Alexis recoil in fright, even more so because almost instantly, Paul's tan coloured cowboy hat burst into flames. As this occurred she remembered Paul saying how his wife could set fires with her mind.

"I'm Debbie." She said as she glared at Paul, who was putting out the fire on what remained of his hat, he was laughing quietly as if he found it deeply amusing.

Debbie had dark blond hair and an oval shaped face, and Alexis knew that she was around the same height as herself, if not a little bit shorter, but her eyes had the odd intensity she had never really understood, it was a maternal look that she wasn't really used to seeing as she generally avoided her own family, and she looked very concerned when she realised that Alexis was not doing so well, Paul had obviously described her as a vibrant, lovely young woman, but the reality was that she was only like that when she was in Xander's company, without him she was a train wreck waiting to happen.

"He will be fine you'll see." She said trying to make Alexis feel better, it was not very successful and Alexis managed a weak smile in response.

"You can't know that." Alexis said her voice was filled with the agony she felt.

"You need to give Alexander more credit, he knows what he is doing, and he knows the Covenant better than almost anyone, he knows that it would be best to settle this peacefully." She smiled as she said it, and she reached out to put her hand on Alexis's shoulder to comfort her.

"I do believe in him, but it's easier said than done though, as everything I have heard about them says that they are cold blooded killers." She knew that her voice conveyed the terror that they had begun to evoke in her.

"They aren't as bad as you think, honestly, they have been our adversaries for millennia, but none one of us would describe them like that. They merely follow a different philosophy than we do." She sounded so convincing, so right, yet Alexis could not understand why of all people she would defend them.

"Easy to say when you're not the one they want dead." She snapped back, but before Debbie could respond she said "I'm sorry, that wasn't fair, and I know you're all doing your best, but I can't help but worry." Debbie smiled at this and she seemed to be debating whether to carry on the conversation or not.

However the choice was taken away when Anthony and Charlotte arrived, no one had told her much about Charlotte other than that she was very gifted, they failed to mention that she was breathtakingly beautiful, she had long light brown hair that was perfectly straight, accompanied by soft eyes and a friendly smile, her eyes carried the same violet hue as the rest of them, but she seemed so much mellower than the others. She smiled at Alexis when she saw her staring, but she did not speak for what seemed like an eternity, they were all staring at Alexis with almost the same sort of intensity that she herself had gazed with.

3:30pm Vienna, Austria

Xander

As he approached the all too familiar building, he knew that they would have already sensed his presence, even if their surveillance equipment had not already detected him, they would be waiting for him.

When he arrived at the entrance he was stopped by a mortal requesting his key card, but before he even had to decide how to handle this mortal, whether he would merely speed past him or even if he would have to harm the helpless mortal, the door opened and a tall figure stood at the door, his expression was menacing.

But he had expected this, Xavier would side with Luccia, and he would want Xander dead as well, but they would at least hear him out and let him have his chance to make his case before they make their judgement.

He knew that if it came to a vote, then he would have to hope that Morgan and Anna would vote on his side, if that occurred it would be a stalemate as he knew that Narcissia would not be back for quite a while.

"Alexander." He said abruptly, his voice displayed the loathing and animosity he obviously felt for Xander, and he opened his mouth slightly to display his fangs, he meant this as a threat, and to show Xander that if it were up to him, he would already be dead.

And as Xavier walked behind him, he could hear the giant of a man clicking his knuckles and tensing his muscles trying to intimidate him. Xander almost laughed in amusement, and at that moment he decided he would return the favour, as he felt time slow around him, his body sped up and in one fluid movement, in the barest fraction of a second, he was behind the other man, before he allowed himself to return to normal time.

Xavier spun round almost immediately, as Xander caught sight of his face he could tell instantly that he was struggling not to launch himself at Xander in one of his violent rages, and Xander knew that he was barely containing his anger. So he decided to smile mockingly, he knew that this would enrage Xavier but he didn't care, he wanted to give the overly confident Immortal a taste of what he would have to face if he got his wish.

But before Xavier's anger could get the better of him, Luccia arrived ahead of them and asked Xavier what was taking them so long, she would not even look at Xander, she acted as though he was not even there, and they led the way down into the depths of the passage that led to an elevator which would take them all to the council chamber, it had been built far below ground level so that it could double as a bomb shelter should anyone be foolish enough to attack.

But now it would be used to decide the fate of one of their own, something that he didn't think had ever happened in the twelve millennia history of the Covenant.

"So" She said bitterly, "you have *returned.*" Her face was masked once more; it meant that she knew that he had provoked her on purpose before, and that she would control herself far better this time so that he would not take advantage of that weakness again.

"I want you to give me your permission to make her one of us." he said sincerely, knowing that he had limited time, so he needed to get straight to the point.

"That cannot and *will not* happen." She glared at him as she said it; her voice was rigid in its tones.

"Then I will turn her anyway, and if I don't, then *others* will." He said others with such deliberate control that caught the attention of everyone in the room. And he continued "*You* are not the only ones interested in her future abilities." He put deliberate emphasis on how he said the word '*you*' so that he would sound as scornful as possible, and he knew he would be tempting the limits of her patience now, but he had no choice, he had to make them see sense, and he had to force them to understand that the repercussions of their actions will reverberate severely if they did not act very carefully.

"So not only have you turned your back on the people that love you, that have always accepted and protected you. But you have left our fold and joined that of our enemies." Her voice was full of venom now her voice said quite plainly that she thought he was a traitor; she appeared to be trying to make a case to justify his execution.

"I will warn you once and only once." Xander said, his voice was unusually low and ominous "Never speak to me like that again." they all stared at him now, as he had never before taken this approach to them. "You have two options, the first which I suggest is to allow me to turn her and give me your blessing, the second is to continue on the course you are on now."

"Neither option will allow you to decide my fate; I am beyond your judgements now. I just want to be left alone with Alexis." The sharp intake of breath from everyone present showed him that they could not believe he would say this. It was totally out of character for him, he had always been so passive when it came to dealing with them.

But now they knew that he was like a caged lion that had been unleashed and that they would have no choice but to take his wishes into consideration. He relaxed as he saw the expressions on their faces change to ones of silent acknowledgement.

"What do you have to say then?" he asked them impulsively, he was shocked that they had been so silent.

"We need time to talk about this between ourselves." A quiet feminine voice said, he turned to face Anna, and the expression on her face suggested to him that she was not an enemy.

He considered this, if she wasn't hostile, there was a good chance that Morgan would side with her which would put the council to a stalemate until Narcissia could get involved, and he already knew her vote. So he decided he would give them their time to deliberate.

As he left the chamber he knew that he would only be returning to the room one more time and then no longer would he return to the only home he had known in his Immortal life. This would be a big step for him, but there were no other alternatives, either they would allow him to change her or they wouldn't, and if they won't allow him to, then he would be leaving, and if they followed, then he would fight to protect her from them.

It didn't take long before Anna came to ask him to return, the look on her face was faintly hopeful, but he didn't have time to inquire, and as he followed her back into the room, he could sense that the balance of power had shifted, as he looked around the room,

Luccia looked livid and Xavier's face was deeply veined and it looked like they were both about to explode, contrary as he looked around at Anna and Morgan, they seemed placid and peaceful.

"Have you made your decision?" he asked, deciding to get to the point rather than let them waste time skirting the subject when he wanted to get back to Alexis as soon as he possibly could.

"We are at an impasse." Luccia said bitterly, she glared at Anna as she said it, as if she felt betrayed by her daughter's actions. And she continued "You will remain here until Narcissia returns."

As he glared back at her defiantly and pushed his chair back as he prepared to leave the chamber, but she raised her hand in a stop motion and said "If you leave here before she returns, we will consider both your life and the *mortal's* life null and void and we will hunt you both down."

"No deal." He replied to her bluntly, a look of surprise spread across her features, but before she had time to anything, Anna spoke up again "Alex, be reasonable, she won't be gone long and then you can return to your mortal lover again."

"Phone her and ask for her vote, I will not stay here as a captive." He said defiantly, even though he knew this would only enrage Xavier more.

"We cannot get hold of her; she left a message saying she would be out of reach for several weeks." Morgan said, his voice quiet and firm and he continued "And besides, we do not ask you to remain here as a prisoner, but we do ask that you remain in this facility, you need to be here for the verdict."

"I already know how she will vote, I saw her when I arrived." And the look of shock and anger that Luccia displayed was surprising, he could almost imagine what she was thinking. She would be wondering why her sister didn't tell her about it, and wondering what else was going on that she didn't know about.

"But I will stay here, but you have seven days before I will be leaving, whether you give me your approval or not. Make your decision by then." He said this with such control and power that they knew this would be the most they could get out of him and he continued "and I will not remain here as a prisoner, I will resume occupation of my old quarters." It was a statement and not a request, everyone present knew that.

Anna accompanied him to his quarters even though he had tried to refuse her; she obviously wanted to talk to him privately so he allowed it. After all he suspected that she was the reason that Morgan voted in favour of his request.

"What is going on Alexander? You have changed so much, you don't seem the same person anymore." Her voice conveyed her concern and wonder.

"I found someone I love, and for once in my life I am not going to stand aside. I am going to chase the dream." She recoiled slightly and he realised he had said it more forcefully than he had intended.

"Sorry." He said, "I didn't mean to be so aggressive."

She smiled again realising that he was only being so defensive because of the recent attacks on him and the one he loved.

They began talking and he explained how they had met and started telling her about Alexis and how he felt about her and by the end of it, he was convinced that she would not harm her, and that just left Xavier and Luccia to convince. After they had finished talking, she quietly departed and left him alone so that he could think about everything that had happened, he knew that he was well on the way to securing both of their freedoms, as long as nothing happened to upset the balance, he just wished that Narcissia would return, but he knew she wouldn't, she would be well on her way to Alaska by now.

9:30pm Paxson, USA

Alexis

As she walked along the frozen street with Charlotte she wondered what Xander was doing now, she hoped he was okay. But she knew she wouldn't be able to contact him until things had settled down. Even though she wanted to, she was beginning to walk slower. And Charlotte prompted her to keep up, as it was getting cold and Charlotte didn't want her to get ill, they had agreed to look after her and they had been doing everything they could in order to keep her occupied and safe.

They had walked for miles under the clear skies this evening, it was warm by Alaskan standards and she had wanted to take a walk to get some air, Charlotte had gone with her to keep her company. Even though Charlotte had been with her, she sensed that Alexis wanted space and just someone to be there with her, without talking huge amounts, and this was something Charlotte did well, she talked when Alexis wanted to, and she was quiet and attentive when she didn't. She was the perfect companion and friend, they had learnt a lot about each other in the brief conversations they'd had on their walk.

But it was getting late and Charlotte was jokingly threatening to pick her up and carry her home if she didn't keep up with her. They both laughed as she said this, even though they knew she was being honest.

Though they had kept her as occupied as they could, she still missed him terribly, she could feel her mood dropping bit by bit, and as hard as they tried they couldn't seem to lift her out of the depression she felt like she was falling into.

He was her sun, and she felt like there was a dark cloud in the way, she felt like there were no rays of sunshine without him and it hurt her more than she could explain to them.

How can I be alive, when I'm dead inside without him? As she thought this, she knew it wasn't fair to burden on her new companions and protectors.

That was why she had decided she needed air, Debbie had realised something was wrong, and she wanted to help her, and even though the woman was so loving and kind, there was nothing she could do, and Alexis didn't want to risk upsetting her or bringing her down too.

When they arrived back at the hotel, Paul and Anthony were in quiet conversation, they looked worried but they went quiet as soon as she walked in the room. She sensed that it was something bad, but half of her couldn't bear to ask in case it was bad news about Xander, but eventually the other half won over and she asked "What's wrong? What have I missed?"

"You haven't missed anything important, nothing you need to worry about anyway, and Alexander is fine." Debbie walked over and glared at Paul and Anthony as if they should have stopped their conversation sooner and not worried her needlessly.

"Tell me." She said quietly and gave Paul a look so that he would know she really wanted to know and that she wouldn't stop asking until he gave in.

Paul looked at Debbie and shrugged and then said the news she really wouldn't have wanted to know if she'd had the sense to not ask.

"We've had a report that Narcissia is on a flight to Alaska." As he said it everyone in the room looked at her with quiet determination. They would fight to protect her.

Chapter 12: Alone In a Crowd
10:50pm Paxson, USA

Alexis

As the Illuminati prepared themselves, both mentally and physically for the battle that they all knew was about to happen, Alexis could feel it in the very air, that they were all starting to get a buzz from the high levels of adrenaline pumping through their systems now, and even though she couldn't quite understand it, she knew that she had felt a similar sensation during some of the most extreme manic episodes she had endured, the feeling of elation and excitement, it seemed strangely familiar to see how they were all acting now.

She supposed it was one of the reasons that mortals could get addicted to adrenaline rush's by doing extreme sports on a regular basis or even risking their lives in whatever job they had.

Even Charlotte who was generally a quiet and introspective figure was starting to look and act as elated as the rest, it was like being surrounded by drug addicts except that they were all in total control of their senses and bodies, they were wired and she could feel it. They were talking in a speech so rapid she couldn't understand a word they said, but she could read the expressions on their faces better than she could understand what they were saying.

Charlotte decided to translate for them, as the rest were in deep discussion trying to plan how they would handle and respond to the Covenant's scouting party.

"We are going under the assumption that they are being devious and searching for you anyway or that they have rejected Alexander's proposal, either option we must be on guard. So far we have only detected one of them, but the others will track her to us, so we must be ready to leave as soon as we have dealt with her." She was talking very fast, and she wasn't appearing to take breaths as she spoke, but she still seemed deeply troubled, almost as if there was another option that she didn't want to say aloud.

So Alexis decided she would ask the unanswered question herself and hope they would be honest with her. "What does this mean for Xander?" she tried her best to keep her panic out of her voice, but she failed.

No one answered her question and she feared what that could mean.

11:50pm Ketchikan, USA

Narcissia

The instructions Alexander had given her were very specific about where to go and who to ask for, so this was very straight forward in terms of travelling. She knew she was on the last leg of the journey now, and that it wouldn't be long before she landed.

The closer she got the more immortal's she could feel. It was beginning to make her feel faintly uneasy, mainly because Alexander had not been willing to risk contacting the Illuminati to warn them that she would be arriving, as it could have been tracked as he was already in Vienna when they had met. So she would be flying into a nest of probably aggressive Immortals that expected her to be there to assassinate Alexander's mortal lover.

She was not looking forward to stepping off this plane, as she knew she would have to talk fast or risk a confrontation. Not that she felt that any of them could defeat her, her gifts were surprisingly effective during combat, she could invoke her opponents to remember memories which would distract them, either memories that they fear, or even using memories which they were deeply fond of. Either could be disastrous during a fight and not many had the mental control to negate it, or even to stop her breaking in, in the first place.

But she would rather not have to resort to that and she wasn't even sure if she could. She could feel them even closer now; she was only minutes away from landing. So she prepared herself just in case. She jabbed the Epi-Pen into the crease on the inside of her elbow, this was one of the softer parts of her stone like body. For she was ancient and strong, the virus had made her body a veritable fortress that nothing but the sharpest blades could pierce, she and the other members of the Covenant had to make use of custom injectors made out of titanium so that they could inject themselves easier, but they also used glass vials of epinephrine, this worked just as well, but they all considered it somewhat less civilised so they rarely used it unless it was all they had, or unless they were already in combat and couldn't risk making themselves vulnerable.

As she felt the spread of adrenaline spread throughout her body, she felt her muscles come alive, and she felt her mental abilities reach out, crossing the distance between them, she could finally sense exactly who would be waiting for her when she stepped out of the plane. And she hoped that things would go well. *This should go well* she thought *if not, then there will be one hell of a war.*

Her plane landed a few minutes later, and as she disembarked she could sense waves of hostility and aggression from the direction of the group standing beside the landing strip. She counted three immortals there now, and another one in the nearby town.

She suspected they had left another one there to protect the mortal, and was pleased, that suggested that they were thinking rationally and she hoped that they would listen to reason.

"Wait!" she called out before they had time to speak."Alexander sent me here; ask him if you don't believe me."

"We have not heard from him since he left." The taller bearded man said, she knew him, but she had not seen him for a long time. She and Paul had never really got along, she knew the reason for this though, she had always appeared to be hidden within her sister's shadow, and even she knew that not all of Luccia's actions were noble.

"Well I have seen him, he sent me here to assist you." As she said it they all stared at her suspiciously. No one moved for several moments and she continued "You have two options; either you accept that I am here to help you, or you can fight me right now. There is no other option." She deliberately made her voice steely so that they would understand that she was deadly serious.

"Fine, get Anthony to use his ability on me, and ask me why I am here." She said bitterly as they didn't seem to like either of her suggestions

Paul stared at Anthony meaningfully and then Anthony stepped forward and said "*Tell me why you are really here.*" His voice was intense, so unlike his usual voice and he was obviously confident that this would invoke a powerful susceptibility in anyone he used it on, and they would obey him. he had demonstrated it on even the members of the Covenant during the Kane Wars, so she was sure that they would believe her when she answered him truthfully telling them how she had met Alexander at the airport, and had delved into his mind, how a piece of it still remained in her mind, and they honestly believed her when she told them that she would give her life to protect Alexis.

05:00am Vienna, Austria

Xander

It felt like time was going even slower than normal to him, he was bored out of his mind, but he didn't dare to risk contacting Alexis in case he inadvertently led them to her, he didn't trust Luccia enough that she wouldn't try and eliminate her out of spite.

So he decided to take this time to relax and attain a state of deep meditation, it was his bodies form of sleep, even though he was still conscious he could direct his mind in any way he wanted during this time.

It was like a controlled dream state, anything he wanted to do was possible for him during this state, and all he wanted was to be with Alexis.

So it didn't surprise him that his dream consisted of him walking hand in hand along the frozen wastes of the North Pole, Alaska. He looked up and above them was the Aurora Borealis. To him this was probably one of the most romantic places on earth, of all the sights he had ever witnessed this was the most beautiful act of nature he had ever seen, he had trekked here every year near the equinoxes so that he could see this spectacle, but not once had he ever had a companion with him to enjoy the sights.

As they walked, talked and enjoyed the colourful array of lights, he marvelled at the colour of her deep blue eyes, they were as blue as his and twice as beautiful, her skin was crystal clear and it was as pale as polished marble, she looked perfect, her deep chocolate brown hair contrasted against the paleness of her skin perfectly, and her eyes held within them the most loving quality he had ever seen. He didn't think about the fact that she might not survive to become an immortal, which would have distracted him from his dream.

As he marvelled at how lifelike she appeared in the dream, he kissed her passionately and powerfully, far more primal and unrestrained than he had ever managed before, as he always had to hold back so that he wouldn't harm her, but in his dream state she was a durable as he was.

He managed to stay in this state of deep meditation for far longer than he would usually sustain it, and it wasn't until Anna came to keep him company that he realised just how long he had been 'sleeping' but this didn't stir him, even though he was awake again now, he still kept the dream going in his head, he longed for Alexis's touch so badly it caused him pain, he missed her terribly and he knew he would be causing her agony because he couldn't contact her.

Anna did her best to comfort him, but she didn't really know what it was like, Luccia had given her permission to turn Morgan when she had fallen for him, so she didn't have to make the same choice. But even so, she appeared to feel deep compassion for him even at the risk of displeasing her mother, and he was thankful to her for it, but he just wished she would leave him alone so he could resume his dream. At least during that he felt close to Alexis again even if it wasn't real.

He wanted to know what she was feeling and doing, he wanted to know so desperately that he couldn't think straight, but he had no way of contacting her, he had left his cell phone in a secure safe at one of his properties in Paris. He didn't want to risk them being able to track her using it. And he couldn't use one of the phones at the headquarters as they were all monitored, and would be monitored even more closely while he was there than usual now.

Anna didn't stay long, she could tell that he needed to be alone, that the only person whose company he craved was the one person he couldn't be near, and the effort it was taking him to remain in the complex was taking its toll on him. And he knew he wouldn't be able to wait long. *They need to make up their minds faster!* He thought in frustration.

He wondered what she was doing right now, and he hoped that she was doing better than him, the effort of him being away from her was eating him up inside.

12:02am Paxson, USA
Paul

As he led the group back towards the hotel, he considered all the things they could learn from having one of the oldest living people on the planet with them. He could only hope that she would tell them all her story, so that they would know what really happened all those years ago to cause the existence of such powerful beings. He had tried desperately to track down what happened but he had no luck. The only people alive who knew were on the council of the Covenant, even Alexander had not known and he had been on the council for over two millennia.

In all that time he had tried to organise a sharing of knowledge several times over the last few thousand years, but Luccia had always turned him down, and he hoped that the only thing her twin shared with her, was her genetics.

They did not however go to the suite Alexis was in when they arrived at the hotel, he wanted to have a talk with Narcissia in private first, without being overheard, he asked Anthony and Debbie to go and check on Alexis and Charlotte and make sure they were okay.

Now that they were alone, he sat down at the table and relaxed a bit, and gestured for her to do the same. He could tell by the way she sat that she was not comfortable, she knew he was going to ask her things that she was forbidden to talk about.

"What is it you want from me Paul?" she asked as she stared into his deep violet eyes

"What I have always wanted, I want to know the truth." He said this politely and they both knew what he was referring to.

"You'll find out very soon. Try to be patient my *young* friend." She said emphasising heavily when she said young, he knew that she was being patronising but he couldn't think of a way to reply without being rude, and that was not something he wanted to do.

"Are you going to tell Alexis your story?" he asked inquisitively, suspecting that was what she had meant before.

"That is a possibility yes, if she wants to know I'm not sure if I could refuse her." before he could reply to her last statement, she said "Anyway, take me to her now please."

As they both got up out of their chairs, and left his hotel room, they could both tell quickly as he led her to Alexis' suite that she was watching the news. The dreary monotone voice coming from the television was what he had always associated with news programs. He caught the last part of the news and it interested him mildly but not enough for him to want to ask what it had been about. *"... Young thrill seeker found dead ... suffered a fatal heart attack while mountain climbing."*

Of course this only interested him a little bit; he had far greater concerns now and he knew that he would have to focus.

As they entered the hotel suite, everyone looked around to face them, and then they heard the crack of broken porcelain. Everyone changed the focus of their stare from Narcissia onto

Alexis now, who was still staring at Narcissia with a shocked look, her broken cup on the floor below her hands.

"I know you." She said, her voice conveyed the feeling of terror she felt. "You were in one of my dreams, along with your twin sister."

Everyone in the room gasped as she said this, they had not told her that Narcissia was a twin, and they all began to stare at her in amazement and wonder what other latent abilities this remarkable young woman had.

"I know." Narcissia said and continued "Alexander explained it to me, and he told me what you saw in your dream, and I know that it is my future." Again everyone stared at Narcissia in shock because of how much fear and hesitation she had shown in her voice.

12:15am Paxson, USA

Alexis

The only thing worse than being alone she thought *is being alone in a crowd*; She knew she wasn't being entirely fair and she enjoyed their company. But she missed him terribly; it felt like someone had cut out her heart and left it just out of her reach.

And the news had not helped her feel better. There had been an increase in the number of deaths of adrenaline junkies in Asia and that unsettled her, because as soon as they mentioned 'Adrenaline' she immediately thought of Xander.

She just wished she had heard something from him, anything would have been better than nothing. But she knew that he wouldn't risk it. Since he had left, she had received three notes a day from him; he had left them with the hotel staff and asked them to deliver them with her food each day. She had been surprised at first, but his poems and letters telling her how much he loved her had begun to make her miss him even more than she already did. Something she didn't think was possible.

And now this strangely pale woman from her dreams was now a reality, Xander had already warned her about the possibility that her dream was real, but seeing a dream become reality was deeply disturbing to her. And once again the one person whom she wanted comfort from was nowhere near her.

This sent a wave of sadness through her that she felt would eventually tear her in two, she had felt depressions like this before, and they had eventually stolen her life for months at a time, and had almost stolen her life completely as her mood delved so low that she contemplated ending things, luckily she had eventually been saved by her health care team and she got better gradually.

But now the only thing which could bring her out of the depths she felt like she was sinking into was the one whose absence was causing her fall.

During this time Charlotte and Debbie were a godsend to her, Charlotte was so quiet and caring, and she would try to comfort her without being obtrusive or bringing up memories that she didn't want to think of.

Debbie had told her the previous day, that the only way to stop yourself from falling into a depression, was to deny it battle. At first Alexis didn't understand what she had meant. But now she was beginning to feel like she did. It meant that if you try to fight depression, it would feed off of that fight and eventually you would succumb to it. But if you denied it battle, and simply moved on trying your best to get on with life, you would stand a much better chance of surviving it than if you tried to fight it repeatedly and lost. No one beats a depression; you can't beat something that has no physical body, you can only survive it or move past it.

She knew that if they were not there with her so much, showing her that she was not out of her mind, that she would have began to suspect that none of it was real, and even now there were lingering doubts in the depths of her subconscious, almost as if they were whispering to her, telling her that none of it was real, that Xander wasn't coming back to her.

As she sat there overwhelmed by her own thoughts, she fought back the tears and stared at the eerily pale woman in front of her, unlike the others here, she had a complexion of polished marble rather than just being very pale. And she wanted to know why Xander had to leave her; she just couldn't understand why it would be so important for him to leave, why these strange immortals wanted her dead.

"Why do you all think I am so important?" she asked, it was a general question aimed at everyone there. The reply was one that she had least expected.

"You're important to us, because we think you are gifted." It was Paul speaking again "And you're important to Alexander because he is in love with you." He didn't allow time for anyone else to speak and he continued on talking regardless of anyone else in the room "and as for The Covenant, I believe that they are interested in you for two reasons. The first is that you're gifted and the second is that they probably think you have subverted one of their own."

"But I haven't done anything." Alexis said frantically, she couldn't believe that she had a death sentence on her head for no reason. She looked at Narcissia for answers and asked the question most on her mind.

"Why are the Covenant so afraid of anyone with abilities?" she had expected the question to surprise Narcissia but she showed little surprise at all, almost as if she had been expecting it.

"It will take a long time to explain, but first I will explain why she thinks you are so much of a threat."

As Narcissia recounted the vision that Luccia had shared with the Covenant, it made Alexis suspect that Luccia was not so much against people with extrasensory abilities, but rather that she didn't like anyone being able to match her.

She voiced this question to Narcissia and she smiled and replied "Luccia is fond of power, but she has her reasons, her visions are not all encompassing, she can only see certain futures and events, and a long time ago, she foretold a prophecy that told of a great war between mortals and a large group of immortals, who were gifted with super human powers, and that they would shake the world as they clashed in a battle for supremacy."

She continued trying to explain it properly. "If I am to tell you my story, it will take a long time, and please do not interrupt me; I will answer all of your questions afterwards. But it is important for me to keep focused as there are a lot of obscure details, and I don't want to miss anything out."

And then she began her story, the story that would shake the foundations of everything Alexis had ever thought she had known, and might also explain to her why she had always been different.

Chapter 13: Predictable

7:00pm Vienna, Austria

Xander

He was getting more and more restless stuck in his room, even though it was fairly large and had every amenity he could have asked for, so he eventually decided he would have a wander around the complex, just to make sure nothing had changed since he had lived there last, but also in part just to annoy Xavier, as he knew that he would not be able to rest knowing that Xander was roaming around unattended.

And the thought of him irritating Xavier made it extremely enjoyable, of course he knew that Xavier would be following his every move using the Covenants surveillance system, but that didn't bother him really, he had expected it and they had always done it, granted they hadn't usually had such a fixation on him, but they monitored all passages and entrances to make sure that no intruders could enter or leave without attracting notice, not that the immortals within the building wouldn't sense the intrusion without the surveillance system, but they all knew that sensing someone wasn't the same as seeing them.

As he walked along the corridors the idea hit him, a way he could occupy himself whilst irritating Xavier even more, he decided that he was going to break into the Covenants secure computer network and leave a load of annoying errors and loops just to irritate the hell out of Xavier, he knew that they would eventually fix it just by using a backup of all the data, but it would cause them substantial trouble before they would take that step.

When he returned back to his room, with the laptop he had 'borrowed' from Xavier's room. *Let him fret on that.* He thought as he laughed, knowing that Xavier had probably watched him do it, granted he would have had to slow the video footage down for him to be able to see him on it, and even then he would not see Xander for very long

It didn't take him as long as he had expected to break into the network, and as he began to reroute all the CCTV camera's so that they were all scrambled and had no order system anymore, he came across Xavier and Luccia in one of her private chambers, which he knew would be deep underground, because the vast majority of her living quarters were due to her irrational fear of attack.

They appeared to be having a heated debate, and he could see that they were both aggravated but this didn't bother him, he would enjoy it more if they were unhappy, neither of them would realise that he was spying on them, the cameras in their private rooms had been secured so that they were not active. Well that was what they believed anyway, but thanks to his efforts, that was no longer strictly true.

He turned on the microphone so that he could listen in on their conversation and see what was causing them to become so worked up and aggravated.

"... is in Alaska." Xavier had been saying to Luccia, and as he listened in, he felt a pang of fear in his stomach, he had been expecting this, but he hadn't expected them to find Alexis so soon.

"But why hasn't she contacted us to let us know what is going on?" Luccia had said, and he knew then that they hadn't found Alexis, relief spread through him, but then he remembered that they must have been tracking Narcissia, a wave of panic spread through him once again, as he knew that if they did manage to track Narcissia then they would soon learn that they would find Alexis if they found Narcissia.

"I think we should send someone there, we can bribe the mortals easily and find out everything that is going on." It was Xavier again

He was beginning to get worried now; he knew that he couldn't stay here, that he had to flee so he could warn the others so that they would be on guard again. *This is bad* he thought. But as the panic spread through his body and he failed to notice that the camera in his own room was still active.

It didn't take him ten seconds before he had gathered everything he needed to take with him, he didn't notice the small unobtrusive tracking device that had been planted on the inside of his jackets seam.

By the time he realised that it had all been staged, it would be too late. He was already on his way to the airport, and had he stayed there watching just a few minutes longer, then he might have realised what they had planned.

He would have seen the smile spread across Luccia's usually composed face knowing that she had achieved her aim; they had provoked Alexander into leaving of his own accord, and thereby forfeiting both his own life and the life of that dangerous mortal.

8:05pm Vienna, Austria

Luccia

She had known that eventually he would try and break into the surveillance equipment; he was so predictable to her, even without her ability to see the lines of the future that would intersect with her. She had never been able to predict the future of random events, her ability didn't work quite like that, but it did allow her to see future events which would involve her, and it had allowed her to foresee many events head of time and plan alternative futures. However she had often found that her own actions caused the futures she had seen as often as they had averted them, this wasn't something she could control.

And when they had realised that Alexander had broken into Xavier's room, they knew it wouldn't take him long, and she knew almost exactly when he would stumble across the camera's which were located in her private suite, and they had planned out their conversation ahead of time, they knew that it was the only way they could make him forfeit his own safety.

Perfect timing had of course helped in this matter as Xavier's investigators had informed him of the location they suspected that Narcissia had flown to judging from her credit card receipts, and they had decided that this would be a very enticing morsel of bait that might just send Alexander on a new course that would get both himself and his new companion terminated.

"He has boarded a plane to Paris." A voice called out to her, snapping her out of her own thoughts, Luccia knew that she should have been expecting him.

"Ah, so he thinks that if he takes a roundabout route then we would be fooled?" she knew that she would have to play along with this game that Alexander had started, and she didn't plan on playing fairly.

"So it seems."

"And is the tracking device working?" she already knew the answer but she felt like verifying it anyway.

"Yes, we can track him anywhere on the planet using the global positioning satellite network."

"Good." She knew that she sounded faintly smug now, but she couldn't resist it knowing that they had played their hand perfectly.

"Right." She said firmly and then after a short pause continued "Alert everyone, including the Acolytes, and have everyone gather in the briefing room." She knew that he would have already planned on doing exactly that as soon as he left her room, but all the same she figured that it would be best to ask him anyway on the odd chance that he was not as predictable to her as she hoped.

As he turned and walked out of the room, she caught a reflection of his face as he walked away, his grin said a lot to her, he was enjoying this far more than he should, he was seriously underestimating Alexander, she knew that he would, he really didn't see him as a threat.

Of course Xavier had the edge in some respects; he was far more ancient, the virus in his system had built up and strengthened his body incomparably more than Alexander's had received. No one alive really understood what it did anymore, but she knew that it was some sort of retrovirus, initially it had infected the host body and then altered their bodies DNA, strengthening it and replicating itself, as the virus built up in the host body, that body was then strengthened by the virus, but the more the virus spread, the more adrenaline it required, and after a few weeks, the original body could no longer produce enough adrenaline to sustain it, and then it had mutated the host body so that it could feed on other beings for its adrenaline supply.

It didn't take long for the group to assemble in the large square room that they used for briefings and conferences, which didn't happen very often, but everyone knew her well enough to know that when they were called to the conference room, then everyone had better pay attention or face her wrath.

Once everyone was there, they numbered a total of nine immortals, although only four of them were the ancient council members, the other five were loyal mortals who had served them well during their mortal lives and were rewarded with the gift of immortality. They knew that their chance of survival was not high, for none of the council would lie to them about the risks in becoming one of them, but they had all accepted the risk and most surprisingly, they had unlike the countless other mortals survived the ordeal. Only one of them William, was over five hundred years old and yet still looked as if he was the twenty six year old mortal he was when she had given him the gift of immortality, and even with this, they were all incredibly weak compared to the council members.

There was a rough way to calculate the strength of an immortal based on how old they were, and it basically equalled to a strength increase of a factor of ten on the initial mutation and then by another factor of five for every century after that. She knew of course that even all five Acolytes at once could not survive combat against Alexander, but they might be able to occupy him long enough that the ancient council could handle him without risking injury. And even that was not as good odds as Luccia would have liked. Though she was not cowardly by nature, she did not like taking chances that were not required, and anyway she already had a plan that would weaken Alexander's resolve.

"Right, as you all know. Alexander has forfeited his life and that of his mortal plaything; we had offered him sanctuary until Narcissia returned so we could arrive at a verdict." She didn't give anyone time to say anything else before she continued, but she noticed that her words had made the eyes of several of the young ones light up, they knew that this would be a time for them to show their worth.

"We know roughly where he has gone, and by the time we arrive in Alaska we will know exactly where he is. However this will be very difficult, you all know how powerful Alexander is, and it will take a co-ordinated effort of everyone present in order for us to defeat him without taking heavy losses." She looked at them severely, so that they understood that by heavy losses, she had meant them.

"His one weakness right now, is his mortal, if we can capture or eliminate her, and then he will be easier for us to deal with."

An all too familiar voice called out before she had the chance to explain the plan of action she and Xavier had decided upon, and it surprised her in how bold her daughter was being to interrupt her while she was talking. "I won't be going and neither will Morgan!"

She had expected this, and had already planned accordingly, but it still stung her as if her daughter had struck her. "I knew that already, now be silent or leave, so I can finish."

"Can I not say my piece?" she asked curiously, the startled younger members in the room were looking back and forth between the two of them, almost as if they expected Luccia to react violently at any moment. But none of them understood her well enough to realise that this was not very likely.

"No, now please leave as you have shown you cannot remain silent."

"I will not, you will hear me out first." Several of the youngest Acolytes gasped at this, and Xavier clenched his fingers, crushing the wood of the table that he had been clasping onto.

"Oh go ahead then, but be quick and then leave." They all knew that this would play out a certain way; there were limits to how much insolence she would take from anyone, even her own daughter.

"I know that you tricked him into leaving, and I know that you never planned to follow through on the agreement that I tried to orchestrate. And I want to know why you are acting like this when you could have handled it with far more subtlety and wisdom."

Luccia recoiled at the tone of Anna's voice and she felt her anger beginning to spill over, she could feel violence building up and she could even feel her body chemistry start overloading and her thirst build up, the unquenchable hunger, and then she felt her venomous fangs extend into position.

. It took all of her self control not to launch herself at Anna at that moment, and she knew that everyone in the room would see how close she was to a rage based purely on her eyes.

Because when an immortal is angered then their eyes are like a weather vane to their mood, and even the whites are consumed by the rage and everyone in the room was staring at her cautiously, because they were consumed by the dark blue shade now.

"Get OUT!"

Even though Anna did not move at all, Morgan beside her rose and grasped Anna just under her shoulder and gently pulled her up, she succumbed and they made their way towards the door to leave.

She had never really considered Morgan a man of action, as he was always in Anna's shade, but in that moment, she caught a glimpse of the man he truly was. He would risk much for his wife, but he would not allow her to be harmed, even if that caused her to be angry with him.

As they left, Luccia glared around the room and said "I trust no one else has any comments they want to get off their chests." She knew that no one would dare to speak up now even if they wanted to, her eyes were still deep blue and her penetrating stare showed everyone present that her anger was still barely under control.

"As I was saying, we need to focus on the mortal girl, this should make it a lot harder for Alexander to function; if we plan our attack accordingly we can defeat him without losses." She left the possibility of defeat unsaid.

"I have arranged for our weapons when we arrive in Alaska, we will be using the usual array of edged weapons. Even though these will not be overly effective against him, if we can severe some of his arteries it will weaken him enough that we can dismember and burn his desecrated body."

"Do not allow him to single you out, or he will tear you apart." Xavier said sternly.

"Remember always, Alexander is one of the most deadly fighters to have ever lived, the only one of us that can come even close to equalling him is Xavier, and you will be practicing on him in order to get used to fighting an opponent that can outfight you on every level." Luccia said calmly.

As she watched Xavier instruct them, and watched them try to assault Xavier from every angle at once, she marvelled at the skill he displayed as he jumped, spun and kicked out at his opponents, even to her he was a blur of movement, and she knew that to the Acolytes he was appearing to disappear and then reappear at different locations. She had only ever seen his ability trumped by Alexander, who could move so fast that it was like he could stop time.

It took the better part of an hour of constant fighting until they could eventually take Xavier down, and she knew that the main reason for that was that he was getting tired. Even for an immortal, fatigue does set in if you exert yourself for too long. However they could sustain themselves longer by biting into their opponents and feeding off of their adrenaline. This was what would give them the edge against Alexander, if they could get their teeth into him, the venom in such high doses would cause him to burn through his energy reserves.

And she knew that if that happened then even a small use of his powers would soon dry up what little adrenaline he would have left.

As they left the room one by one and went to gather their bags before they departed, she stopped Xavier so that she could talk with him privately. They both knew what she would have to say. It was very likely that none of the Acolytes would survive the encounter, but they had to accept the losses. Anna and Morgan sitting out of the fight was a big hit to them and she knew that he would try to talk her into persuading them into coming.

"No my savir, they will not come. It will just be us." She knew that using their ancient word for 'love' would soften him somewhat, and they only ever used their ancient language when they were alone, even Anna and Morgan did not know of it.

Then she remembered her last vision, of Xavier lying dead in the snow and she suspected for the first time that the vision might be coming true, but she held her tongue.

9:50pm Paris, France

Xander

He knew he was in a race against time and that he really needed to fly back to America as fast as he possibly could, but he also knew that he needed to contact Alexis and warn them that the Covenant knew their location. This would give the Illuminati time to prepare and they already had the upper hand because Luccia did not know about their involvement and they would be expecting to be going into combat with a lone immortal and a supposedly harmless mortal.

This gave him little comfort as he knew that Alexis would still be at great risk, as would he. But he could not allow the Illuminati to fight this battle without his aid or it would cost them heavily in blood.

As he arrived at his apartment which was located in the centre of Paris, right next to the Seine River, he rented this under one of his aliases and used it occasionally when he needed time alone to think, none of his associates were aware of it. Well he hoped they weren't aware of it. He immediately went to the safe deposit box located behind the bathroom mirror and grabbed the mobile phone he had stashed in there on his last visit.

Within seconds he was on the phone to Alexis, he knew that the time difference would make little difference as it would only be the early afternoon for Alexis and her newfound companions. The phone rang and time seemed to hang forever as he waited for her to answer the call, he didn't have to wait long and Alexis sounded almost as frantic as he did when he heard her voice, it made him yearn for her all the more.

"What happened? How did it go? I've missed you so much. Where are you?" she didn't give him the chance to answer her questions or even allow him to say a word.

"No time for that, *they know*." The effort he put into saying it calmly was very difficult and he knew that she would realise the severity of the matter, and her reply did not surprise him.

"WHAT??" the sound of panic in her voice and the fact that she was barely controlling her breathing was apparent to him.

"They found out earlier today, they tracked Narcissia, I'm on my way, and I fly out in a few hours time. I will be arriving early tomorrow morning."

As he left the apartment, he ran to his car and begun the drive back to the airport, he paid little attention to road safety and had to swerve in and out of traffic frantically, the whole time he was still on the phone to Alexis.

He could hear Alexis's rapid breaths on the other end of the line, as well as the faint sound of her voice whilst she informed everyone there what he had told her, but he also wanted to give her time for the information to sink in, before he said anything more.

"Are you still there?" she asked

"Yes my love I am." His voice trying to maintain a sense of calm that he hoped would sooth her.

"Paul wants to know how long we have." She asked him in a harried voice.

"My best guess would be 24 hours at most."

"Really? How did they find out so soon? Can we not get away before they arrive?"

"No, that would be bad, we need to head them off before they realise that Paul and his family are aligned with us."

"I don't understand. You said they know."

"They know very little, but I had to leave before they had time to learn more." He continued without taking a breath. "When I left it would have made them stop trying to find out more and they wouldn't dig further, they would just assume they were right."

"So they don't know about the Illuminati?"

"No, I am hoping they don't know that, it will hopefully give us the edge that will force them into finding a peaceful solution. If not, then the involvement of the Illuminati will at least give us a fighting chance."

"Paul wants to talk to you, can I put him on?" he could tell by the sound of her voice that she didn't want to hand over the phone, so he was determined to speak to her again afterwards.

"Yes but I want to talk to you again before I board the plane."

"Hello old friend." the voice was strangely familiar and yet friendly

"Evening." He said to Paul promptly.

"Can you explain the situation and give me as many details as possible please? I need to prepare my family."

As he explained everything he knew, what he had already told Alexis and then he went into detail about how he had got bored and hacked his way into the security network and overheard the conversation between Luccia and Xavier. Paul remained silent while he briefed him.

"How many will we be facing?"

"There were nine of them while I was there, but that would be counting their Acolytes." He then explained that the Acolytes were all relatively new to life and were created in response to the Illuminati; however none of them were particularly gifted as far as immortals go.

"How much of a threat are they?"

"I could handle all five Acolytes at once without much difficulty. However the real danger would be the council. They are truly ancient."

"I know, but we have *gifts* to our advantage"

"Indeed" he knew that Paul was including him in his assessment and for the first time he really considered what it would mean to fight alongside the Illuminati. Technically they were his intellectual and psychic equals, they were not like the Covenant and didn't react so negatively and violently upon gifted immortals.

"I'll put Alexis back on, fly safely my friend."

"Hello?" she said frantically, almost as if she were worried that he would not be there.

"I love you; I cannot wait to hold you in my arms again. I have missed you so much."

"I've missed you too; I've been so down since you left, I've been so worried like you wouldn't believe." He could hear the pain emanating from her voice as she said it, and it sent a wave of guilt through him.

"Trust me. I understand, and I feel exactly the same."

"Right sorry my angel, but I'm going to have to go, I'm arriving at the airport now and I will need to go and check in." But before she could say anymore he wanted to tell her exactly what was on his mind

"I will be with you soon, take care and know that I love you."

"I love you too."

And then he ended the call, he knew that if he didn't end the call then, he probably never would, and that would have attracted unwanted attention, when he needed to be as fast as possible so that he could get onto the next plane to America he could.

He had to fly to New York first, but he knew that was something that couldn't be avoided, he needed to get to the United States mainland first and then he could head for Alaska once he arrived.

Chapter 14: Narcissia's Story Part One

9:37pm Paxson, USA

Narcissia

I was born around the year 10'200BC; I can't give you an exact date anymore as we used a totally different calendar system back then, but by our Calendar I was born in the year 3507SA. Our civilization had thrived for over three millennia when I was born, and my sister and I were the first born children of our family, who were one of the Noble ruling families in the caste system which consisted of four different castes, a rough translation of them would be Noble, Scientist, Warrior and Worker.

When we were born, we were praised highly as twins were seen as a good omen, and we were named after the two most famous twins in our empires history. The two twin sisters Narca and Lucca, whom had founded two of our oldest settlements.

However when we were sixteen a pandemic began ravaging every population centre on the planet, it spread like wildfire and affected not only our own Empire, which was known as the Az'nor but also our rivals, the Indusi. The plague had a 100% mortality rate, and while it took years before it finally killed whomever it had infected, as it completely decimated their immune system until the point where even a common cold was fatal. Our civilization which was at a similar rate technically to the United States, a little more advances in some respects, and very far behind them in others, struggled to cope with the onslaught of the virus, no matter what we tried, however strict our quarantine measures were, the plague spread further, we soon discovered that it was an airborne virus that could survive in the open air for weeks without a host.

Eventually those that were not infected sealed themselves off from the outside world, and we tried frantically to find a cure, but our Scientist caste had been hit very hard by the virus, in their attempts to cure the sick they had inadvertently exposed themselves to the virus.

One of our scientists, Revik who had been working on a cure for a disease which caused children to age rapidly, stumbled upon a possible solution to the virus, however before he could perfect it, he fell into a deep coma. By this time around 30% of our entire population, around five million people had died and another eight or nine million people were infected with the virus and had months left to live. All of our remaining scientists began work using Revik's retrovirus as a baseline for their research. Two months later, one of our youngest scientists, a student of Revik known as Genus stumbled across a viable serum that could render the host immune to the virus along with almost every other ailment which had ever affected humanity.

Widespread testing began and even though under the best laboratory conditions possible, nearly 75% of the people who were given the retrovirus died from it, the remaining 25% were physically and mentally far stronger than their counterparts, the retrovirus which we designated ReGenus in honour of the two scientists that had created it. Between the original virus and the 'cure' our civilization had crumbled, our population dropped from over twenty million down to under three million within five years. Our rival empire the Indusi soon discovered that we had a cure for the virus when several of our citizens attacked and killed members of an Indusi empires patrol, but our Warrior Caste, whom had discovered that the retrovirus had strengthened their warriors by a factor of ten, did not want us to supply our rivals with something they could use against us.

In response, the Indusi used one of their last resort weapons in an attempt to force us to give them the serum. They used one of their experimental atomic warheads on two of our biggest remaining population centres, over two million people died in the nuclear explosions. In response, our Military caste did not even wait for a response from the Noble caste, they launched our own atomic weapons and biological plagues at every single Indusi city they could. And overnight a catastrophic war had begun and ended which had almost caused the extinction of all human life on the planet, other than the scattered villages spread throughout various areas unoccupied by either of our empires.

During that night, my sister convinced me to go along with her and a few soldiers who were there for our protection to hide in our empires best kept secret facility. It was a refuge in the event of an atomic war, something we hoped would never happen. It was an enormous underground facility that stretched for over one million square miles underneath what is now Europe. It was over five miles deep underground and heavily secured, with its own massive hydroponic farms systems that could feed and supply fresh oxygen for over half of our entire civilization. However our civilization didn't have time to hide its civilians, we barely had time ourselves to retreat into the facility which was code named 'Lantis'.

And so what remained of our once great civilization were my sister and I, Xavier and the four other soldiers. We never found more survivors from our empire, and overnight the Az'nor and the Indusi Empires were extinguished.

We remained within Lantis for months, but we found no other survivors within the complex, though we could not access most of the network due to cave-ins because of the explosion of so many atomics overhead. So we eventually had to resurface due to dwindling supplies of food.

It took human civilizations millennia to build up to a point where it was once again widespread, and we wandered aimlessly for many years. During that time our numbers dwindled, two of the soldiers deserted us, as they no longer wanted any part of Luccia's dreams of reforming our lost empire. And so we were down to five, the last survivors of an empire that had existed for millennia, it was a dark times for us. Luccia eventually fell in love with Xavier, and they soon discovered one of the other side effects of the retrovirus which no one had considered. She tried for decades but could not fall pregnant. This was a painful period for all of us, as we saw ourselves as the last remnants of an empire that could never again walk the earth.

It was during this time that we also realised that we had to stay close to human populations in order for us to feed as our supplies dwindled. For a time we settled in what is now Africa, as it was relatively untouched from the nuclear war. We forged our own kingdom there and we prospered for a time, however boredom soon set in. We had been alive for over one thousand years before we finally began to understand the more terrible effects of the retrovirus, we could not die, we had not grown a day older, and

Adrenaline Rush

Xavier had in fact appeared to grow younger. Our skins grew paler each year; we began to seem less human with every passing decade.

After a thousand years of living, I fell into a deep depression, I could not stand being alive any more, and I felt totally and completely alone. I tried so very hard to die, I starved myself for years, but nothing seemed to work, it caused me grievous pain and suffering, and I was eventually found by a young man, who could not have been much older than seventeen. He attempted to nurse me back to health, he was not overly successful, because the one thing I needed was human blood, but I refused to harm him, eventually I fell in love with him. His name was an ancient form of the name Marcus.

I lived in peace with Marcus for over a decade, I eventually had to leave him at night to feed, but I never let him know my true nature. I was deeply afraid that he would leave me or become frightened of what I was, however eventually I was forced to, he had begun to notice that while he was aging, I had not aged a day since he had met me.

And then I explained our history, he had heard legends about our lost civilizations, but he thought they were myths, the more I told him, the more he seemed to understand why I was, the way I was when he found me.

Back then we didn't know how to infect others with the retrovirus which was slowly strengthening every cell in our body. We suspected that if we could somehow transfuse them with some of our blood that it might work, but we didn't dare to try. Eventually I went back to visit my sister, with Marcus by my side. Luccia was livid; she could not believe that I had told our history to a common mortal. She forbade me to see him again and even threatened to kill him, when I tried to persuade her that he was not a threat and even suggested that I try to turn him into an Immortal like us. We argued so much that we eventually ended up fighting violently, I eventually defeated her and she submitted to me, having no choice but to give me her blessing to try and turn him into one of us.

However I did not have a clue how to do this, and though he begged me repeatedly, I was afraid to try; as I knew that the chances of him surviving would not be very high. But I was torn, I loved him totally and completely, eventually I agreed, and I bit into my wrist and allowed him to drink my pure undiluted blood. This was the first time we had ever attempted to infect anyone with the virus, and at the time I did not know that I should have bit him as well so that the venom in my fangs would make the virus work faster.

It did not work, and he died an agonising death, he died in my arms two days later, his skin had began to form the white lesions which should have spread across his body eventually encompassing him but his heart gave up before the virus had changed his body. I was distraught and returned to my sister, where I tried once again to end my life, but to no avail, nothing I could do would kill me, I tried to burn myself but it didn't work, although it was agonising, it just didn't do any long term damage, nothing the virus couldn't repair relatively quickly.

Eventually I went into a kind of slumber, even though we cannot truly sleep, we can go into a kind of meditative hibernation which allows our bodies to rest and repair. I went into this state after a while. This is very rare, and we call it 'the peace' and I lay dormant underneath the ground for several centuries, it was during this time that I first developed the Telepathic gift I have had since then. I began to venture out of my body telepathically and enter the minds of the few mortals that were living near where I lay dormant.

It was such a strange occurrence to me that I couldn't understand it at first, and within a few years of its development, I left my sanctuary and tried my best to track down Luccia again and explain this all to her. It didn't take me long to find them again and as I told her about it, she looked at me knowingly and told me that she already knew. She also had psychic abilities, and then she explained that the reason she persuaded me to leave and go into hiding at Lantis in the first place was because she'd had a vision which showed her the impending atomic destruction of our civilizations and she didn't have enough time to warn anyone else so she had no time to lose.

This knowledge astounded me; it made me wonder what else she had been keeping secret from me and what else would happen with the passing of time that could extend our abilities further. None of our companions developed any new abilities for quite some time.

The next major event in our immortal lives happened at around 7800 BC, when Luccia had a vision which showed her the impending disaster that would be raged against them by Enigmas, one of the soldiers that had originally fled with us, and we thought him deeply loyal. But in this future vision that Luccia told both myself and Xavier about. He had chosen to defect against us and use his abilities for world domination. His abilities he had developed in this future were remarkable, he could set almost any substance on fire with his touch, and he began to ravage the mortal communities in this future, and even threatened the immortal community as well.

Once we had learned this, it was my turn to use my ability, and I probed Enigmas' mind to learn whether he already knew about his ability, it was the first time I had ever forced myself into the mind of an immortal, and it took me a considerable amount of time, he didn't realise I was doing it to him, but he began to get frustrated with the state of daydreaming that I was inflicting upon him, but after considerable effort, I uncovered he truth, that he had been experimenting with this power of combustion that he had.

I immediately left to inform Luccia and Xavier about what I had learned, they were incensed at once, as it proved to them that Luccia's vision like her previous one was going to come true. We did not know how long it would take for this vision to occur and we dared not risk letting it happen so we immediately called in Brakh, the other surviving soldier and explained the situation to him, he was deeply loyal to Xavier and so we formulated our plan, we had no idea how to kill an immortal and we improvised.

We decided that if we could all bite and tear at him at once, we could dismember and desiccate his body, so that he couldn't hope to recover, and once he was dry of blood we would attempt to burn his remains.

We all attacked at once, and we managed to inflict severe wounds on Enigmas but he managed to get his hands around Brakh's torso and he used his gift on him, it was the first time we had ever seen an immortal really shriek in unbearable pain. Brakh turned into a fireball so bright it was like a small sun, we had never seen anything like it. The rest of us quickly retreated, not wanting to suffer the same fate, but Brakh did the unexpected, he hurled himself at Enigmas and wrapped himself around him, burning him whilst he himself was being slowly burnt alive. We watched from a distance, and it took over nine days for the hideous screaming to subdue, and another month before the fires went out.

At the time, we didn't know if Enigmas had survived or not, we had not seen him leave, but when we finally checked once the fires were under control, all that remained was deep black ash and scorch marks. We mourned our lost companion, and it gave us all the shock we needed, we now knew that we weren't indestructible and that we could be killed, even if it was only by other immortals.

It was in the ensuing years after that, that we formed the Covenant, we all agreed that we could not allow superhuman powers to ever threaten ourselves or humanity ever again and that we would rigidly control whichever new immortals we would bring into our fold, if we could ever transform anyone else.

We were at peace for a long time, with just the three of us, but to all of our shock and awe, Luccia fell pregnant, even though her pregnancy was incredibly slow and seemed to last over a decade, it still showed that we could still bear children. Luccia was overjoyed, and Xavier was content, he had begun to suspect that the problem was him, but when Annaccia was born, we all knew that we were truly alive.

Xavier was deep in thought for many years over what had happened and he eventually guessed that our bodies had been slowed down to an incredibly slow rate of what was normal for a human, and because of this slow rate of decay amongst our cells, even a girls menstruation had been slowed down significantly, and occurred once every few thousand years rather than every month.

Anna breathed new life into the Covenant, she had her mother's temper with her father's intelligence, her growth was totally normal up until she reached maturity, and then her body clock slowed down the same as the rest of us, and we all knew then, that she was immortal too, and while she looked a great deal like Luccia, she did not always see eye to eye with her, and eventually she found herself a mate, Morgan whom she told Luccia flatly that she would be infecting him, and it was she who came up with the method of infection that we currently use now.

She experimented for several years before she found out a method that had a higher success rate than purely giving them some immortal blood. The exchange needed to be mutual, they would exchange bodily fluids in a much more primal way, by biting the intended target as well as giving them some of your blood, you could infect them far quicker as the venom in our fangs would speed up the process much faster and provided some much needed extra cellular endurance, and although the mortality rate was still incredibly high, it was significantly more successful.

It was around 6300 BC when she finally managed to infect Morgan, she was successful, and even though he was under threat of death if he should develop any psychic abilities that would threaten the Covenant, he was welcomed among them warmly.

"And that I think is enough for tonight, you must be getting tired and I think you should rest, I will continue with our history soon."

12:52am Paxson, USA

Alexis

As they all left her hotel room, she was once again alone, and deep in thought, her mind was reeling under everything she had heard, and she had so many unanswered questions. She wanted to know what happened to the two soldiers who left them at the start of her story and of when they were wandering. She wanted to know what happened to Lantis; the vast underground cave network which she said had once spanned most of Europe.

The new information on immortals fascinated her deeply and she couldn't wait to find out more from Narcissia about what else has happened in the past eight thousand years she has lived.

As she lay in bed, she wondered what Xander was up to, she hadn't heard from him since his phone call earlier that day, she knew that he would have probably arrived by the time she woke up, but that didn't make it any easier for her to sleep. She couldn't get it out of her head that he was getting closer and closer as she lay there waiting.

She tossed and turned for what seemed like hours, not able to sleep, her mind was running through too much information, she lay there not quite dreaming, but not quite awake, it felt like she was daydreaming about the story Narcissia had told her about the two ancient empires. She wondered what it would have been like to have lived all that time, and how no one had any idea, she had never heard of either of those ancient peoples, everything she had ever read about history said that the earliest recorded history was a few thousand years. It made her wonder how many times civilizations had formed and died out, in much the same way that Troy was rebuilt upon the same grounds repeatedly.

She turned and looked at the clock on the wall, it said the time was 4:26am, she stared at it, not believing she had been unable to sleep for so long, it felt like she had been awake for days now, but she'd only been laying in bed for a few hours.

As she lay there in the dark, she wished so much that he was there with her, but she knew that even he could not transport himself from such a vast distance instantly, it was a shame really, it would have been so much easier for her if he could, she was beginning to think she wouldn't be able to sleep until he was there with her.

She could hear the faint voices of the people in the rooms adjacent to her, but she couldn't work out what they were saying, they were obviously being quiet on her behalf, hoping that she would be able to sleep. No doubt someone would come in to quietly check on her later some time, they had been doing this every few hours whenever she was sleeping, they didn't feel comfortable leaving her alone while she was at risk.

And while at first she had found this a bit unexpected, eventually she began to realise that they were generally decent people, who cared deeply about the safety of others. One day she would have to ask them why they haven't tried to solve more of the world's problems.

She heard the door open slowly and ever so quietly, and someone walk quietly into the room, she didn't bother to turn around to look, she knew that it would just be one of her new found friends come to check on her, probably Charlotte, she was usually the one that came to check, or Debbie, who was quickly taking on a motherly role to her, and the more she tried to fight it off, the deeper she fell into place, so she had decided to surrender her reservations and merely live contently with it.

To her surprise whoever it was had not left the room yet, she had expected them to quickly check on her and then leave, perhaps they were seeing if she was awake, they knew she had a lot on her mind and they could probably hear her tossing and turning. Maybe they would bring her something to help her sleep, but then she heard the soft sound of a coat or jacket being placed silently on the couch in the other room.

As much as she tried not to think about the other possibility the more she did, she thought she was dreaming as she felt the soft presence of someone else walking silently into the room, the faint smell of a familiar cologne and then the pressure that their body was exerting on the mattress she was laying on, and then she felt the cool touch of skin against her shoulder, it was not uncomfortable, it was perfection itself, it sent a shiver down her entire body as she surrendered to her dream that he might really be their right next to her.

As she lay there she was torn, she didn't want to risk turning round and finding out she was imagining it, but she had to know if he had really come back to her. It took her a while to decide, but before she had the chance to act upon her decision, she felt the soft moist breath on her neck and felt the soft pressure of lips on her neck gently kissing her and then she heard it. The voice that she had dreamed about every night since he had left, telling her the one thing she needed to hear.

"I love you, and I will never leave you again."

Lee Michael Harris

As he clung to her, she didn't want to risk ruining the dream by waking, so she lay their silently and just enjoyed the moment, *nothing could be better than this* she thought to herself. Not wanting to say it aloud in case her imagination was getting the better of her. And now that she finally felt safe, she drifted slowly off to sleep. Not really believing that he was there with her, but pleased that her imagination had provided her with what she needed.

Chapter 15: The Uneasy Wait

10:00am Paxson, USA

Xander

He had laying down next to Alexis since he arrived back at Paxson, he hadn't wanted to get up to talk to Paul and the others, but he knew that he really needed to, so he could get it over and done with, so he got up as quietly as he could and left the room without a sound

As he crossed the brief passage in the hotel towards Paul's suite, the door was already ajar, so he suspected that they knew that he would be going to see them.

"Morning." He said as he walked into the room, and glanced around the room ay each of them as they sat very still looking at him with a mixture of curiosity and concern.

"Welcome back." Paul said cheerily as he stood up and then ushered Xander into a seat at the table they were sitting around.

"We need to discuss how we are going to handle them." Xander said anxiously.

"Indeed." Paul continued before Xander could say anything else "Firstly, we need to know exactly what they are capable of."

"Right, well I'm sure you are all fully aware of how deadly Luccia, Xavier, Morgan and Anna are, but the others are likely to be unknown to you. The eldest of the small group that are known as Acolytes is around 500 years old, he is known as William, the other four of them range from 300-400 years old; their names are Ruth, Sebastian, Nathaniel and Ryan."

Saying their names made him recall them all, in the way he had seen them last.

William was built in very much the same way as a bulldog, he was a very stocky man, with mousy brown hair, Ruth had a thin mouth and an overly long nose, with jet black hair, her brother

Sebastian looked very much like her, and shared her dark black hair, and her widows peak hairline. Nathaniel was a small man with hair so light it was almost white, he had a very unremarkable face and Ryan was overly large and somewhat out of proportion which gave him a top heavy appearance with his broad shoulders and wide set chest.

"They have been taught to fight using knives primarily, and they usually try and sever as many arteries as they can, it is the only tactic we have found to be effective in fighting more powerful immortals, as a last resort they will attempt to distract you, and working in groups, one will attack you head on, while the other attacks from one of your blind spots and will attempt to bite you." He didn't feel the need to state outright how to kill another immortal, they all knew that the main ways in which that could be done, was by decapitation or totally destroying the heart, and even that wasn't always guaranteed, which was why they almost always drained and burned their opponents afterwards.

"The bites won't be fatal, but it will send you into an enraged state where you will burn far more adrenaline than normal, none of us can last for long under those conditions, even more dangerous it would supply the one who bites you with a large quantity of your own adrenaline if you can't get them off you."

He continued as their expressions changed which told him that they understood what he was saying.

"As for the council, they will be a different sort of challenge all together, as they won't be fighting to slow you, they will be trying to kill you. Every single one of them is so ancient that they are magnitudes stronger and faster than any of us. However the only threat is Luccia as far as any special abilities which would be harmful to us."

"Xavier is the most dangerous of all of them; he is the fastest and strongest immortal I have ever seen, myself not included of course, even he cannot match my speed, however his strength is enough to rip me apart if he can lay his hands on me."

"How would you suggest we handle matters?" this time it was Debbie who was curious enough to ask.

"We will need to split into small groups. The Acolytes are not the main problem, and can easily be handled with two or three of us fighting the entire group."

"However, the other four will be a different matter."

"I will take my sister, I have beaten her before, and I can beat her again." This time it was Narcissia who was speaking up. A confident expression spread across her face. This unnerved Xander quite a lot, he couldn't help but suspect that she was being overly confident considering she knew full well that she had seen a future where she might not be victorious.

"I will take Xavier." Paul said in a tone full of reservation.

"No, he is mine; I'm the only one who can match him without putting myself at risk. You, Anthony and Debbie will need to take on the five Acolytes, you should be able to dispatch them fairly quickly and then aid the rest of us."

Everyone was paying him there full attention now, he had expected this, they all wanted to know who would be at risk, and who would be taking on the most dangerous of their adversaries.

"Charlotte, I want you to stay here with Alexis, I know you will be able to keep her safe, and I suspect you are one of the few people who could keep her occupied so that she doesn't worry too much." As he said this, Anthony looked at him and ever so slightly nodded his head thankfully.

"Michael, Celeste." As he caught their attention, they looked up at him with their deep violet eyes, no trace of fear in them, but one of deep understanding and a trace of boredom.

They stood as he spoke to them, and for the first time he got a real impression of them. Michael was tall, taller than he was, around 6ft4 at his best guess, he had short ash blond hair, and had a rugged leathery look about him, which looked oddly strange considering his pale complexion.

Celeste was the exact opposite, she was just over 5ft tall, and had a rounded face that looked surprisingly young and baby like. She had dark black hair that was cropped in a short bob around her head. Her hair was a perfect contrast considering her pale face.

"You two will need to take on Anna and Morgan, you should be an even match with them, the Elixir should have strengthened you enough to hold them off until Paul, Anthony and Debbie finish off the young ones."

They both nodded at him and then turned to face to face and looked into each other's eyes, before walking hand in hand out of the room. Xander assumed that they wanted to spend some time alone, in the off chance that they might not make it out alive.

"What are our chances?" Debbie asked him curiously, but without the slightest trace of fear in her voice.

He looked into her eyes as he replied. "I won't lie to you, we are going to be very evenly matched, and it will be a difficult struggle at first, but as long as you, Paul and Anthony can quickly deal with the five young ones, we will be able to use our superior numbers and abilities to maximum effect."

"The other possibility is of course, that they won't even fight, that as soon as they see us, they will decide that such an even fight would not be a good idea." Everyone in the room looked at Narcissia when she said this, not quite believing that it was an option.

1:20pm Ketchikan, USA

Luccia

As they arrived in Alaska after the three flights it had taken them to get there, she eyed the younger ones so that she could get a good grasp of how they were holding up. She knew that William at least would be a grave loss, and that he was intelligent enough to know that they might be on a suicide mission and that the only ones who were guaranteed survival were Luccia and Xavier.

Adrenaline Rush

It didn't take her private investigators long to find out where Narcissia had gone, she hadn't been trying to hide her destination; she had taken a small private plane to a town called Paxson. As she drove towards the small private airport on the outskirts that her sister had used to fly to the town, a distance some twelve hundred miles north-west of them, she thought about how, soon this whole annoyance would be over and done with, she didn't see this as overconfidence, she knew what Alexander was capable, but she also knew Xavier and his capabilities, as well as knowing that the five young ones would give them an added advantage, she didn't anticipate that she would even have to get her own hands dirty.

The pilot was a short stubby kind of man, he was balding slightly and was barely taller than she was, he had a very thick accent and a name tag that read Cole, she sighed as she saw this and thought *How utterly human.*

Mr Cole it turned out was very helpful once she had demonstrated with a few hundred dollar bills that she wasn't there to waste his time. He told her that he could only fit five people in his plane, but that he was more than willing to make two trips, of course he added that he would require payment in full for both trips before they left, he reasoned that he would need the money to arrange for the fuel needed.

She told him that she would consider it and get back to him, and gave him another hundred dollar bill, money mattered very little to her, she had more than enough to last her eternity, she had so many identities with numerous accounts tied to each one that unless she was exceptionally narrow minded and greedy she would be able to live exceedingly well off of merely the interest.

It only took her another fifteen minutes to drive back to the hotel the others had arranged to meet her at, and she already knew that they wouldn't be taking the plane there, she couldn't risk dividing the group into two, they needed everyone there at once so they could secure a quick victory and then leave, she didn't want to have to deal with anything too messy, that she would have to spend time and money cleaning up after.

It was hard enough covering up battles between immortals a few hundred years ago, or even a few thousand, but with how the world had changed in all that time, it would cost hundreds of thousands to silence local populations if they ever really witnessed what can take place when immortals come in violent contact with each other.

When she arrived she explained to them that they couldn't take the plane, which would have only taken them just over four hours, instead they would have to go on foot, she knew that this was probably for the best anyway, it meant they could carry the assortment of swords and knives that Xavier had purchased before they had even arrived and had stored away in a garage in the outskirts of the city.

While the young ones didn't seem daunted by this, they knew that the journey would be a little harder for them than it would be for herself and Xavier, they had far more experience with exerting their bodies to their maximum potential, and they were a lot stronger and faster, so much so that they would likely barely exert themselves in order to keep up.

She estimated that the trip would take around four to five hours, not too bad she thought considering the 1200mile journey, but she knew that the cold weather and rough terrain might slow them a little, she was very thankful for the cold weather, it would make the extreme temperatures their bodies wouldl raise to more comfortable, the young ones were not used to extended periods of adrenaline overdrive, and they would likely have to consume massive quantities in order to fuel themselves adequately, she knew this was a dangerous risk, but there were no alternatives available to them.

As they began the run to Paxson, she considered this a leisurely stroll, she hardly had to exert herself at all to reach speeds that most mortals would consider extreme, and as she thought this she remembered just how fast Alexander was, he made every single one of them seem like a tortoise, he could traverse the distance in a fraction of the time it would take even Xavier and herself to travel even at their fullest adrenaline fuelled high. He was just that fast, it was incredible to watch, he could move so fast that he could almost appear to be at several places at once, camera's couldn't even catch him on a single frame if he really pushed his abilities.

It was a sobering thought as she ran, not really paying attention to the scenery she was ignoring on the journey, if she had paid it the attention it deserved she would have perhaps noticed just how striking it was, it was a land that was so secluded and quiet that few mortals had ever really explored it, it was unlike anything she had seen in thousands of years.

It took them nearly six and a half hours to get close enough to sense Alexander's presence, Ryan was considerably slower than the rest of them, and he held the rest up while he had to stop for repeated doses of epinephrine to sustain himself, she didn't really consider the impact this would have on the whole plan, she had anticipated the problem and they had all brought copious supplies with them, just in case. Ranging from epi-pens to capsules full of adrenaline. And while the capsules were generally only really used for combat situations, the pens were very useful for pre-combat boosts.

It took another ten minutes before she noticed that Xavier was beginning to look deeply uncomfortable, she wondered at this, she knew his senses were far keener than hers ever were. He was a warrior after all and he had learnt to be sharp. She tried to talk to him, but it was difficult to make sound travel at the speeds they were running at, so she decided to use their silent hand signals to call everyone in for a quick stop so they could all top themselves up and really prepare themselves for combat, as they stood there, the snow around them was melting rapidly, the heat they were generating was substantial.

"What's wrong Xavier, you seem tense?" She knew that look, and it made her worry for the first time since they had settled on their plan of action.

"I can sense a lot more than just Alexander there." She knew that none of the Acolytes would have heard the concern in his voice; it was only because she knew him so well that she could detect the faint trace of it.

"How many?"

"Eight... but one of them is several miles away from the main group." The young ones looked at each other nervously; this wasn't going how they had hoped, and they suddenly realised that they might not even have a fighting chance at surviving this.

"Who?" She asked, trying to hide the concern from her voice, she knew that it would not have done the young ones any good for them to see her worried.

"I don't know, but my best guess is that it's tied to the vision you had, I think it's the Illuminati." The silence that followed his last word, almost made the wind stop, an ominous chill spread throughout the small gathering.

"Then they've already killed my sister?" She asked in a low resigned voice.

"That is likely." He said quietly, his eyes were shifting around the group, almost as if he were trying not to look Luccia directly in the eyes.

"We should have forced Anna and Morgan to come, we're underpowered without them." They all knew that hindsight was not something that could ever be counted on to turn the tide of battle.

"Well." He said, and she could hear the steel returning to his voice as he continued "We are only slightly outnumbered, and none of them can match us."

"Could one of them be my sister? She might be severely wounded? I need to know." Luccia knew that this was a long shot, but she felt that she had to ask.

"No, I'm sorry we're too far away."

"Right, you all know the plan, stick to it. We need to use our numbers decisively, work in pairs and William; you should be able to take on one of them alone." He nodded promptly as she said this; she thought he looked confident enough and as she watched the responses of the rest of the group she suspected that they were all feeling confident. This didn't surprise her, as they had never really had to fight against the Illuminati so didn't see them as that much of a threat, but she knew in that instant, that only Xavier and herself would survive the battle that would take place.

But the thought that her sister was there had guaranteed their response, she couldn't allow Narcissia to be held hostage or worse, and if they had really harmed her then she would not rest until the entire Illuminati had been wiped off the face of the earth.

As they got closer, she knew they couldn't be more than ten miles away from the town now, she could almost sense her sister's presence ahead of them, and she hoped that Alexander had been smart enough to not harm her. She kept running her vision over and over in her head, unable to shake the feeling that something might have happened.

They were about five miles away from the town when they came into a clearing, they could all feel the others ahead of them, they would be in eyesight any time now, the snow was falling gently, and it was almost sunset, they red and golden hues were giving the falling snow a rainbow effect that she would have usually stopped to look at because it was so beautiful, but she had bigger problems ahead of her now and she couldn't let herself be distracted.

The snow was still obscuring their vision, they could barely see fifty feet ahead of them, but they could sense the immortals ahead of them, they were not moving, they were holding their positions steadily, spread out in a way that she thought meant they were making sure they could fight without hindering each other.

They were now so close that they could see the shapes ahead of them, she could almost pickup the features of them, and she was certain that one of them was Narcissia, this didn't register at first, because the way she appeared to be holding herself suggested that she was tense and waiting in a combat stance. She couldn't understand why on earth her sister would possibly feel threatened by her arrival; it just didn't make any sense.

As they got closer they withdrew their sheaved weapons, Luccia had chosen two short knives which she kept in her leg sheaves, she looked to her right and saw Xavier was pulling the heavy broadsword which he kept in an enormous sheave that hung over his shoulder, he lifted it effortless with one hand as if it weighed no more than a kitchen knife. He swung it in front of him demonstrating remarkable dexterity. She had never understood his need to show off like that, but she supposed that it was just a male thing. She noted that with his other hand, he placed a small glass vial into his mouth, as he looked at her she could see that his eyes were totally blue now, and in the sunset's light they seemed so dark that they were black, though she knew they were not.

They were now so close that they could see the faces of those that were in front of them, she recognised them all immediately, though she had not seen them face to face in a long time, and she saw them all now, Alexander, Paul, Deborah, Anthony, Michael, Celeste and finally Narcissia. *What is she playing at?* She thought irritably.

To her surprise a voice called out, though it was not what she had anticipated, she had expected Alexander to call out and try and reason with her, but it was not him, and she almost wished it had been him, as the reality was far worse to her.

"I won't let you kill her."

Luccia glared at her sister now, and noted that she had hefted a small Katana in her hands, held with its edge facing up, rage took her now, and she couldn't possibly believe that her sister of all people would side against her. Especially with them, of all the things she could do, she had decided to defect to the ones that Luccia most despised.

She didn't even bother to reply, she raised her right hand and then dropped it suddenly, and they all knew it was the signal that meant 'attack'.

She lunged at Narcissia now, not even paying attention to what her companions were doing, at that moment she did not care.

Her rage was feeding off of all the adrenaline in her system and she was feeling a blood lust so strong that she could barely contain it.

Her outstretched dagger clashed against her sister's sword and she felt the vibrations spread across her arm, her blade was deflected forcefully and she almost lost her grip on it, the vibrations were under control now, she pulled back several feet and began to prowl around Narcissia now, circling slowly, waiting for any opportunities to strike.

Narcissia just stood there observing, waiting for Luccia to make a mistake or to attack, she was baiting her now. And Luccia felt the rage build up again and she channelled her adrenaline for another attack.

This time she struck in a flurry of slashing attacks that clanged loudly against Narcissia's blade, but she felt one blow strike home in what felt like slicing granite. She knew that she hadn't really harmed her sister, it was a mere flesh wound, but first blood had been hers, the smell of her sisters blood filled the air, and she could smell the thick concentration of adrenaline within it, and with that smell, she was further enraged.

She didn't let up on the attacks, she continued on moving as fast as she could attacking relentlessly, but most of her blows were parried by her sister, she backed off again, wanting to get the measure of her sister and see what damage her blows had done.

She couldn't be sure how many had actually struck her sister, and it was then that she realised that she was bleeding herself. She felt a faint trickle of blood running down her calf muscle, but she ignored that, it wasn't important to her and she couldn't risk focusing on anything but the present, lest she give her sister an opening.

As she backed away she looked at Narcissia again, and a feeling of grudging respect was beginning to fill her, but she forced this away and once again allowed anger to fill her, she couldn't afford herself the chance to really think about what she was doing. Her sister had several deep wounds, mostly along her arms and she could see that her clothes were beginning to show the ravages of combat, they were ripped and torn.

She heard a loud clash to her right and she looked towards the scene for a split second, in that second she saw Alexander fighting Xavier, she didn't have time to really see what they were up to.

Because in that instant Narcissia had launched herself at her and had sunk her katana deep into Luccia's left shoulder, so deep that when she had attempted to pull it out, she had been unable to.

Luccia was once again enraged, the pain shooting through her didn't bother her anymore, she knew that he needed to end this fast, and that she couldn't allow her mind to register the pain.

Luccia turned her whole body sharply to the left, so that Narcissia lost her grip on the hilt of the katana, and then she swung her right arm with as much force as she could manage, the blow struck home and sunk deep into her sister.

She didn't know where it had landed, but she quickly pulled back and as she withdrew the blade she saw the blood erupting from her sister's chest, the extremes her sister was pushing her body to was causing her further damage as she had raised her blood pressure and heart rate considerably.

Spurred by this she launched herself at Narcissia again, but just as she was about to strike, Narcissia dodged her to her left side again and with both her arms grasped the hilt of the blade and swung.

The force of this dislodged the blade from Luccia's shoulder and sent her sprawling across the ground.

As she looked up, she was surprised to see that she was almost thirty meters away from Narcissia now, which told her just how much force she had used against her.

They both knew that they couldn't keep this up for long now, one of them would have to submit, but neither of them was willing to. They both knew that they were edging dangerously close to mortal wounds. Not mortal in the sense that it would kill them, it takes more than loss of blood for that, but mortal in the sense that they would be totally incapacitated.

They looked at each other now, it had the eerie feeling of a calm between the storm, they could both hear the simultaneous fights going on all around them, but neither of them would risk taking the time to look around them and really grasp what was happening.

Luccia knew that she was running out of adrenaline, she could feel it in her muscles, the slight sluggish feel, and the blood loss was beginning to affect her now as well, their bodies were diverting a lot of their strength into repairing the wounds they had inflicted on each other.

She knew that she could only handle one more assault; she primed herself and decided how she was going to handle this.

Moving as fast as she physically could, she collided with her sister in a colossal crash that sounded like the clash of thunder, the force of it sent both of them flying, but she refused to let go of her sister so they rolled along the ground together.

Narcissia had lost her sword along the way, and Luccia knew she had won now; there was nothing her sister could do.

Except the unexpected, she felt her sisters teeth sink deep into her injured shoulder, she felt the venom spread into her system, and she felt the rush of adrenaline flowing once more, it was so powerful it was almost pleasurable.

She lost herself in this for several moments, before the adrenaline gave her the rush she needed to finish this, not bothering to try and pull Narcissia off her, she drove her knife cleanly into her sisters exposed neck, she felt the blood pour onto her hand and she withdrew the blade in one swift motion.

Narcissia dropped to the floor and blood began to flood out in a vast torrent of dark-red almost black liquid that was causing steam to rise as it poured onto the snow on the ground, she stood there for several moments before what she had done began to really sink in and the horror of it began to surface, as she realised that she had almost severed her sisters spinal cord.

She heard a loud shout behind her and turned to see Alexander turning to face her with cold fury in his eyes, Xavier was staggering behind him, barely able to keep himself off of the floor, and she could see just how much his exertion's were costing him to keep himself from succumbing.

Chapter 16: When Gods Collide

6:07pm Paxson, USA

Xander

He barely had time to think as he saw Luccia's hand drop in the signal that he knew meant they were going to attack. Xavier leaped at him and landed a heavy blow on the ground where Xander had been standing a split second before it could strike its mark.

He felt the pace of the battle slow now as he used his ability to its fullest, Xavier was still crouched over with his sword buried deep in the ground, and his rate of movement, while it would really take him a fraction of a second to withdraw it and attack again. It would seem like minutes for Xander now.

He couldn't sustain this for long he knew that, but it would give him the edge in this fight.

While Xavier had all the brute strength and lightning fast reflexes, he on the other hand, could slow down the pace of battle to suit himself, so it seemed like he could react so blindingly fast that no one had ever been able to match him in combat, even though it was not how fast he could move, but rather his ability to slow all time except for himself.

In the brief space of time, he withdrew his own blades, they were similar to what he had used for millennia, he had designed them early in his immortal life, and while to most they would just look like bladed knuckledusters. Others would see them as a work of art, and Alexander's art had always been war, he used them because to him they were the most intimate weapons he had ever used, they forced him to get as close and personal as possible in order for him to win a battle.

They could cost him any chance of victory he knew, because he would have to expose himself in order to attack with them, but to him that was all part of the allure.

As he looked at Xavier, he appeared to have moved a few inches now, he was moving backwards very slowly and Xander used this opportunity to move at him as fast as he could and strike him as hard as he could directly into Xavier's exposed kidney, it sunk in deep and for the first time he really understood just how much tougher and stronger the ancient ones really were. It felt like he was stabbing solid rock, but he managed to force the blades in with brute force rather than the finesse that he had always preferred.

He allowed time speed up again now so that it returned to real time, and he watched Xavier recoil in shock, looking stunned as he eyed Xander wearily.

He smiled at Xavier now, knowing that this would force Xavier into some foolish gesture that he could exploit.

Once again Xavier swung his blade in a diagonal motion that if it had landed, would have cleaved Xander in two, but before it got close to him, Xavier fainted quickly to the left and in one furious slash he tried to gouge Xander's eyes.

He knew that Xavier was obviously trying to trick him into allowing him to strike him with a heavy blow. Xander didn't kid himself; he knew full well that if Xavier managed to land an attack, then it would cut through him like butter. Xavier would not face the same tough resistance when he cut into Xander's flesh; with his strength would make it cut through him like a hot knife through butter, not that it comforted Xander to think of it like that.

Even though the duel had only taken a few seconds so far, but it felt like an eternity to Xander, he needed to finish Xavier quickly but he couldn't figure out how to do it, and he was worried about his companions, he knew that he would have to wear Xavier down, before he would have any chance of ending this battle.

And for the next few seconds he dodged every blow that Xavier swung at him, each attack was enraging Xavier more and more, he could see the vein on Xavier's forehead pulsing under the strain, he could smell the adrenaline running through his veins and it made him ache to launch himself at him, but he resisted this as he knew that if he gave into the desire then Xavier would have the chance he needed to literally rip Xander apart with his bare hands.

He knew that Xavier could only keep this up for so long; this was not like a normal sparring match where neither of them would really push themselves to their limits, it was a no holds barred fight for survival.

And then he decided that he would finally go on the offensive, he felt time slow around him once more as he pushed his body to its limits and he unleashed a flurry of devastating attacks, each of them sunk deep into Xavier's granite like flesh, and while none of them were anywhere near fatal, each successive blow slowed his opponent slightly and by the time he had ceases his attack, Xavier's chest and face looked like a bloody pulp, he had shredded him apart and even his eyes were covered in blood.

He backed away again quickly and surveyed the field of battle, he could see that almost all of his companions were handling their adversaries with ease, all except Narcissia; even though both of them were bleeding profusely, it appeared to him that Luccia was getting the better of Narcissa.

And then he saw Luccia launch herself at her sister, and after they had finished rolling across the field his eyes followed them and without realising it he let out a loud yell

"NO!" he screamed, turning to face Luccia, he didn't care about Xavier for this moment, who was staggering around now, barely able to stop himself from stumbling after the previous assault that Xander had unleashed upon him.

As he ran up to Narcissia's body, he knew she was seriously hurt, blood was pouring out of the wound in her throat and he didn't know what to do about it. He kicked out as hard as he could and sent Luccia sprawling across the field before she would have a chance to attack him while he tried to assist Narcissia.

He heard footsteps running behind him now, and he turned round as fast as he could, he wasn't able to use his ability this time as he was filled with grief.

As he turned around to face his attacker, he dived towards Xavier and plunged his right fist deep into Xavier's chest, cutting straight through his ribs, far deeper than any other blow he had managed that day, as he withdrew his fist from Xavier's chest he realised that it had landed just to the left side of his heart. He knew that Xavier wouldn't be getting up from that anytime soon, that he had most likely severed many of his major arteries which would take him a considerable amount of time to repair.

He reached down to the ground beside his opponent and grasped Xavier's heavy broadsword and pulled it from his outstretched hand. He hefted the sword in his hands as he got a feel for its weight and then raised his arms above his head, preparing to strike the killing blow, Luccia had probably killed Narcissia, and so he decided to even the score.

A deafening piteous scream caught his attention from the direction that he had kicked Luccia, and he looked over to see her on her knees looking at him pleadingly. She mouthed the words "Please, No I beg you."

"How could you?" he asked as he looked across at Narcissia

Luccia broke into tears and said "I had no choice."

He dropped the sword and heard it drop with a loud clang as it landed heavily on Xavier's head; he didn't care if it caused him pain.

"Order them to stop" it was not a request and she obeyed. Though only one of her companions was still standing, and he would not have been standing long, if she not ordered him to submit to them just after he spoke.

As the fighting ceased around him, he looked around to see the scene surrounding them, the blood stained snow half melted in some spots was the primary indication that there had been a battle there.

He looked over to see Narcissia laying just a few meters away from Xavier, neither of them were moving, and the traces of life were very dim on both of them, they were both in a very weak state, and they would require quite a lot of care to be revived.

Paul and Debbie were moving around checking their defeated opponents; he shook his head to Xander after they had checked the remains of the four young immortals and gave him a deeply regretful look.

Xander understood his misgivings, they had not wanted to kill the young ones, but during the heat of battle it is hard to be restrained when facing people who could and would have killed them if they had the opportunity.

He then looked down at Luccia, who appeared to be trying to nurse Xavier back to health, she was frantically injecting him with Epi-Pens, which reminded him of the need to do the same for Narcissia, but first he had to make sure that Luccia understood the terms of this cease of hostilities.

"I want your word that you will not try to harm either myself or Alexis." His voice was edged harshly with scorn and contempt.

"You don't understand, she will cause a disaster if you turn her." her response was higher pitched than usual.

"I won't let her, I swear to you I won't." He knew that she would have to trust him, but he could see that part of her had deep reservations about doing so.

"But..." she was still leaning slightly on the side that had a deep wound, but it was healing rapidly, and would likely be totally healed within an hour.

Before she had time to complete her sentence he cut her off by raising his open hand in a stopping motion and she fell silent. "No ifs or buts, you will give me your word, NOW!"

"I... "She hesitated slightly as if she were about to say something else but then reconsidered. "I swear that I will not harm you or her."[1]

"And neither will anyone from the Covenant or on behalf of the Covenant." it was not a question; it was a simple fact that he expected her to agree to regardless of how grudgingly she felt about it.

"As you wish." She looked like she wanted to say more but then she simply raised her wrist to her mouth and bit down on it, causing a deep flow of dark blood, it was almost black due to how much oxygen was in it, and put it gently to Xavier's mouth.

Xander glared at her briefly one more time, and then ignored her so he could assist with Michael and Celeste who were trying to resuscitate Narcissia; she had lost a lot of blood, so it would take time.

It took a massive amount of epinephrine to revive her, that would have been enough to kill at least twenty healthy mortals, and that much had barely made her conscious, it would likely take several hours before her central nervous system had regenerated enough so that she could even move her muscles, and she would not be capable of speech for several days at least.

The wound had caused heavy damage to her vocal cords and nervous system, and it would take a substantial amount of time to repair itself. They carried Narcissia back into town slowly, so that they didn't attract any more attention.

Paul and Debbie stayed behind at the scene of the battle so they could clean up the evidence. Debbie had agreed to do a full scorch of the entire area; no traces would survive to even hint that a massive battle between immortals had taken place. Paul would use his abilities to dig a deep pit for the four corpses of the young immortals, he couldn't risk any mortal ever finding there remains, once they were in the pit, Debbie used her gift to ignite them.

He didn't care about how Luccia would get back home, she assumed that her lone surviving initiate would bear the brunt of the load, he almost felt sorry for Sebastian for surviving the battle. No one from the Covenant would forget in a hurry just how painful it would be to fight the Illuminati again, and he did not expect them to try it for a very long time.

The Covenant had always seen themselves as equal or better than any force on the planet, and while tonight they had not been at their full strength, they had been dealt a heavy blow, one that would take centuries to recover from, and he suspected that they would never truly make up for the loss of Narcissia and himself.

Charlotte opened the window to allow them to get Narcissia into the hotel suite without them needing to take her past the mortals, her face was stricken with worry, and he felt a wave of compassion sweep through him, she must have thought that Paul and Debbie hadn't made it. He shook his head and mouthed the words "No, they're fine." Her face lightened almost immediately and then he made the jump.

It was easy for him, even though it meant jumping over 30ft through a small window to get back in the room. As he pulled himself through the window, he saw Alexis again, and he felt happy almost immediately, she was safe, and he had ensured that she would stay safe. He longed to drop Narcissia to the ground and grab Alexis in his arms and hold her and never let go. But he knew that Narcissia didn't deserve that, she needed urgent attention now.

6:32pm Paxson, USA

Alexis

Paul and Debbie arrived about fifteen minutes after Xander had returned with Narcissia, Michael and Celeste, and while Xander had no wounds at all, Michael had suffered a few deep wounds to his abdomen and Celeste had a deep cut along her cheek that looked enflamed and very sore.

The state of Narcissia worried Alexis deeply, she looked like she was barely alive, and she looked so empty and drained, almost as if she had lost all of her blood, the wounds on the rest of her body looked severe, but there was nothing she could do for her, so she did her best to keep out of the way, so that they could do whatever they could for her.

Once Xander had made sure that Narcissia was comfortable, he came over to the table they were all gathered around, she looked at him in desperation, hoping that he would explain to her what had happened.

No one had told her the details yet, as no one really knew everything that happened and they wanted to wait for Xander before they spoke of what had happened to them, so as to not be forced to repeat it again later.

As he sat down at the head of the table, he smiled briefly at Alexis but didn't say anything for several moments, and no one else spoke up, they all appeared to be waiting for him to speak. Charlotte seemed to be focusing on his every movement almost as much as Alexis was, this didn't surprise her as Charlotte was the only other person in the room that wasn't present at the battle and because of that, didn't have a clue what had happened.

"First I want to thank you *all*." He looked around the room so that they all knew he was talking to everyone "If you all hadn't helped today, both Alexis and myself would likely be dead by now."

This sent a shiver down Alexis's spine and the hairs on her arms and neck arose, she hadn't really considered just how much danger they both had been in.

"It was our pleasure." Paul said speaking for everyone, Anthony and Michael nodded silently and Debbie grinned at Alexis, before she turned her attention back towards Xander.

He began telling everyone his part of the battle, piece by piece detailing exactly what he had seen going on around him, and how he had defeated Xavier. Paul looked at him approvingly, clearly impressed that Xavier had not even managed to scratch him, and then he came to the end part and Alexis winced as he told everyone what he had seen of the fight between Narcissia and her twin.

She had of course already witnessed that particular fight, and he described it almost exactly as it had happened in her dream, she didn't bother to explain what she suspected had happened before that, it wasn't her place and she would wait for Narcissia to be back on her feet.

Paul spoke up next and he recounted how he had fought hand to hand against the one known as William, how he had eventually been forced to kill him, even though he found such a waste of life deeply regrettable.

Michael spoke for both himself and Celeste who had fought against Nathaniel and Ruth, and though they had both suffered minor flesh wounds, they were otherwise unharmed.

Debbie was next and she told how she had kept Sebastian at bay mainly by setting walls of fire around him, and he was so confused by this that he didn't think to risk breaking through it, and that it was by this method that she had managed to defeat him and yet keep him alive. Paul seemed impressed by this; he hadn't thought to restrain his opponent using his gifts and he seemed faintly sad because of what he deemed as his own personal failure.

Anthony was the last to speak and he explained that he had fought against Ryan, whom he suspected was a weak link among the Covenants forces, as he had not troubled him at all, but that he would not submit, so he eventually had been forced to kill the young one.

After they had all finished, almost everyone at the table looked around towards the room that Narcissia was resting in, there was one story that they all wanted to know, but the only person who could tell it, was the one who had suffered most out of all of them.

Paul eventually spoke up "Now that your safety has been guaranteed, how you all would feel about coming to my home for a few weeks, so you can all recuperate in safety."

Alexis looked at him and blinked several times; she hadn't really considered that the death sentence that had hung over her head for the last several weeks now, was finally over. It seemed like an eternity since she had been locked away in the psychiatric ward back in her old home town. She didn't even consider it her home anymore.

Her home would now be wherever Xander was, where he goes, she would follow him, and when he looked at her, almost as if he wanted her approval on whether they would go with Paul and the rest of the Illuminati.

She looked at Paul and said "If Xander is going with you, I would love to join you." She then looked back at Xander and looked deeply into his sparkling blue eyes and he nodded.

"We will come with you then, where are we going?" he asked him curiously

"To my home in Utah, I assure you, you will enjoy your stay, and while we are there we can discuss a few other matters." He nodded at Xander gravely, and she didn't understand what he had meant.

"I don't understand what other matters are there?" she said in puzzlement.

Once again, everyone at the table looked directly at her and smiled, Paul stood up and walked round to her, and placed his hand gently on her shoulder and said in his loud but friendly voice "You my dear, we must discuss *you*."

Sensing the puzzled look in her face he continued "We must discuss whether you will join the Illuminati, but more on that later. There is ample time my dear, we have eternity."

"You all have eternity, I do not" she remarked quickly

"Not yet you don't, but you will."

10:32am Utah, USA

Alexis

She had been at Paul's home for several days now, and she almost felt at home, she hadn't been this relaxed in a long time, as she started to climb out of bed; a hand reached out from behind her and gently pulled her back down.

They had been spending the days talking about anything and everything, their time together was more like how it had been when they had first met all those years ago, and he was a totally different person when they weren't both carrying a death sentence over their heads. The change was remarkable, but she loved him all the more for it.

She hadn't believed she could love anyone quite this much, and he had been doing everything he could to keep her occupied so that she could not worry about Narcissia, who even though she was recovering, still could not talk for more than a few minutes.

They went hiking together and he showed her some of the most amazing sights she had ever witnessed, she had never dreamed that anywhere quite so barren could be so beautiful, they went horseback riding on Paul's horses, Xander even wore one of Paul's cowboy hats, when she had first seen him wearing the hat, she had burst out laughing, and she laughed so much that she went weak at the knees and ended up rolling around on the dusty ground, and had to be dusted off by Xander shortly afterwards.

In the evenings they had gone to Salt Lake City, where the people were so friendly towards the pair of them that she could barely believe how lucky she was. The food they had eaten while they were there was breath taking. And after they had eaten he had taken her to watch the Ballet on their first night and to the theatre on the second, it was nothing like she had expected or even hoped, it was infinitely more amazing than anything she had ever dreamed of.

She had no idea what they would be doing that night, and she couldn't wait to find out, she suspected that they would be going to the symphony orchestra, but he had not given her any hints to suggest this. It was a big advantage that Paul's mansion was so close to such a massive city, with such a wonderful history, it was less than an hour's drive away and he had lent them one of his limousines every night so far.

They still however had not discussed the two of them joining the Illuminati, and she almost suspected that Paul was in absolutely no hurry at all and that he was waiting for Xander to bring it up. And to her great relief they had not heard at all from the Covenant, not that she had expected to, from what everyone had told her, they had just suffered their worst defeat in the past twelve millennia.

As she lay there with him, he leaned over and kissed her gently and whispered in her ear "I will love you forever"

He then he finally allowed her to get up, so she could go and get dressed in the bathroom, she could hear him waiting patiently for her, but she didn't rush, she didn't want to forget anything, and she wanted to make herself look perfect for him.

When she had finished, she walked into the bedroom again to find that he had also changed, he was now wearing khaki trousers and a white shirt, she found that the colours made his paleness less noticeable, she guessed that it was mainly to make him fit in easier.

As he escorted her downstairs, he explained to her that they would be going on a tour of all the local museums that she wanted to, and that there was a new Spanish restaurant that he wanted to try out.

This surprised her at first as she had not expected to see him place himself so close to so many mortals all at once quite so soon during the daylight hours, but he had managed it. He always seemed so completely at ease around her now and she didn't want him to be forced to put on an act again. He smiled at her noticing her reluctance and said "I've always done it, so I am used to hiding what I am, it is you who needs to practice pretending to be mortal, my love."

Before they left, he told her that he wanted to go in and say good morning to Paul before they left, and also to tell him that they would be back in the early evening and that then they could have their little chat about everything.

She was shocked at this, he hadn't mentioned this since that night back in Alaska, and she was amazed that he said it now so casually. The thought of this made her quite nervous, she had wondered why the whole of the Illuminati were still here, she knew that this was Paul and Debbie's home and that the others lived in various parts of the world, according to their own tastes.

Noticing her change in mood, Xander spoke to her again and said "Don't worry my angel, everything will go fine, they will accept you, they already consider you a member of their family."

He continued after he saw her confused expression and said "Joining them is a mere formality at this point." He laughed after this trying to lighten the mood and make her feel better. But before she could say anything more, he gestured towards the front door and then he went and opened it and waited patiently beside the open door until she had walked through it.

He then walked closely beside her as they made their way towards the limousine and he opened the door for her, he kissed her hand gently as she got into the car, and he followed close behind her.

"It will all be okay, you know that right? Just enjoy today and tonight will turn out fine, if anything it will turn out better than you expect. Trust me, I love you."

He kissed her again after this and she smiled, as they were driven quietly and steadily towards the city again, he held her in his arms and caressed her head close to his chest. She could feel the beating of his heart, and even through it was substantially faster than anything she had ever heard, for the first time she realised that he was truly alive, as alive as she was.

Chapter 17: The Rules

1:57pm Vienna, Austria

Luccia

She was still reeling from the defeat that they had suffered in Alaska, and she was angry at herself for nearly killing her twin sister and even more so, she was furious at herself for allowing a momentary lapse in control that had resulted in the loss of lives of four of her companions that she had known for centuries, they were almost like family to her.

And to make matters worse, Anna wasn't talking to her because of the state that her father had been in when they had returned. She couldn't believe that Luccia had risked not only her own life, but the lives of everyone with her just to get even with Narcissia for siding against her.

Xavier was however recovering well now, she was thankful that he would be totally fine within a few days, he was still grim and sulking because he had been defeated by Alexander, she knew that it had been a big hit to his ego and as far as she was concerned, that was the smallest price they had paid.

Not only had Alexander left the Covenant, but so had her sister, and now they were enthralled with the Illuminati, things couldn't get much worse for the Covenant, they had lost two of their most powerful members, and their loyal core had been decimated.

She had suspected that her visions could be a self fulfilling prophecy in the past. But the more she thought about it, the more she realised that had she not received the vision where Narcissia and Xavier were lying on the ground almost dead, then Narcissia would have never left to try and stop it from happening, but the very fact that she tried to stop it, led to its cause.

Because of this, she was determined to be a lot more careful with how she handled her visions from now on; after all she now knew that trying to stop a prophecy from occurring could be the catalyst which would make it occur in the first place.

What happened to her next was a complete and total shock to her. Her vision went blank, the strength of the vision she was being forced to watch was so powerful that she collapsed to the floor.

And then with her sight returned, she knew instantly that she was not in her room any longer and she saw it happen, she could see the mortal armies gathering just outside the sprawling metropolis, could see that they were accompanied by mechanised vehicles which she have never considered much of a threat so she didn't care enough about to know the names of the machines. At first she didn't realise what was going on, but then she saw what was happening, they were being slaughtered by a large group of immortals, she couldn't see their faces, but she had guessed roughly that there were dozens of immortals of varying strengths, as they tossed the massive machines around and tore them apart piece by piece.

They decimated the mortal army that must have numbered in the thousands, and as the immortals fled the battlefield together, time appeared to speed up to a rapid rate, and then it happened; the explosion was catastrophic and massive. She had witnessed this sort of explosion several times in her long life time, and every time she saw the mushroom shaped cloud, it sent a shiver of terror through her.

Atomic weapons were one of the most destructive forces that had ever existed, they were powerful enough to wipe out all life on earth, and she couldn't understand the mortal need to build them, let alone use them.

The vision began to fade and her eye sight returned to her, she was still feeling shaken by the strength of it, and even more shaken because of what had happened in the vision. In the past she had received three other prophetic visions which had scared her quite this much, the first time was when they had barely managed to evacuate to Lantis before her entire race had been extinguished. And she didn't even want to think about the other two prophecies she had suffered, she didn't even want to risk thinking about it, in case there was a link between those ancient prophecies and the newest one.

She tried to pull herself together; she knew that she needed to focus, so that she could sift through the vision meticulously so that she could decipher every detail of it. She would also need to talk with Xavier about it, and then she sighed deeply, knowing that she would have to force Anna to make peace with her, this was too important to allow such petty squabbles to get in the way.

She could tell that Xavier was still in his quarters, so she decided to go and see him, it didn't take her long, even though he was on one of the higher floors of the complex, they had a direct connection to each other's rooms via an interconnected elevator system, as neither of them liked being out of easy contact with each other.

And even though she had not really spoken to him much over the past few days, there was nothing bizarre about that though, they had on occasion gone weeks without talking to each other, but that was generally when one of them was deep in thought, and the other did not wish to intrude. They respected each other's privacy, and they knew how much they cared about each other, that it just didn't matter whether they expressed it verbally.

As she entered his room, he turned to face her and she knew that the expression on her face would tell him that there was something deeply distressing her, it didn't take long for him to ask "What's wrong?"

Her reply was however not what he had expected "I have had another vision; this one involves not only an immortal army slaughtering mortals." But this had not been what he had anticipated, he was visually shocked by her words, and she continued "worse than that, someone is going to use an atomic weapon, I suspect it is connected with the immortal army."

He stood speechless for several moments after this; atomics had always been something they all feared, when they had been reinvented decades before, he had begged Luccia to allow him to wipe out anyone connected to the research of the bombs. He had even asked her if they could not set up residence back within Lantis, however they had not been able to follow up on this.

That was mainly because Lantis was buried so deep underground now, none of the access points would be uncovered, over twelve millennia of sediments had built up and they were not even sure of the precise locations of the entrances.

Luccia did not want the complex found for other reasons, she knew that if they found it, then there was a chance that mortals might find it, and it was far too large for them to ever defend it from mortals, and buried deep within the complex was a vast armoury of weaponry, both atomic and conventional. Well conventional as far as Az'nor technology was at its height.

As well as a vast array of research material that could possibly lead them to creating their own Regenus Virus, and that was something Luccia did not want to become common knowledge, it was too dangerous a risk to take.

"What perspective did you experience this vision from?"

For a moment she was shocked by him, it was a very perceptive question for him to ask her.

"I was not one of the attackers, if that's what you meant; I was watching it from a distance." She snapped back at him.

"I didn't mean that, I just wanted to know how close you were to them, and whether you recognised any of them."

"No, I didn't, which means they are very young or very old."

Neither of them liked the way this conversation was going, but they couldn't avoid it any longer.

They both knew that one possibility was that they were not the only survivors left of the Az'nor, the other possibility was that there former companions were involved. Companions they had not seen for millennia, this possibility was deeply unnerving.

"We must contact the Illuminati; this could only be the result of someone creating a lot of immortals. Someone who doesn't follow our rules."

Luccia smiled at this thought, in her mind, it would make perfect sense for it to all be down to Alexander's new mortal plaything, and if turning her into an immortal could cause this future, and then she knew that she must contact Paul and Alexander and make sure that they wouldn't risk trying to turn her, they must think of the rest of the immortal community and what would happen if mortals became aware of them all.

This thought sent a shudder through her, she knew that they would attempt to hunt them down and kill them, and while she didn't really fear that they could manage it, the blood retribution this would cause among the immortals would be cataclysmic for the entire human race.

Immortals had almost completely ceased feeding on humans now, and most of them were glad of this, while they wanted to continue living, they did not like having to kill others so that they would be able to survive, well at least not if there were other options.

"It might not be her though; it could still be someone else, we have never had proof that Kane was really dead, and I would hate to imagine if Enigmas was finally deciding to resurface again."

"Oh come on Xavier! You know that neither of them are alive or they would not have waited this long before they made another attempt at gaining power." She snapped back at him, not even wanting to consider the possibility.

"Or they could have finally realised that they have eternity, and that they could afford to take their time." He retorted with uncharacteristic sarcasm in his voice.

She dismissed this, she didn't want to consider either of these options as she knew that if he was right, then they would not be able to stop it from happening, nothing had been heard of either of them for millennia, and they had not heard from Enigmas for nearly half her life time. And because of this, she assumed that he must have died, there was no other reason for him to have kept silent for so long.

Xavier continued trying to get her to consider other possibilities for several hours, he was obviously adamant to not have to face Alexander anytime soon, and she believed that this was impairing his judgement. But she eventually decided to ignore him and she decided that she would at least try to contact the Illuminati, and make them aware of the risk.

7:27pm Utah, USA

Alexis

They were almost back at Paul's mansion again now, they had spent the entire day in Salt Lake City, and they had gone to visit as many of the sights and museums that they had time for. This turned out to be a lot, and it surprised Alexis with just how many exquisite pieces if artwork and local monuments had in them, she had no idea that the city had so much to offer.

She was beginning to feel quite nervous now; even though Xander had done his best to keep her mind occupied throughout the day, but now as they were mere minutes away from Paul and the rest of the Illuminati, she couldn't do anything except worry.

It was difficult for her knowing that they would be discussing her future life in the next few hours, knowing that if they don't agree to her joining them, then she wouldn't stand as much of a chance in surviving the process to become an immortal like they all were, and spend eternity with Xander.

Xander put his arm around her empathically, if she didn't know better she would have suspected that he had Narcissia's gift, but she knew that he was probably just worried, her fears were displayed on her face, and the tension in her muscles that would make her fears and doubts like an open book.

As the limousine pulled into the drive way of Paul's home, he was there standing at the front door ready to escort them into the large conference room. He was smiling broadly and he asked her briefly about their day, even giving them tips on where to go and what to see the next time they go to the city.

This made her a bit more confident, she knew that Paul wouldn't have been acting like that unless he at least believed there was a strong possibility that they were going to allow her into their highly selective family.

As they walked into the conference room, she marvelled at the artwork on the walls, she had not been in this room before, there had been no need. Paul pulled out a chair for her as they entered and then she looked around the table, expecting to see a lot of grim expressions on the groups faces.

But to her surprise they were all looking at her with expressions of amusement and kindness, Charlotte grinned at her as she caught her eye, and for a few moments she was mesmerized by her violet eyes which were sparkling in the bright almost luminous light.

Debbie smiled at her and Anthony nodded his greetings, Michael and Celeste both seemed fairly quiet, but out of the whole group they were the two she'd had the least contact with, during the time they had all spent in Alaska they had kept to themselves most of the time, almost as if the problem had interrupted them from something important, and she wasn't feeling bold enough to ask them.

"Right shall we get this started?" everyone looked at Paul as he spoke, his voice echoing a bit off the walls, and he winced a little as if he hadn't realised how loud he was talking.

Everyone around the table nodded and murmured their approval and he sat down at the head of the table, and she felt Xander come to stand beside her, he bent down and kissed the top of her hair before he took a seat beside her.

"As you know, we're here to discuss whether both you and Alexander will join us." He said to them all in a matter of fact type tone.

"I still don't understand what the Illuminati is, or what it does." She said honestly, expecting everyone around the table to laugh at her, but she was pleasantly surprised that they didn't.

Paul smiled as she said this and nodded and began "As you know, we were founded around three thousand years ago, but in essence what we are is very simple."

"We are a family, an extended family of gifted individuals." He said cheerfully.

"But what is it you do? And what do you require of your family?" she asked him curiously

Again he smiled and nodded agreeably, so she knew he would answer him momentarily.

"Well unlike the Covenant, we are not a rigidly controlled group, everyone is equal within the Illuminati, and while we are passive by nature, we all rise to defend our family when threatened."

"Also unlike the Covenant, who steer human affairs whenever they feel the need, we do not get involved unless we have no choice. We will of course protect ourselves."

"And as you experienced before, we will aid other gifted individuals that we believe might one day become part of our family." He said subtly in a way that made her very curious.

"But what do you mean by gifted?" she asked him, honestly not sure how she could fit into that category.

"I mean people such as yourself, or Alexander, or any member of my family." As he said this, she didn't understand how he could place her in the same league as Xander; he was someone who was infinitely more capable than she ever could be.

For a while no one spoke, they could all see that Alexis really didn't understand why they had helped her in the first place, she didn't see herself as gifted in the way that they were, she could never do what they do.

"But I'm ordinary..." she said in such a quiet voice that she didn't think they would have been able to hear, she realised shortly afterwards that they could all hear her very clearly as they looked at her with looks of astonishment and concern.

"No my dear, you are more extraordinary than you could possibly imagine." Anthony spoke this time, shocking her yet further, but it still didn't make sense to her.

"I don't understand..." she said politely.

"I know you don't, and I will try to explain it to you." Anthony continued shortly afterwards in an attempt to tell her why they were so adamant.

"Since we formed all those years ago, we have searched for gifted and wise mortals who might someday join us, even if they do not join our immortal family, we learn much from them and they learn from us. However they never learn the truth about us, unless they do join us."

He continued "and in all our history, we have never felt the call to someone over such a massive distance, with as much power as you called to use and you my dear called to us without evening knowing."

"That is phenomenal to us, and all of us are deeply curious to see what sort of abilities you will receive once you are an immortal, even more so if you decide to join us and taste the Elixir." He looked at her deeply, hoping that she would understand what he was trying to explain.

And then she understood him, it was not whether they would accept her; it was whether she and Xander would accept their offer to join.

"How much of a difference would it make if I took the Elixir?" she asked curiously

"It would make a massive difference, and I mean massive, it would give you many millennia's worth of strength which you would normally have to gain slowly over time, this has always been our greatest secret, it's something which we will not allow to someone who is unsure." Paul spoke again, putting deliberate emphasis on his words as he spoke.

"But you said that it also increases the chance of becoming an immortal in the first place?" she looked around the room as she said it, to see the resounding nods of "Yes" from everyone sitting at the table.

"There are however some risks." He said looking at her gravely, she didn't understand what he meant by risks and she decided to ask him.

"You will be immensely powerful straight away, there will be no gradual natural growth of power that is common for immortals, and you will have to deal with that. It might take you quite some time before you can fully control your abilities." He nodded at her as the information began to sink in.

"At any rate, I would advise taking the Elixir, several weeks before you are infected with the virus, so the elixir would have time to strengthen your body as well as give you a small taste of what abilities will come to you fully when you are one of us." He said and she couldn't deny the wisdom that seemed to shine from his voice as he spoke.

She looked to her right, to look into Xander's deep blue eyes and asked him the question that was bothering her.

"What do you think my love? Do you want to join the family?" she knew that she couldn't join them unless he decided to as well, no matter the risk it would pose to her.

"I owe them much my love, they saved your life and for that I will forever owe them a debt of gratitude which I will never be able to repay." His voice was calm and he nodded solemnly.

"But do you want to join them?" she asked him curiously.

The rest of the occupants around the table kept silent and allowed them to have their discussion; they were all so patient she couldn't even begin to comprehend just how much time it would take for her to ever develop that sort of ability.

"I want to be with you, and yes I do like them and enjoy their company." He looked at Paul and nodded towards him, she could see that they had bonded surprisingly well, but she knew that fighting on the same side, risking their lives for each other would create a strong bond.

She had suspected this already, as he seemed to have a deep relationship with him and appeared to have always enjoyed working alongside the Illuminati; it was his loyalty to the Covenant which had prevented him from joining them millennia ago.

"But what about Narcissia?" she asked and the mood around the room dropped, they had obviously been avoiding bringing this up until Narcissia was healed and could talk for herself.

"That will be down to her choice, and whether she too agrees to our rules." Paul said resolutely.

"But what are your rules?" Alexis asked bluntly, far more bluntly than she had intended and she almost wished she could have taken back her words.

"They are more obvious than you would think." He smiled as he said it, and then he continued and said the rules.

1. That you keep our secret from all mortals.

2. That a member must actively seek out gifted mortals and alert the rest of the family if they find a potential member.

3. No member may use their gift to harm another member.

4. No member may create another immortal without first consulting the family.

"But that all seems simple, how would that be so hard to follow?" she said curiously, careful to keep her voice passive and controlled.

"It is very easy to follow, right up until the time that it's not." Paul said humorously, and she didn't quite understand.

"I don't understand..." she looked around still feeling very puzzled.

"Well it is simple really, the rules are very easy to follow, but there are always circumstances that could make anyone lash out if they don't agree with it, an example of that would be, if part of your mortal family were to become very ill, what would you do? And would you respect the rules." He nodded at her knowingly, almost as if he could see she was beginning to understand.

"Ah, I think I understand." She replied truthfully.

"Indeed, but the question is, do you think you could follow the rules?" his voice was uncharacteristically serious as he spoke.

"I'm not sure, I think I could, but I can't ever really know." She hesitated, but he smiled as spoke and then he said "I'm glad you answered honestly, that is a very good place to start."

"Honesty is something we value highly, especially when dealing with other family members." Anthony said, with a cheerful tone to his usually placid voice.

"What about you Alexander? How do you feel about the rules?" Paul asked him and the room seemed to drown in silent anticipation.

"They are far easier to follow than the Covenants; however we all saw how that ended when they refused to allow me to turn Alexis." He said somberly.

"Yes but we, unlike the Covenant, would never deny you the right to turn someone you were in love with, we merely wish to know when someone is going to be turned into an immortal, we are at our core a family, we share information within it." Anthony said, with surprising compassion in his voice.

As she considered this, she thought about what he has said, about her mortal family, what she would do if one of them did become ill, she knew that she couldn't try to turn all of them, someone would notice and most of them would not survive it. Even with the elixir of life the survival chances were not what anyone would consider generous.

It was still a virus after all, and that it was not a guaranteed immortality serum, but could well kill her.

"I will do my best to follow your rules." She said with as much confidence as she could muster.

"That my dear, is all anyone could ever ask of you." He nodded gravely

"But you still need to fully understand that even if we give you the elixir, you may not survive the transformation when he shares his blood with you." Debbie said gravely.

He rose from his chair to signal that the meeting was over; she thought that he wanted to give her time for everything they had discussed to sink in before they gave their final verdict over whether they would give her the elixir or not.

She walked with Xander hand in hand up to their new bedroom, which was on the third floor of Paul's massive mansion, the room had a floral aroma when they entered and she noticed that someone had placed fresh flowers throughout the room, she looked at Xander but he raised his hands and said "it wasn't me angel."

The bedding had been changed and it was now a rich creamy colour tipped with a rich chocolate brown, she had to admit that whoever had decided on the colours had a fine eye, but she had bigger issues on her mind and she really needed Xander's advice.

"What do you think I should do?" she finally decided to ask him.

"Whatever makes you happy my love." He said to her with a sweet tone to his voice, which made her melt inside.

"But I want to be with you, forever." She told him honestly.

"Forever is a very long time my young angel." She could tell he was putting deliberate emphasis on his words as he spoke.

"It's not long enough, not nearly long enough for me." She said, and she could feel the tears welling up in her eyes, and she tried her best to hold them back.

He looked at her now, and she was sure that if he could have cried he would have, he was not used to anyone really loving him as much as she did, and he obviously had a hard time believing it when it did happen.

"I love you, you know that right?" she asked him pulling herself close to him

"Yes angel, I know." He said "but I love you more."

"That's not possible, you have no idea how much I love you." she grinned broadly at the defiant look on his face.

They both laughed at this and rolled around playfully on the bed, neither of them willing to give in, but she knew that neither of them were ever really going to have an argument over whom loves the other the most.

"You will survive, you know that right?" He said forcefully, she knew that he couldn't bear to think otherwise.

"Yes, but I am a bit worried about it. I don't know how much it will hurt when I'm infected." His eyes lit up as she spoke, and she could see he was feeling nervous.

"You'll have the Elixir, that will protect you a lot, but yes my love, it will be very painful for anything from thirty minutes, to three days." He said, barely more than a whisper.

"How painful?" she asked inquisitively, trying to hide the fear she felt.

"It will feel like all of your muscles and your skin is being ripped apart, you will be almost completely paralyzed by the pain of it, and once you're infected by it, it won't stop until it has converted every cell in your body, and while that might sound like a lot." He continued sensing the confused look in her eyes.

"It takes time, but it also varies person to person, some people's cells fight the process, and that is when it becomes painful, it will feel like every cell in your body is ripping itself apart."

"But don't fear my love, I will be there at your side the entire time, I promise you I won't leave you." He said finally, trying desperately to allay her fears.

"Is there anything you can do to speed it up?" she asked in desperation, she really didn't know how she would be able to endure the pain if it was really that bad.

"I'm not sure, we could try flooding your system with Adrenaline, that might make the conversion go faster, but it could also kill you." She could tell by the tone of his voice that he didn't want to risk this option.

"I'm willing to try it, if it will make it quicker, I don't fear the pain myself, but I know it would be torture for you." As she spoke, she was barely containing her emotions.

"You have no idea, but I'm willing to endure it so I can spend forever with you." His voice conveyed the anguish that she knew he was feeling.

He smiled and kissed her gently; she surrendered herself to him and allowed him to pull her close to him in a tight embrace.

Chapter 18: Narcissia's Story Part Two

4:05pm Vienna, Austria

Luccia

She had spent over a day deciding just how would be the best way to approach Paul and Alexander, she just didn't know how Paul was going to react, she knew that Alexander wouldn't believe her, but she had to try anyway, the future she had seen was just too terrible to allow to happen.

Finally she decided to get it over and done with, and she dialled the direct line to Paul's mansion, she'd had the number for a long time, her contacts in the telecoms industry had given her it, but she had never needed to use it before now.

It rang for what seemed like an eternity to Luccia, but finally she heard the dull click that meant someone had picked up the receiver.

"Hello, this The Norse residence, how may I help you?" her voice had a polite musical quality about it that she supposed would have put most people at ease. But Luccia knew better than to allow such a human trick of the senses to control her.

"I would like to speak to Paul please." Her high pitched tones cut through the air like a knife.

"Who may I say is calling?" Luccia noted that her voice didn't quite have the same ring to it now; it was almost like the woman was off guard and didn't know why.

"Luccia." She knew that saying more than this would have been pointless, as Paul would know exactly who his housekeeper meant; it wasn't a very common name after all.

"Okay thank you, I will put you on hold for a few moments." The housekeeper had obviously given up all pretences this time, and Luccia knew that this time she was not using a show voice, but rather how she would talk ordinarily.

She had to wait the better part of a minute before the irritating sound of the melancholic music finally stopped and the handset was picked up again, she recognised the voice instantly.

"Hello Luccia, how can I help you?" his deep voice was as calm as always and was the perfect exact opposite of Luccia's high, frantic voice.

"I have had another vision, it was a disturbing prophecy." She said hastily, the nervousness in her voice was apparent to both of them.

"And you want me to sing you a lullaby so you can sleep at ease?" he said sarcastically and then he burst out laughing in such an uncharacteristic fashion for him, and Luccia wondered whether he was reacting like this over his annoyance with what had occurred in Alaska mere days ago.

"I'm serious Paul; someone is going to set off an Atomic warhead." The silence that ensued could have been shattered by the drop of a pin and no one spoke for several moments.

"What is there that I can do to avert this?" as he spoke she could hear in his voice that he was paying her, his complete and undivided attention now.

"I fear that it is something to do with *that* mortal." She was barely controlling the scorn in her high pitched voice.

They both knew who she was referring to; Alexis would forever be *that* mortal to her.

"And why would a nuclear attack be the result of her? She is harmless." He said offhandedly, and she knew that he would need to think outside of the box if they were to avert the coming disaster.

"But she won't be once you have made her one of us." At that moment, they shared the same mutual thought. Luccia's biggest fear was that Alexis would cause a devastating shift in the balance of power of all immortals.

"Did you see her in your vision? Are you positive that it will happen because of her?" Paul asked uncertainly, almost as if he was in two minds about whether he wanted to know the answer or not.

"No, I didn't see her, but I saw an immortal army, it was a large group, over thirty of them, and they massacred a large mortal army, they left no survivors, and then they left and a nuclear device was detonated shortly afterwards and it destroyed the entire city." It almost sounded like she heard a sigh of relief on the other end of the phone, but Paul spoke again before she could force the issue.

"I see." He said hesitantly, and she suspected almost instantly that he did not believe that Alexis was part of the problem, and this was beginning to worry her profoundly.

"I hope you do, I hope you see and that you don't risk turning her." She could tell by his breathing that he was weighing her words before he spoke, but she heard a voice in the background which was muffled heavily, but she could pick it out quite clearly, as she had known the man whom the voice belonged to for millennia.

"Alexander wants to talk to you; he is understandably an important part of this." She had expected him to want to hear what she had to say, and she knew that he would be even tougher to convince than Paul was.

"Hello Luccia." His voice was harsher than usual; he obviously had not forgiven her for trying to kill him and Narcissia.

Did he not understand that those things didn't matter anymore, that none of that really mattered? She only wished now that she had killed Alexis, at least then they would all be safe. She thought bitterly.

"You cannot turn her, it is not safe, and she will create an army of immortals." She knew that he would be able hear the panic in her voice as she spoke.

"You cannot know that, she would never do that, your vision must be incorrect." His voice was strangely different as he said this, it was almost comforting.

"Possibly, but are you willing to take the chance?" She implored him in her most contrite voice.

"I promise you that we will not turn her until we are *absolutely* sure, but forgive me if I don't take your word for this." She could hear his deliberate emphasis on absolutely, as well as the disdain in his voice as he spoke.

"What do you mean by that?" she couldn't understand how he could be so petty at a time like this, it was driving her insane, she wanted to shout and scream at him and beg him to listen to her.

"I mean that your vision might have been because you wanted an excuse to kill Alexis and that you might have an ulterior motive for all of this." She knew instantly that he honestly believed what he was saying, and for a moment she began to feel an unusual feeling. It was one of despair and she had not felt it for such a long time that she didn't know how to handle it.

"You have to believe me, please Alexander, you have known me for most of your life, and I have never lied to you." She knew as she said this that it would hit home hard with him.

"No, you haven't, but you have betrayed me." This stung her, but she knew she had always done what she thought was best to do.

"You do not understand Alexander; I refused her entry into the Covenant because she is dangerous, far too dangerous to allow her to become one of us." She could hear the despair in her own voice now, and she knew that he would also be able to sense it.

"You thought the same of the Illuminati, and look how that turned out."

That retort stung her, but before she could counter it, he merely said "Goodbye Luccia, we will consider what you have said."

And then he put the phone down on her and the connection went dead.

She was lost for words, she was desperately trying to control her temper, and she knew that if she was to function she couldn't risk her temper getting the better of her, not again, this was far too important for that.

She decided that the only thing she had left to do was to convene the Council of the Covenant again, *what remains of it anyway* she thought. With Alexander and Narcissia no longer among them, it left the council with her, Xavier, Anna and Morgan, she almost considered calling for Sebastian, but she decided not to at the last moment.

She knew that they would not be safe living inside any city for the next few months at the very least, so once she had got them all together, she was adamant that they must all leave the city so they would at least be safe in case the nuclear attack was planned in order to destroy them.

Her mind was still considering all the possibilities, she almost wished that she still had Brakh around, he had at the very least been loyal to the end, as for her other comrades during the early years, Arafaz and Ptomaas, they had left so long ago that she didn't really believe that they were still alive, they couldn't be, no one had heard of them or from them in so long that the only possibility was that they were dead.

Unless of course they had returned to Lantis, but she seriously doubted this, because if they had, then they would not be able to leave now even if they wanted to and they would have likely died in there.

12:38pm Utah USA

Narcissia

She was finally beginning to feel better, the wound on her neck had not quite healed fully, there was still a deep scar there along with a large amount of deep bruising, but she could at the very least talk now without feeling like her throat was being scratched and torn.

And she knew that she would need to talk with Alexis again soon, she wanted her to know her story, and she really didn't understand why, in all her life she had only known one other person who made her want to tell her life story before and he had died.

Of course she realised that this was in part due to her touching Alexander's mind, but that didn't bother her, the traces of his love for Alexis had affected her so deeply that she wasn't bothered about it anymore.

When she finally decided to walk downstairs, they were all gathered in the large lounge area, Paul was talking to them rapidly but she wasn't paying attention to it, she caught her sister's name and winced. Nothing involving her sister could be good.

They then appeared to notice that she was there, and as they saw the blank expression on her face, they began to explain, what Luccia had said earlier that day, just hours before.

When she had heard everything her sister had said and everything they had discussed since, they had agreed to accept Alexis into the Illuminati's extended family and that though they wanted Alexander to wait a while before he turned her, they would give her the Elixir of Life so that she at the very least would be more resilient and she would not age further.

Overall they said it didn't make any difference, because it would have been safest if she waited several weeks to a month after taking the Elixir before they tried to infect her with the virus, to give her the best chances of survival.

They explained their new ideas as well, no one had been turned in a considerably long period of time, so modern science had changed many things, and they all suspected that from a scientific viewpoint that if they injected her with epinephrine as well that her body would be converted by the virus far easier.

As they discussed the different possibilities of what Luccia's vision could have really meant, Narcissia understood that she really needed to continue the history, she figured that if she did then they would explain a lot of things Luccia had not mentioned to them.

"I think you need to hear the rest of my story, which might open up some other possibilities." She said hesitantly, her voice still sounded scratchy, but she knew that she needed to continue no matter how painful it was for her. And she knew that she had everyone's full attention now as they looked at her in apprehensive silence.

Narcissia's story part two.

When I spoke before, I told you our history up until about 6'000 years ago, how we thought the threat from Enigmas was over but there was still some doubt about his fate, how Morgan had just been successfully brought into the Covenant.

We lived in peace for a relatively long time, but we eventually heard news that a man who had magical powers to start fires had appeared in what is now Asia; he had begun terrorising anyone who opposed him.

He had built up quite a strong empire by the time we had finally realised that it was Enigmas, he had built up a small core of immortals to protect him and we were forced to retreat from them, even though we were a lot stronger than his bodyguard they outnumbered us heavily and we could not get past them to get to Enigmas, he sat on his throne and mocked us, not even entering the battle himself.

This taught us a very valuable lesson; even though we were powerful we could not rely merely on our own strength, our response was to track down Arafaz and Ptomaas, this search took us nearly three years to find them, as they were both living in one of the most remote parts of southern Africa, they were living a life of relative peace there where they were worshipped as gods of the forest, occasionally coming in contact with other humans but on the whole they survived off of the blood of wild animals, as they produced copious amounts of adrenaline, until then we had not realised that we could use animals for this, without at least some human victims to supplement our diets.

However we had no real way of harvesting it until modern scientists developed the technique, but I get ahead of myself.

We had just tracked down Arafaz and Ptomaas and we explained about the danger of Enigmas and the death of Brakh, they were both furious to learn that he had killed their friend, and they agreed after some time to work with us to bring him to justice.

We spent a long time gathering an army together, and while they were only armed with spears and rudimentary swords they were nonetheless very deadly, we recruited heavily from some of the local African tribes which remained almost unchanged for countless millennia afterwards.

And we even converted almost a dozen of them into immortals like us, and while they were not as strong as the seven of us that made up the core they would even the score against Enigmas' bodyguard.

As our forces approached the outskirts of his empire, he had already realised what we were planning to do, and had responded in force, he marched his army out to face ours, his forces were strengthened by his own elite bodyguard.

The ensuing battle was catastrophic, and while all of our core survived all but three of our newest immortals were killed in the battle, Enigmas surrendered to us and we held a meeting to decide what we would do with him, none of us could figure out a way to kill him without one of us dying alongside him, so eventually we decided to exile him, with the understanding that if he dared to bother us again, we would find a way to execute him.

Arafaz and Ptomaas agreed to go with him and keep an eye on him, where they went we never found out, we had our suspicions but we were never certain, and in case you are wondering, we suspected that they had gone and tunnelled their way back into Lantis, that was something Arafaz had hinted that he would like to do. And though it might have taken them time, we never really knew.

Adrenaline Rush

Once again we were enjoying a time of peace and quiet; we had all agreed that the knowledge of Enigmas' actions must remain taboo, and we forbade everyone involved from talking about it, lest anyone else get any ideas about creating an immortal army and conquering the world. None of us ever spoke about it after that, and we retreated back to our European kingdom.

After that we decided that no more immortals should ever be created, we all swore that none of us would ever infect another mortal unless it was a matter of life and death for the entire human race.

Our numbers were still bolstered by the three surviving African warriors; they stayed with us sensing that they would no longer be welcome among their own people, while it took them many months to be able to communicate with us fully, they enjoyed their time with us and they showed no desire to ever leave us.

During the peaceful years that followed we tried unsuccessfully several times to find a way back into Lantis, but none of us ever managed it, it was buried far too deep and we did not know the precise locations to dig.

However unknown to us at the time, one of our Africans named Kuni was infatuated with a young mortal girl, and while he did not try to turn her into an immortal, he eventually got her pregnant, and most unusually, he did not infect her when they had intercourse.

He didn't tell us about it until many years after the girl had died, he had done his best to ensure the safety of his child, and we agreed to not harm his mortal son. Had we realised the consequences of allowing him to live, we probably would not have been so lenient.

For you see the consequences were that a small part of the virus had mutated into a dormant strain and while his descendants were not immortal, they had within them the chance of developing latent psychic abilities. And those who had gifts were far more likely to be able to survive the infection and become an immortal.

By the time we realised our mistake, the damage had already been done, we never knew the name of his son, but we found out that he had lived for over two hundred years, and for over one hundred and fifty years of it, he had bred indiscriminately, and had spread his genes throughout a very large portion of European and African bloodlines, and we could not solve the problem without destroying a large part of humanity.

This was something we were not willing to risk, so we did not do anything about it, and while the bloodlines grew more and more diluted, with his descendants that exhibited gifts becoming far less common, we breathed a sigh of relief, we thought the problem was sorting itself out naturally.

However his bloodline never truly died out; much to our dismay, even though it became very rare for anyone to manifest the abilities, some of his descendants did, and they went on to form the Illuminati.

Kuni's bloodline exists in a direct line even to modern times; his genes have spread throughout an enormous portion of mankind, growing weaker with each generation.

Three millennia ago we learned about the existence of a group of immortal humans, we had heard rumours that they were exceptionally gifted, Kuni begged us to leave them alone, but we knew we couldn't risk them being like us, so we sent Kuni's brother Halaka to investigate the group.

He spied on them for several months, and realised that they were not like us, that they had found their own way to achieve immortality, he returned to us to explain and once again we were relieved that our secret had not been compromised, and once again Kuni begged us to leave his family alone, he cared for them deeply but we had to learn more, so Halaka went back to find out everything he could.

He never returned to us again, and at the time we were very worried, we had no idea what had occurred, we eventually went searching for him, but the location where he had been before was empty, they had left long before we ever got there.

It wasn't for many years that we found out what had happened, Halaka it seems had attacked one of them, and they had responded in kind, they had captured him and they had used their abilities on him until he gave in to them and told them what they wanted to know, and then they had found out how to become true immortals just like we were, and by then it was too late, once again our deepest fears had arisen, we were no longer the sole masters of our secret.

Shortly after that the wars of Kane began, he was a rebellious member of the faction we came to know as the Illuminati, I believe you already know the story, but what you don't know is that we had already seen the tactics he used so effectively before, but we had sworn to keep the secret.

We were terrified that he was in communication with Enigmas; we knew that if Enigmas ever found an ally who was as gifted as he was then we would all be in terrible danger. For many years we ignored the threat as long as we could, but we eventually had to deal with it. And you know how that went so I won't bore you with the details of it, as I'm sure that Paul told it accurately.

With Kane vanquished and now with a new young immortal in our ranks, we had to make decisions about the future of the Covenant, we were breaking our own rules by allowing Alexander to live, we all knew that should he defect like Enigmas did then we would all be in serious trouble, we debated for a long time whether to execute him or not.

And as you've probably guessed we finally decided that his loyalty had warranted his survival, for a time at the very least, but that still left us with the Illuminati, we had seen them in action during the Kane wars, and we were so deeply worried about them that we contemplated attempting to wipe them out, but we had seen them fight, they were as capable as we were and Luccia and Xavier arrogantly believed that they were no match for the Covenant, however Anna, Morgan and I held deep reservations about fighting them with such insufficient information.

And so we allowed them to live in peace as long as they followed the rules we had imposed upon them, we never told them about Enigmas, worried that they would go looking for him or that they would gain inspiration from him.

"And that just about covers the important bits, I think." And as she finished she smiled and looked around the room.

Everyone around the room was staring directly at her, they were all clearly stunned, she knew that they must be thinking about the things she had said, how they were all related to each other through Kuni's genes, but none of them even attempted to speak.

2:21pm Utah USA

Alexis

She sat there in total amazement, she was struggling to really comprehend everything that Narcissia had said, how she was actually related to almost everyone in this room, and she had never even suspected it.

As she sat there she knew that she needed to ask the one question on her mind that she had no answer for.

"I'm confused, why do my abilities get triggered by Alexander when he is close to me? And how could the Illuminati have been drawn to me?" Narcissia smiled at her almost instantly as if she had been expecting this question.

"Because you are all Kuni's children, some of you carry the gene stronger than others." Alexis could hear the emphasis that Narcissia was putting on her words, and this worried her deeply.

She continued sensing Alexis' bewilders expression "Don't worry you're not that closely related, but sometimes the genes are stronger than others, and if I'm not very much mistaken, your genes Alexis, are the strongest mortal of your bloodline in the past two thousand years, if not longer."

"But..." she was lost for words, she didn't know what questions to ask, or what she should say.

"This is why Luccia did not want Alexander to turn you, everything he had said to us had hinted that you were of Kuni's bloodline, the very fact that he was so infatuated with you concerned her deeply because should the two of you procreate it could produce an incredible child, and that was why she forbade him from turning you."

And continued sensing Alexis was still totally lost in her own thoughts, but as much for everyone around her as for Alexis' own benefit.

"And that my friends, is the reason Luccia has been hunting down and killing any gifted mortals she ever hears about. She is deeply afraid that sooner or later, the genes will be strong enough to breed another immortal, and that the virus will spread out of control into the general population."

No one spoke for quite a while, everyone was in a state of deep shock, and she suspected that she knew why.

The illuminati had considered themselves a family for millennia, but it was still a big shock for them to find out that they are truly related in ways that they had no knowledge of.

"Why has no one ever told us this before?" it was Anthony this time, and as he spoke Paul nodded his agreement but didn't voice his own thoughts.

"Because Kuni died during the Kane wars, and Luccia did not want anyone else knowing, because if the Illuminati knew the truth, she was afraid that you might try to organise a breeding scheme to strengthen the bloodline."

"I don't understand..." it was Paul this time, and he seemed honestly surprised, it was the first time Alexis had ever seen Paul like this.

"I suspect, and this is only a hypothesis; that Alexis was descended from an incredibly strong genetic line of Kuni's bloodline, it is the only thing I can think of, and Luccia suspected this almost at once, when Alexander had spoken to us about her."

"And is that the reason she could call to us subconsciously?" it was Anthony again, and she was surprised to see him speak to Narcissia so much, he was usually fairly silent towards her.

"I believe it is yes, and I am almost certain that she will be able to survive the virus, even more so should she partake in the Elixir of Life, which I believe you have discussed as a possibility." Narcissia said knowingly.

"But why didn't I call to you sooner?" she asked in a tone laced with not only curiosity but also of fear. And when no one answered she said. "From what you have all said, you didn't hear my call until Xander had already rescued me."

Paul nodded and spoke up next. "I cannot answer your question, I don't know the answer, and we must assume that something changed once he returned to you again."

They all stood in silence, no one spoke for quite a long while, but then it was Alexis that spoke up again "but there is nothing special about me, how could I be of Kuni's bloodline."

Narcissia stared at her for several seconds and then answered "Don't believe everything doctors tell you, several of the manifestations of Kuni's bloodline are often misdiagnosed as mental health problems."

Alexis still didn't quite understand what she meant, she wondered if her diagnosis could have possibly been misunderstood, but she couldn't be sure.

"So you're saying that Luccia wanted me killed because I have a psychiatric disorder." Alexis said bitterly, none of it really making sense to her.

"No child, she wanted you killed because you carry the gene, we have done research into it, and it is an inert form of the Regenus virus, and close contact with an immortal who shares your bloodline can occasionally spark those inert cells and make them active."

"So your saying that close contact with Xander or someone else who shared common ancestry with me, will cause me to hallucinate?"

"They are not hallucinations; your dreams will occasionally be prescient, and some of them will be of the past or even present." She could see the blank expression on Alexis's face and said "Prescience is the ability to see the future, my sister Luccia has this gift, though hers is very limited, she can only see visions of things which will directly affect her, and even then only on a grand scale."

"An example of this was that she saw a vision of both Xavier and I dead on the ground." As she said this Alexis finally realised what she was getting at, she knew that she had received a similar vision in the form of a dream and she decided to ask Narcissia about it.

"Yes I believe that your dream was a prophecy, and I'm curious to see what other latent talents you have, I believe Alexander suspects that you occasionally receive visions when you touch objects as well, is that correct?" Narcissia said, a smile touched her lips as she spoke.

As she said this, everyone around the room once again looked at Alexis, she wasn't sure what she should say, they were all staring at her as if they were penetrating her every secret, though she knew that only Narcissia could do that, and she trusted her to not invade her privacy.

"I have hallucinated when touching objects yes, they are sometimes very vivid and I can see things that can't possibly be real." Alexis said in a tone that displayed her misgivings over their theories.

"They aren't hallucinations; it's a gift that mortals call psychometry, which means the ability to see visions connected with an object or person." She said, once again with a knowing smile that mildly irritated Alexis.

"But surely I would know if I had all these gifts?" she asked, positive that they were mistaken; she couldn't really believe that there was anything special about her at all.

"You were diagnosed by mortal doctors, who are trained to discount anything which they don't understand, and they have almost no idea what most genes can do." Narcissia said with a tone of finality which Alexis took to mean that she did not want to discuss it further.

"I have so many questions I don't even know where to start..." Paul nodded as Alexis spoke, and she could tell that he was feeling the same way, he held his tongue for several seconds, but she could tell that he would not be able to do it for long.

"Whatever happened to Arafaz and Ptomaas? And how come we have never heard about Lantis?" Paul said broadly and then everyone was focusing so intently on what Narcissia's reply would be that the only sound any of them could hear was the slow breathing of Alexis, she almost wished that she could stop her breathing so it would be quiet.

"We haven't heard from Arafaz and Ptomaas since they left with Enigmas, I honestly don't know what they are doing or even if they are still alive, it's possible that Enigmas murdered them, but I don't think so."

Everyone stared at her again now, waiting for her to react to the final part of Paul's question.

"You have heard of Lantis, however mortal legends are not always accurate, it was never technically a city, and it never sank beneath the sea."

Alexis' mind went wild at this, she had been too preoccupied with everything else had had learnt, to put two and two together to realise that the underground complex she had spoke of was the same as the tale of the lost city of Atlantis.

If she didn't know better she would have suspected that she was having one of the most vivid hallucinations of her life, not only had she met Alexander the great, but now she had finally realised that Narcissia was a survivor of the lost city that almost every human alive had heard of. *If I didn't know better, I will be waking up in a sectioned ward anytime now.* She thought with amusement, and a slight tinge of fear.

They all started firing questions at Narcissia again now, and she answered them patiently, every time she went to speak, the entire room went quiet, everyone was totally absorbed by what she had to say, and Alexis could tell that most of them had waited their entire immortal lives to hear of these things and that they were amazed that Narcissia had finally agreed to tell them her history.

Chapter 19: The Explosion

6:31pm Vienna, Austria

Luccia

As she finally took her seat the room they were all gathered in, the artificial lights masking just how deep underground they truly were. Once again she was in room that they used as their council chambers, where they had discussed some of the most important issues that had arisen over the past few centuries, as she looked around to see the two empty spaces she knew that the council had been severely weakened, but she was determined to not let it fall into complete disarray because of this.

Anna and Morgan were sitting across from her, Anna was glancing at her suspiciously, as if she were trying to figure out why they had been summoned again, and it would be the first time they had spoken since shortly after she and Xavier had returned from America. Morgan was focusing intently on Anna, and he looked faintly uncomfortable with all the aggression that was flowing between mother and daughter.

The room was well lit and the there were two doors connecting to it, one of them faced north while the other faced south, she had only used northern door so far, the one which allowed them to get to the elevator which would take them to the ground floor, the other one led to an emergency escape exit, which they had built to ease her own fears that they would be attacked, they never had been of course, not many people were foolish enough to attack them. The exit led all the way to the outskirts of the city, she had originally requested it because of the underground network from Lantis, as that had saved her life once before she hoped that it might do the same once again.

She had been deep underground ever since she had seen the vision of a nuclear attack, mainly because of her paranoid fear that she was the target, Anna was tapping her foot impatiently and she knew that she would need to explain to them soon or Anna would end up leaving in defiance.

"Are you going to explain why we are here?" Anna said, her impatience finally winning over her better judgement to remain quiet.

"I have had another vision." As she said this, Anna rolled her eyes in disbelief and Xavier scowled at their daughter.

"If you don't believe me I'm more than willing to let my blood speak for me." She said bitterly.

"Oh I believe you; I just find it a bit *too convenient*." Luccia felt strangely off guard because of this statement, it was the second time someone had said that it was convenient and she didn't like it.

"As I was saying." She continued disregarding her daughters comment "I have had another vision, one which if it is true, will cause catastrophic repercussions for us all."

She had everyone's attention now and she knew it, and even Anna didn't supply them with any more useless comments, so she decided to continue.

"I saw a very group of immortals, there were over twice as many of them than the combined forces of the Covenant and Illuminati together." She gave them several moments of silence before she continued, she knew that it was a lot for them to take in and she knew that she would need to convince all of them of the dangers.

"Did you recognise any of them?" it was Morgan this time, and she was surprised, he rarely ever spoke up in council unless he was very curious, which wasn't often.

"No, I did not, but there were over thirty of them that I saw, and I suspect that most of them were newborns, but worse than that, was the fact that my vision ended with the detonation of an atomic." The silence that exploded after that simple statement was eerily similar to the aftermath of an atomic explosion, and she found this rather ironic.

But that had done it, everyone was now in rapt attention, they all held a very deep fear of atomics, as they all knew that it was one of the only foolproof ways of killing an immortal, and they would all consider this a danger, as they all valued their lives.

"Do you know what city it was?" everyone looked at Morgan again, they were obviously surprised that he was still voicing his questions, rather than losing himself in introspection.

"No, I didn't recognise it, so it could have been any, and that is why I think we need to relocate to a home outside of this city, the bomb could have been set as an attack on us."

"Do you have any suspects as to who could have been the source of the army?" it was Xavier this time, of course he would want to know who the perpetrator was; he was always fond of clear cut missions.

"The only one we know about who will be a newborn will be Alexander's plaything, I have contacted them and requested that they not turn her, they have agreed to postpone it." she said, with the subtle undertone of resentment that allowed everyone to see that she still blamed Anna and Morgan for not joining them and turning the tide of battle in their favour.

"Are you sure no one else could be at fault?" it was Anna this time, and Luccia couldn't quite understand why she would side against her own mother in favour of a mortal.

"There is no one else, you know that. Who do you think it could be? Kane? Or Enigmas?" She snapped viciously at her daughter, who recoiled in shock at the anger in her mother's voice.

She continued and allowed her anger to taint her voice faintly. "If either of them were involved they would not have left it this long before they had taken their chance to get revenge."

"You can't be..." Anna's voice was cut off in a cascade of loud explosions emanating from above them, the force of it was so great that the ground shook; they could hear the floors above them buckling under the strain of the floors which had collapsed in the initial explosion.

Adrenaline Rush

Less than a second had gone by since they had all heard the explosion, a thick layer of dust had been stirred up by the vibrations caused by the explosion, and it was slowly falling back down, gravity once again winning over the small particles.

Everyone in the room stared around blankly for what seemed like an eternity, but to a mortal's senses it would have been under half a second as their bodies had been shocked into overdrive by the threat to their bodies, it was Xavier who spoke first, his voice barely cutting above the noise of concrete collapsing and crashing down several floors above them, and he shouted "OUT!"

None of them needed to hear anymore, they had all been thinking it, all they needed was to be pulled out of the shock they were all in, and one by one, moving as fast as they physically could, they ran towards the southern facing door, the one that led to the emergency exit.

Xavier led the way, not bothering to open the door, he kicked it with so much force that it crumpled under the pressure and fell to the floor, its heavy metal hinges were torn from the brackets on the wall, they had all left the room before the thick steel bolts landed on the floor, no one could hear the loud clang as they stuck the concrete floor.

Barely a second after that they were all running as fast as they possibly could, they were now almost a hundred metres from the room, they all knew they couldn't keep up with the pace they were putting their bodies through for long, but they knew they had done enough when they felt the tremor behind them, where the entire building had collapsed and sent a shockwave through the tunnels.

For a moment they thought they were safe, but then the tunnel began to buckle and the metal groaned, they knew it was not going to be able to take the pressure for long, they ran as fast as they could, but they knew they had over another mile left of the tunnel to run through before they were out of it.

And while that wasn't a long distance for them, it would put a lot of strain on all of them, especially Xavier who had still not fully recovered, but they had no choice, the tunnel began collapsing piece by piece, the sound of it was a deafening cascade of loud explosions as it crashed to the ground.

None of them had time to look behind them to see how close they were; they had to push their bodies to their maximum abilities. Luccia could feel her muscles burning as they consumed every miniscule bit of adrenaline she had in her body.

She was running mere feet behind Xavier now, and she could sense Anna and Morgan behind her, she couldn't hear them because of the deafening noise behind them. And then she saw it, she could see light ahead of them.

She couldn't possibly slow down in time, so as soon as she left the tunnel she was travelling at such velocity that she went flying through the air and crashed hard into a large mound of earth, had anyone been watching from the distance they would have suspected that a meteorite had collided with the earth, the collision sent a shockwave of earth for over fifty yards all around them, and the simultaneous eruptions of earth from the holes left by Anna, Morgan and Xavier.

As they all dug them self out of the earth, they looked around at each other, and then back at the tunnel's exit, it had finally collapsed now, they had been mere seconds away from being trapped within it, and it could have taken them months to dig out had it not killed them, which was a distinct possibility.

Silence enfolded them now, they were all far too busy recovering their breath to talk, and they all looked at each other once again, the silence was ended by Anna's voice "You know mother, I think you might have been right about us leaving the city."

The next eruption of sound was that of laughter, both Anna and Morgan had broken down and were laughing so hard that they fell to the floor, even Xavier chuckled lightly and Luccia had to admit to herself, things could have gone a lot worse, then the pang of loss hit her as she remembered that they were not the only ones in the building when the bomb went off.

Adrenaline Rush

6:59pm Wolfsgraben, Austria

Luccia

They had finally made it to the small house that they owned in one of the nearby towns just outside of the city, and even though it was very small and quite dingy, and they would not be able to stay there for very long in any degree of comfort, but they did however have a small supply of epinephrine there which they all needed urgently after their recent exertion.

Once they had one by one, all showered to get rid of the dirt and dust that their bodies were caked in, and changed into fresh clothes, Luccia knew that they would not be able to stay here.

She knew that someone and she didn't have any idea whom, had tried to kill them, if she didn't know better she would have immediately blamed the Illuminati, but she knew that they were not brave enough or cowardly enough to attack them in that fashion.

She was trying desperate to not take in what had happened, they had lost their home, and they had also lost Sebastian, he was in the upper levels of the complex, and they all knew that he couldn't have hoped to survive the blast and subsequent collapse of hundreds of tons of metal and stone.

No one had spoken for quite a while now, they were all relaxing in silence, and all in a little bit of pain, in a way that is similar to when athletes exert themselves when they are tired, if immortals do the same, it makes their muscles ache and burn for several hours afterwards, but the recent influx of adrenaline had helped them all substantially.

"I'm going to contact the Illuminati and ask them for assistance." Her words cut across the quiet room with such force that had they been making any noise then it would have silenced it. Xavier grumbled and she knew that he would not be happy about it.

"Are you sure that's a good idea?" He asked cautiously.

"What choice do we have? Who else can we turn to?" she snapped at him

"But." However before he could say more, she cut across and said "No ifs, no buts, someone is trying to wipe us out, someone almost did, we cannot go to any of our own houses, our entire security may have been compromised!" She saw him take a deep breath and then he breathed out slowly.

"Our only chance is to get outside assistance and you know it." She said in a voice of enforced calm and tranquillity, though she knew that none of them believed her act.

"But." He winced but when she didn't cut him off he continued "would they help us? Mere days ago we were fighting them, why would they want to help us now?" he said timidly.

"It's simple; they need us, not quite as much as we need them, but still..." Anna said with an unusual strength of will that surprised everyone in the room.

Everyone turned and stared at Anna now, she had not said anything since her comment as they left the tunnel, and they were all surprised that she had said something so constructive.

Once again the room was filled with silence as they considered what she had said, Luccia knew she was right, they did need each other, they would need every immortal they could to be able to survive the coming storm.

"What do you plan on saying to him?" Xavier's voice was cold and low, she knew he wasn't pleased about this, but she knew that they didn't have any other options.

"The truth, we need them, they need us, and we will need to work together if any of us are to survive the coming war." Bitterness edged her voice, as she thought about the irony of that statement.

"Do you have any idea how bad this war is going to be?" it was Morgan again, asking the question that was on all of their minds.

Of course they would want to know if she had seen anything which could help them, but she wasn't really paying attention to that, she had just realised something that she caused a very strange feeling in the pit of her stomach.

"It's nothing to do with *her*..." they all stared at her for several moments now, none of them speaking up, they all knew that she didn't like not being right, but they all knew that whoever had attacked them, couldn't have been Alexis, as they knew she was still in America.

"Why is that such a shock? You said you didn't recognise anyone in your vision." It was Anna again now, and her voice carried a trace of scorn, they were both thinking the same thing, had she not refused the mortal's entry into the Covenant, and then they would have been a lot stronger and more able to handle the crisis.

"I..." her voice broke and seemed to get higher pitched "I thought it would have had to have been her."

"It would appear to be someone else; the question is who could it be?" She looked at Morgan as he spoke, waiting for him to provide any examples that he had thought of, but he remained woefully silent.

"It could have been mortal's that attacked us." It was Anna this time, and Luccia almost laughed at what she had said. Luccia knew that this was all connected to her vision, and that vision had a lot of renegade immortals in it.

"Yes... it could have been, but it wasn't." Anna glared at her now but she raised her finger so that she would remain silent. "It is all related, the vision, the attack, everything."

"Okay." Anna she said impatiently and when didn't Luccia interject she continued "so if it wasn't mortals, it wasn't the Illuminati, then who was it?"

"I don't know" Luccia answered honestly, and she could tell they could all hear the truth in her voice.

Morgan spoke next and said what they were all thinking. "It was someone new, or someone very old."

"So it would appear." Xavier nodded his agreement as he spoke.

"Phone him then." Xavier said bitterly, she knew that he didn't want her to contact Paul, but they all knew that they had no other options.

She left the room so that she could have some silence while she spoke to him, she knew that they would all be able to hear what she said, but at least she wouldn't have to put up with them staring at her.

She phoned the number she had for Paul's mansion and once again she was put on hold by the housekeeper while she went to find Paul. It didn't take very long for him to get to the phone this time, barely thirty seconds had passed.

"Hello again Luccia." He said coldly

"We need your help." Her normally haughty voice was unusually contrite, so much so that it took him several moments to respond.

"Why what is wrong?" His voice showed that he was obviously very puzzled by her request, but she was thankful that he was treating it very seriously.

She spent several minutes explaining everything that had happened since they had last spoken, how she had convened the council to discuss the threat that was indicated by her vision, and how their complex had been destroyed and how they had barely escaped alive through the tunnels. He listened with rapt attention, not speaking so that she could explain everything as briefly as possible.

"I see." He said and then "I take it none of your other facilities are secure?" His voice showed that it was as much a question as it was a statement of fact.

"No, I think we have been compromised." A slight twinge of humiliation edged her voice, and she felt even more embarrassed that she had allowed such a human emotion to taint her voice and show her weakness.

"Do you have any ideas on who might be doing this?" she knew that he was hinting about whether it was anything to do with Alexis, and she answered his question.

"I have no idea who it is, but I know who it is not." She knew her pride was getting the better of her, and that they both knew that she didn't want to say it aloud, but they both knew what she meant.

"So your reservations about her are over?" the silence that unfolded after his question was almost painful to Luccia, she hated admitting she was wrong, and he obviously knew that.

"Yes." She replied, barely more than a whisper.

He didn't say anything for several seconds, it seemed like an eternity to Luccia.

"Could it be anything to do with Enigmas?" This statement blew her mind, of all the things she had expected, this was not one of them, she was so shocked that her sister had told them at least in part the history of the Covenant, they rarely spoke his name aloud anymore because of the trouble he had caused.

Her mind reeled as she tried to think of an answer to his question, she knew that if she spoke she would not make very much sense and she didn't want to risk displaying more weakness.

She was in total shock that her sister had betrayed them so completely. It took her a while to calm her thoughts, Paul waited patiently for her to reply to his question, he obviously knew the effect it would have had on her and he didn't care.

"We haven't heard from him in a long time." She knew he was waiting for more from her, as he remained quiet, and then she continued "Even if it was him, why would he have waited so long before..." they both knew what she meant be before, she didn't want to voice it and he knew it.

"Something has changed; we just need to find out what." He said politely and she knew he was right, but she didn't feel the need to tell him that.

"There is something else, I need to ask a favour of you." Once again he went quiet for several moments, she suspected he had been waiting for this, but she had no way of proving it.

And then he finally replied "Go on." She smiled for a second; at least he was allowing her to get to the point.

"As you know, none of our facilities are safe; we're going to need somewhere secure to stay, outside of our own network." she heard the very faint sound of "hmmm" on the other end of the line, and she knew that he must be thinking of where he could send them.

"I will have to speak to Michael, his place is closest to you, and can you hold? Or should I phone you back once I've spoken to him?" she knew that if she had to hold the line she would have to put up with the irritating music that would flood the line, she had never understood why they chose such horrible music for lines on hold.

"Phone back would probably be best, you don't know how long it will take." And then she gave him the number to contact her on and they both said their polite goodbyes.

Her mind was still shocked about the betrayal of her sister, even though Luccia knew that she had probably done the right thing, Luccia still felt a twinge of guilt over the circumstances that had led almost to the murder of her own sister.

She walked into the other room where her companions were all seated, they looked at her apprehensively, and they could tell by her body language that she had learnt something which she found distressing.

They did not ask her what was wrong; they all knew her well enough to know that she would tell them when she was ready to. She tried to relax for several minutes before she finally managed to get her thoughts under control.

As she told them what they hadn't heard from her conversation with Paul, they all reacted in a different manner, Xavier as she could have expected broke the table he was resting his hands on, and Anna sighed at him in a bored fashion, while Morgan placed his hand on Anna's shoulder ever so gently.

She wasn't really paying that much attention whilst Xavier and Anna began their debate over how Narcissia could betray them, the only thing on her mind was how long it would take Paul to contact them, and who had it been in her vision that was planning on using atomics.

Her phone rang and she was quite surprised at how little time it had taken Paul to get back to her, she had expected him to take at least an hour, but while it had felt like forever to her, while she was lost in her own thoughts it had only really taken him a mere fifteen minutes to talk with Michael and then phone her back.

She walked into the kitchen once again before she answered him, she didn't want Xavier's tooth grinding to get in the way.

They dispensed with the usual pleasantries they both knew they were on a tight deadline. "Michael has agreed to your use of his home, you'll need to book tickets to the UK, and then arrange for a car to take you to Cambridge." He stopped at the harsh intake of breath that had escaped her.

But before she could comment that she really didn't want to be in a city until this threat was over with he said "The mansion isn't in the city, it is outside of it, so relax and let me finish."

"We have also decided that we need to organise a meeting so that we can discuss this, it is far too important to ignore It." she nodded her head in agreement but then realised that he couldn't see that gesture so she voiced her opinion instead.

"Where?" she asked curiously, not really wanting to travel too far as she knew that they would be in danger wherever they travelled.

"At Michael's place, its ideal and we can make it there by tomorrow, Anthony is organising it all as we speak."

As he gave her, the exact directions to Michael's mansion, she was grudgingly impressed by how calm and composed he was, she had never seen him unnerved before, he always remained completely in control and she wondered how he had managed that, given how young he was compared to her.

Once he had finished giving her the directions, they said their polite farewells and she walked back into the front room so that she could tell them the news, Xavier was still in a foul mood because of Narcissia, but she ignored him, he would have to get over it.

Anna and Morgan were pleased that there would be a meeting to discuss the impending disaster, she had expected this, neither of them were quite as adamant as she and Xavier were, about how dangerous it was to have such a large group of immortal's as powerful as the Illuminati were, while they remained out of their control

Even more so when that group were the descendents of Kuni, and they seemed to be unconsciously be drawn to his other mortal descendants, they had been forced to execute quite a large number of those mortals in the past, as their abilities had grown too strong to allow them to become immortals as well, to embrace the virus completely. The mere thought of it was anathema to Luccia, and she felt her anger flare as she considered it.

While she did feel a small amount of remorse for those mortals, she knew that it was for the best, they wouldn't all be harmless like the Illuminati, if you could say they were harmless, but at the very least they were not overly aggressive, but even they had had their own black sheep in the family. And how shockingly alike Kane was when you compared him with Enigmas, they both started out as good people, but they were drawn to the allure of power and that had caused their own downfall.

As they booked their flights and arranged to be met by a limousine at the airport in London, she began to feel calmer; soon they would be able to enjoy at least a small amount of security.

Chapter 20: The Gathering

3:20pm London, UK

Xander

As they arrived in the busy London airport, he had the uncanny feeling that he was forgetting something, he couldn't think what it was, but he couldn't shake off the feeling.

Paul had already arranged for transport for the four of them to get to Cambridge, and so he, Paul, Anthony and Michael all climbed into the limousine and prepared for the long drive to Michael's long term residence in the secluded countryside that was on the southern border of Cambridge.

No one spoke until they were well outside of London and the tension was apparent in the air, none of them wanted to talk about what was weighing heavily on their minds, least of all Xander, he knew that he most of all would receive the most scrutiny from the Covenant, *well what was left of it*, he smiled as he thought to himself bitterly.

Finally not being able to stand the silence any longer, Paul spoke up "So what are the possibilities then?"

The reply came not from Anthony like he expected, but from Michael "There are three possibilities." He said calmly and with surprisingly delicate control that it impressed Xander.

He continued on, not letting very much emotion fill his voice, his vocal control continued to be astounding, Xander was shocked, Michael didn't often talk in his presence, so Xander knew that he must finally be beginning to trust him. "The first possibility is that it is Kane *again*, but that doesn't seem likely." As he said this he glanced at Paul knowingly and then said "Is it possible, Paul?"

It took Paul several moments to recompose himself before he said "Yes it is possible, but it just doesn't make sense."

Michael disregarded the last part of the statement and continued on in his strictly controlled monotone voice "The second possibility is that it is Enigmas, but if it is him, why has he waited for so long before resurfacing and why now?"

No one spoke until Anthony looked at him and said "But what is the third possibility?"

Silence filled the passenger cabin of the limousine again and for what seemed like eternity to Paul, Anthony and Xander no one spoke, no one breathed and then Michael spoke again. "The third possibility is that Luccia was right."

"I don't follow you." Paul looked around to see if comprehension had spread to anyone else, or if he wasn't the only one who wasn't sure what Michael was leading to.

"I mean she might have been right to fear Kuni's bloodline." And he continued when he sensed the dawning comprehension spread across Paul's face. "There is a very small possibility that the virus could have manifested itself naturally in one of Kuni's bloodline, the real problem with this that I can't figure out, is how we haven't heard about this before now."

"I don't think that is very likely." Anthony said breaking the silence.

"Neither do I, but the possibility remains." Michael replied to him.

They sat in silence for quite a while after that, no one really wanted any of those possibilities to be correct, but they knew that it could be any of them, they had seen from Alexis the strength of that bloodline, and she had no idea of it, they all wondered at just how powerful she might become once she was given the Elixir and then the virus.

Xander couldn't get rid of his feeling of apprehension, he knew that he would have to restrain himself or face the possibility of violence from Xavier again, he expected him to be severely angered by his defeat in Alaska and he would likely seek any opportunity to claim himself a victory, even though by attempting it he would cause this meeting to fail.

As he looked out of the window, he could see that the sun had almost set, the colours were radiant and beautiful, and he couldn't help but think that the only things in this world that were more beautiful to him were the aurora borealis and of course Alexis, he wondered wistfully about how amazing it would be to spend it with her, but he knew that he had to do this, or the world he was bringing her into would not be safe and that was something that he could not allow.

"Are you going to give her the Elixir?" he asked impatiently, determined to break the silence.

"Later my young friend." Paul placed a hand on his shoulder in an attempt to calm him, it didn't work at first, but he began to feel calmer in the ensuing silence.

He knew they were probably right to delay, but he couldn't help but fear how fragile she was in her current state and the sooner she was given the elixir; the sooner he could share his blood with her.

7:05pm London, UK

Paul

As their limousine pulled into the gates that secured the boundaries around Michael's home, he could feel a sense of unease spread through his companions, he knew that none of them particularly wanted to have to discuss matters with the Covenant, that none of them had wanted to come, but they had felt obligated to because if they hadn't, then Paul would have gone alone.

Michael was grinding his teeth over the fact that he had allowed the Covenant to befoul his home.

He could feel Alexander's unease in how rigid he was sitting, it was almost as if he felt that his presence was going to compromise what Paul hoped to achieve here, but Paul felt confident that he would be an asset, after all who knew the Covenant better than he did.

As the car finally stopped, they climbed out the door one by one, Paul led with Michael close behind them, and they were met by Luccia and her companions who were standing just outside the doorway that led into the country mansion, the house that Michael had owned for centuries, they all knew that he prided himself in how well preserved it was, and he had grudgingly allowed the Covenant to use it as a temporary residence.

Paul and the others were beginning to feel more at ease, they had known as they approached the outskirts of the mansion that Luccia had told the truth about their numbers, but it had been touch and go before that.

They couldn't have been sure it wasn't an attempted ambush, but now that they could see and feel the location of the Covenants leaders they began to relax, he could see the tension in not only Alexander, but in Xavier as well, and he knew that Xavier had better keep himself under control or Alexander would be forced to incapacitate him once again.

As they made small talk and discussed where the meeting should take place, Michael spoke up and suggested that they use his patio, and as they walked there, he could tell that Luccia hadn't even considered holding the meeting outside, he knew that she was more comfortable inside, but she was willing to give it a try.

They all sat around the rectangle room in the soft patio chairs, they were silhouetted by the moonlight, and all of them could see perfectly clearly even though there was very little light, they all had the ability to see clearly, even in the dark so it didn't bother them.

Xavier was busy flexing his muscles and cracking his knuckles loudly, so loud that everyone in the room stopped and turned to look at him, Luccia made a stopping motion at him, but he did not see it, he was focusing on Alexander and only Alexander.

Paul was impressed that Alexander was not rising to Xavier's bait, but he knew that his resolve would only last so long, he cleared his throat loudly in an attempt to gain the attention of the group, but it didn't have any effect.

He knew what was going to happen as soon as he saw the smile rip across Alexander's face, as soon as he had done it Xavier arose and was about to fling himself at Alexander when the sound of a loud crack sent a shockwave that stirred up all the dust in the room, and caused birds to fly away in fright from the nearby trees and bushes.

As the dust settled, Xavier was on the ground, with Luccia standing above him, she had obviously felt the need to intervene, she glared at Alexander now for giving Xavier the excuse to start a fight, but then she aided Xavier to get to his feet and they both walked back to their chairs.

Now that they were all calm Luccia decided to go over every detail of what she had seen in her vision, she recounted every tiny detail she could think of, from the local landmarks to the exact shade of colour on the soldiers uniforms as well as any insignia's she could remember.

Anthony recognised not only the uniforms but also the local landmarks that Luccia had seen, and he knew that it must have been on the outskirts of Vienna, and he also knew that there was a parade of the Austrian armed forces scheduled to take place in a couple of months time, on the outskirts of Vienna.

For several moments nothing could be understood because everyone had begun talking at once, and while some of them were not overly concerned by this, they were being blinded by their prejudices. Alexander and Luccia attempted to calm the group so they could continue the discussion in a controlled manner.

"Right." Paul said now that they once again had silence in the room

"We need to decide how we're going to handle this; we cannot risk fighting them in front of witnesses." He looked around the room at everyone sitting there one by one so that they all knew he was referring to all of them.

"What choice do we have?" Xavier growled, and without giving Paul a chance to answer his question he said "You would rather we allow those mortals to get massacred?"

"That was not my intention, but I do not see how us charging in head first into battle while there is a whole army gathered around us watching." Xavier pulled back at his words as if he had been slapped across the face by them.

For several minutes they discussed it in within their groups, Alexander was talking to Anthony about how they could handle the two on one odds and he remarked "Well by then we will be one woman stronger." But before he had the chance to continue his sentence Xavier had rose from his chair and had pinned Alexander up against the wall by his throat.

Luccia shouted at him to let him go but he refused, she had to prise his hands off of him in order to break the potential fight up before it escalated into something that could not be stopped. Alexander was still smiling, obviously unconcerned by it all.

"So you're going to turn her after all?" it was Luccia again, her voice carrying venom again.

"You have already said you were mistaken and that it wasn't down to her." Alexander wasn't helping matters talking to them in such a baiting tone, but Paul knew he couldn't stop him from doing it.

"I have been known to be wrong, but surely you can see what a risk she is?"

Anna and Morgan looked at each other and nodded, as if they were communicating without words, they seemed completely in tune with each other that it distracted him from the debate going on between Luccia and Alexander.

"We need her." Alexander was protesting to Luccia now and she responded fiercely "No, you need her! We do not!"

Paul decided that he had let them argue more than enough now, and raised his hand and said "ENOUGH!" they both fell silent now, and allowed him to say his piece.

"You yourself said she was not the one responsible, if she is not a danger, then her abilities might well be helpful to us, you know full well that the mortal descendants of Kuni make exceedingly strong immortals."

His words cut into Luccia, she was not used to him knowing on his ancestry and he could tell that she did not like it at all.

She looked as if she were going to make a retort, but every time she seemed as if she were going to speak, she stopped just before, like someone who was battling for the right words to use. And then she simply nodded, so Paul assumed that she had given up trying to make a case against Alexis.

He decided to change the subject to get her off of the course she was on "The real question is who is responsible?"

"Indeed." Anthony agreed quickly almost as if he had been waiting for it.

Michael was the first to speak "We have come up with three possibilities."

As he said this, Luccia, Xavier, Anna and Morgan all stared at him; this had caught them surprisingly off guard as he knew it would. Anna spoke next "Three?"

"Three." He said answering her question but not elaborating on it, murmurs spread across the room again and he raised a hand with his finger extended and waited for silence again.

"The first possibility is that Kane has come out of retirement, if this is the case then he has spent over two millennia planning this, and we will find it very difficult to stop him."

He surveyed the room slowly before he continued "However, if it is Kane then we are very fortunate." Xavier glowered and muttered that he didn't consider this a fortunate event at all; they all knew that Kane had a grudge against the covenant.

Michael ignored him "This would be fortunate because he would not be any stronger than anyone present, if anything he would be a bit weaker."

"And the second possibility?" this time it was Anna who spoke up trying to keep the conversation going in the right direction.

"The second possibility is that it is your old friend Enigmas who is responsible, and if that is the case and we had all better hope that we're wrong." He looked around the room again before he went on "Then we would all in serious danger as he is stronger than most of us here and remarkably powerful. Not to mention he would have spent the better part of seven thousand years preparing for this moment."

No one spoke, so Michael continued speaking his mind "The real question if it is Enigmas is why now?"

He looked at Luccia now who was deep in thought, she couldn't allow herself to believe that it was him, because if she admitted that then she would know that it was her problem, and if it was Kane again she could be free to blame the Illuminati for it all.

Anna spoke again, shaking them all out of their own thoughts and back into the real world "What is the third possibility?"

Michael's reply shocked them all as he knew it would. "That it is someone or something new."

"New?" Luccia asked curiously, she hadn't even considered this.

"Yes, new, there is a chance, and I am not certain, but it could be possible that what you have feared for millennia has finally come true, like a self fulfilling prophecy."

"I don't follow you." She said blankly

"Yes you do, I am referring to the children of Kuni, you have feared for millennia that someone of his bloodline would be strong enough to make the immortal gene activate."

Silence spread across the room, it was so quiet that you could have cut the very air with a knife, no one wanted to speak, and

Paul grinned quietly, no one breaking the silence until Michael finally said "Well? Have you nothing to say?"

Morgan spoke now for the first time since they had arrived "If that is the case, then how has that individual infected so many people in such utter silence, we haven't heard anything about it, and you know we keep watch for such things."

"My dear friend, you know full well that if it was someone powerful enough to activate the gene, then they would likely be gifted enough to hide from your eyes, the real problem for them would have been hiding from us, for we can often sense them."

Paul spoke then continuing what Michael had said "Indeed, until recently we had no idea how certain gifted people seemed to call out to us, we now know that it is because they are of our bloodline."

"But overall, I suspect that it would be the first or second theory that would be most likely, as the other option is very remote." Paul said vehemently.

"What can we do to combat the threat?" it was Anna again, asking the question they were all thinking.

"Well we have the same tactic we have always used." Anthony suggested, but the look on his face told anyone paying attention that he didn't really believe they would try it.

"No, that cannot be allowed." Luccia shot him down immediately, but Xavier beside her had a curious look on his face and then he spoke up "It is an option though, my love"

Luccia glared at him as if he had betrayed her, everyone in the room new that Luccia was very adamant against creating new immortals, and they all knew the risks if they did.

"The risks far out way the benefits." It was Anna again, and Luccia looked at her in what could only be described as shock, she obviously hadn't expected her daughter to side with her.

"Perhaps" Paul said "But we do need to keep our options open, and if it is the only way we can keep the human race alive, then we will have to consider it."

"The more immortals there are running around, the higher the chance that mishaps will occur, we cannot afford another Kane and heavens forbid another one like Enigmas." Luccia looked around the room, as if she were waiting for someone to disagree with her.

They all knew that she made a very good point, they would have difficulty trying to control a large group of newborn immortals under the best of circumstances, but to expect to use them effectively to fight a war against an almost unstoppable army would be foolish at best, suicidal at worst.

"No we will have to deal with this mess ourselves." Anthony looked grim as he spoke.

Sensing that this meeting was over and that nothing would be gained by continuing talking in circles, Paul arose, followed by Anthony, then Michael and Xander.

Paul spoke after several moments and said "We will be in touch, we need to discuss this with the rest of the family, and we will be in contact with you very soon."

As they left, the air felt oddly chilly as if it was enchanted to carry all the misgivings that they themselves carried with them about the coming storm.

They arranged for tickets while they were driven back to London and they would be ready to fly back to America early the next morning, the time they would travel meant very little to them, they would not get jetlagged and they knew it.

Paul had been expecting Alexander to bring up Alexis for several minutes before he actually did, and when he spoke up Paul almost smiled knowingly, he knew what he would say before he said it.

"Paul, I want to talk to you about Alexis." He said quietly, even though he knew that Michael and Anthony could hear him.

"I know you do." Paul said, with a hint of curiosity in his voice that he knew would make it appear that he didn't know why Alexander wanted to talk to him about her.

"You're not going to make this easy for me are you?" Alexander said, with the faintest hint of annoying in his voice, Paul's lip twitched as he heard this and he let out a loud laugh and then he replied to him "No, I guess I'm not."

"We need her, and if we have less than two months before we're going to be in a state of war..." Paul could hear the sound of desperation in his voice and he knew the reasons behind it.

"I know, but there is no need to rush these things my young friend."

Xander looked at him for several moments before he replied "I am not that much younger than you." He tilted his head slightly and smiled back at Paul.

"Indeed."

"So will you give her the elixir?" his voice was conveying the desperation that he felt now and he knew it.

"Yes, we will." Paul turned to look at Anthony now, and once Anthony turned to face him he nodded his head.

Anthony then picked up the phone and ordered another set of airline tickets, he would be flying to his home in Connecticut before joining them in Utah, Alexander looked at Paul curiously, and he didn't understand what Anthony change of plans meant.

Paul decided to let him know what was going on "Anthony is returning to his home to collect a vial of the elixir, we only keep a very small supply of it, and we never allow it to be in the same place as our guests."

"I'm sure you can understand." He said politely and then continued "I had the supply that was secured in my mansion moved to Anthony's before we travelled from Alaska."

"So you're going to give her it?" he asked, a hint of impatience slipped out

"Yes I guess we are."

There was silence again for several moments before Xander finally spoke up, and said "Thank you."

Paul looked at him for several minutes and then said "Don't thank me yet, we might be putting her in grave danger, if she is one of us when the storm hits, she might not survive it."

"I know, but we have to try."

The trip home was fairly quiet after that, none of them were really interested in talking, they all had a lot to consider, everything they had heard and suspected.

Paul knew that they were all extremely worried, and by the time they arrived at the airport, they had not spoken for several hours. This didn't surprise him much because the meeting with the Covenant had not gone according to plan, they had expected to figure out some sort of plan, but all that had occurred had been fairly inconsequential, they had not learnt anything they didn't already know, the only ones whom had benefited from it were the Covenant, or more to the accurately, what was left of it.

Chapter 21: The Elixir

2:50pm Utah, USA

Xander

They had been at Paul's home for several hours now, everyone except Anthony who was due to arrive sometime later that day.

He was feeling very apprehensive as they all gathered in the meeting room, he knew what this would be about, and they needed to discuss everything that had been said during the meeting with the Covenant, he didn't expect them to come to anything new, but he was expected to be there anyway.

They were all seated now, with Paul at the head of the table and he begun the meeting in much the same way as he always did, he explained briefly everything that had happened in Cambridge and then went over everything we had suspected.

Alexis was looking around strangely curious for a while, she was not used to being part of meetings of this type, and she had expected them to keep her at arm's length because she was still a frail mortal. Xander had not been able to get her alone to tell her that as soon as Anthony had returned then she would be given the Elixir of Life, which would increase the abilities of her mind and body to a state vastly more powerful, still not as strong as someone infected with the vampire like virus, but far superior to that of a mortal.

She would cease to age, and she might even grow slightly younger, Paul had explained to both of them that each person is different, they all stabilise at different ages, and while one might be at their peak at the age of 18, another might not be at their physical and mental peak until they are around 35, this was the case with Paul and Anthony, yet they did not look it, because their skin was perfectly clear and smooth, almost marble like in its shimmer.

As Paul explained the new situation and told everyone exactly what had been said during the conference and why, he went over what Michael had said, detailing every facial expression that had spread across the faces of Luccia and Xavier.

There were several different sets of chuckles around the table as Paul demonstrated the expressions on their faces, but once they had finished going over everything that had happened during the conference the silence that settled over the table was filled with tension.

Xander knew that Paul would have to bring up the reason why Anthony had not returned yet, he suspected that they already knew, but Alexis didn't and she was looking around curiously, obviously wondering why everyone was so silent.

Paul broke the silence after several minutes, when he felt that the tension had reached a peak "We also discussed Alexis and whether we would give her the Elixir of Life."

Alexis stared at Paul as he said this, the expression on her face was plain for everyone to see, she was very shocked and they all knew it, but he carried on talking "Anthony should return sometime later today with the vial, and when he does we will perform the ceremony."

Reverent silence spread across the table now, and it was plain by the look of confusion spreading across Alexis, Narcissia and Xander that they had no idea what sort of ceremony they were talking about.

Before they could say anything, Paul broke out into a loud laugh and said "Had you there didn't we?" a loud eruption of laughter echoed throughout the room now, he could tell by the way Alexis winced that the noise was slightly painful to her ears.

Once the laughter had settled down Paul began explaining what would happen when Anthony returned, first both Paul and Anthony would perform some tests on the sample to make sure it was pure and then they would allow Alexis to consume it.

8:15pm Utah, USA

Alexis

She had been relaxing in her room with Xander, it felt like time had slowed down, and they had been waiting for Anthony to get back since they left the meeting room, her nerves were beginning to get the better of her now though, she couldn't sit still for long and she was feeling very anxious.

Nothing Xander did would keep her occupied enough to forget about what would be happening to her once Anthony returned, she would be one of them, she would be immortal, and while she would not be a vampire like them, she would be one step closer and she knew it.

As she began to pace up and down the room, Xander took her by her hand onto the balcony, and he lay down on the floor and pulled her down to join him, this was the first time since they had arrived at Paul's mansion that they had been out on this balcony, there had always been something more pressing to deal with.

As they lay there on the floor, looking up at the perfect, clear sky Xander began pointing out the different constellations, she had no idea that he had liked to gaze at the stars, but then again she didn't know that he was 2300 years old.

In that moment she realised how little she really knew about the man she hoped would be the love of her immortal life. So she promised herself there and then that she would learn everything about him that she possibly could.

She began firing questions off at him asking him everything she could think of, from his favourite food, to his favourite time, he had shocked her when he had replied to that with "My favourite time is any time I'm with you." She had blushed at this and she asked him whether she would still be able to blush once she was a vampire.

His response was not really what she had expected. "Yes, you'll still be able to blush, but it will be far less noticeable, you see, as your skin will become a lot stronger, and far less translucent."

"Will I become pale like everyone else?" she had asked him inquisitively and he answered her as he looked into her eyes. "In time yes, but it is different with everyone really, some people merely turn a few shades lighter than they naturally were, while others will turn very pale."

She thought she understood this, as he explained how their skin was immune to the damage that ultra violet light caused on their skins, so they no longer produce melanin and because of that, they turn paler over time, until they reach their natural shade.

They talked and talked for what seemed like hours, until Xander told her that he could hear the sound of a car's engine in the distance, he said he could feel the presence of an immortal coming towards them from the same direction, so they assumed that it would be Anthony.

There was a knock at the door several moments later; it was Paul letting them know that Anthony would be arriving shortly and that she should probably change into something more appropriate, she did not know what he meant by this, so she asked and he explained that she would require loose fitting clothes, otherwise she would end up ripping and tearing them.

This frightened her and Paul seemed to sense it and said "It won't be painful, but it is a curious sensation, and you will likely tense your muscles involuntarily, you will be strapped down to a chair until it has passed."

She asked how long it would take, her voice was quiet and he answered her "It will take a few hours."

He led the way down to a chamber deep underground, she was amazed at the level of security that the room was secured by, and it could have been a room in a bank vault, but she knew that it was not.

Anthony arrived several minutes after they were in the vault, she had been looking around the room, to see the ancient parchment and manuscripts that were behind transparent windows, it was like walking into a museum.

With everyone there now, Paul directed her to sit down on the chair, it was surprisingly comfortable considering it was made out of solid metal. They strapped her in slowly now, her arms, then her hands, then her legs and feet, it wasn't painful at all, the straps were very comfortable, obviously a lot of thought had gone into its conception to make sure that the person it held was not harmed.

Anthony was carrying a big leather suitcase, that had two locking mechanisms on it, she knew Anthony had the code to one of them while Paul had the other, once he had finished unlocking his part, he walked away giving Paul the space to sort his part, Paul then walked up to it and inserted his own code, once he imputed his code correctly, the locks popped open and inside it there was a vibrant red liquid, it was almost luminous.

Paul spoke then "Once we give you the elixir, I'm sorry but we're going to have to put a gag in your mouth to make sure you don't bite your tongue."

This frightened her once again and she said "But I thought you said it wouldn't hurt?"

Paul and Anthony looked at each other then Anthony spoke "It won't be painful, but until it has spread throughout the whole of your body and settled down, you won't have any control of your body, and we don't want to take any risks."

She relaxed again and Paul walked up to her, the red liquid in a vial he was carrying, she felt like every step he took towards her was taking an eternity, she wanted this to be over and done with so that she could continue on with her life.

Terror was beginning to grip her fully, but Xander picked up the chair he had been sitting on, and moved it next to her, and he began to hold her hand gently, she felt less anxious almost instantly, but she was still worried.

Adrenaline Rush

Anthony was holding the gag in his hand, and she could tell that he himself was feeling apprehensive, she felt glad that she wasn't the only one who was worried.

Paul placed the vial to her lips and she felt the cool liquid pour into her mouth, in the coming months and years, no matter how hard she would try to explain this very moment, she never would, in one instant it tasted like Aniseed but in the next instant it tasted completely different, her taste buds felt like they were on fire with new senses.

It was like she had never really tasted the flavours in anything she had consumed up until that moment, and the feeling began spreading throughout her body slowly, it sent an eerily tingly sensation down her throat, for a moment she thought that she had gone blind because she couldn't open her eyes no matter how hard she tried.

it made its way slowly down her body, so slowly that she thought it was going to take forever to reach her hands and feet, but she knew that she would have to endure it until it had done its work, as it reached her ear drums, she felt like she was going to scream because of how loud everything sounded, she could pick out the distinctive sounds of the heartbeats of everyone near her, she could hear them swallow, it was so loud to her that she felt like her ears were being swallowed by an enormous mouth every time she heard the sound.

Several minutes passed before her ears had adapted so that the sounds around her weren't causing her an immense amount of pain.

As it reached her arms, she almost believed that she had been lying there for several hours, it felt like an eternity had passed, and yet no one near her had moved an inch since she had first tasted the liquid on her lips.

She could feel her chest convulse as it reached her lungs and her heart, it felt for a second like her chest was going to explode, she could feel every muscle that it had touched now, and she began trying to concentrate, she could make each individual muscle tense and relax now, but she still could not move most them, the feeling was amazing and she almost lost herself in the very act of feeling her muscles for the first time.

Her hands were beginning to feel the tingling sensation now, she could feel the muscles along her upper arms come alive, and then on her forearms and finally her fingers, she could feel them so deeply that she could move single muscles along them without moving anything else in her body, she had heard of this before, but she had never expected to ever experience something as deep as this.

She was so lost in thought that she didn't realise that even her brain had been affected, she was thinking with more than one train of thought, she was multitasking to such a degree that she didn't notice for quite a long time after that.

As the sensation spread down her legs, she felt them tense and relax, as she gained control over her nerves, she felt the material of the jogging bottoms she was wearing split along the seam, but she didn't care, she couldn't help it, and before she could focus her attention on the sound of the material ripping, the sensation spread further down her legs and into her feet and toes.

As the sensation began to fade, she could still feel the individual muscles and tendons on her body, they were still under her control and she knew that it would take her quite a long time to get used to this level of control over her senses.

Paul and Anthony seemed to realise that she was coming out of it, and they removed her gag and asked her how she felt, she couldn't explain how alive she felt to them, and even with her now increased mental cognitive abilities she couldn't describe to them how amazing she felt, but they seemed to understand and they had begun removing the bindings that had held her in place.

She blinked several times and then finally opened her eyes and looked around, she was amazed at the depth of colour in everything around her, and the difference was like watching something that was two dimensional turn into something three dimensional, the new level of definition her eyes seemed capable of was incredible.

10:45pm Salt Lake City, USA

Alexis

They were hurtling along the road towards the city now, the speed that the car Xander had borrowed from Paul was phenomenal, she had never been this fast in a car before. She was absorbing every minute detail as they sped down the motorway at over 150mph, nearly three times the legal limit, but she didn't care, to her new heightened senses it wasn't very different than travelling at 30mph.

They arrived in a fraction of the time it had previously taken them in the limousine, and she was impressed, she knew that before Xander hadn't wanted to risk endangering her, but he now knew that she was far more durable now, and when he had asked her if she wanted to go out for the night, she accepted readily.

As they both got out of Paul's dark green Jaguar, she was curious to know what sort of car it was, so she walked round to the back of it and saw the Jaguar logo in the centre, with the words Supercharged, underneath it, and to the right of the logo were the words XKR, of course she didn't really know what any of this meant, but she was determined to find out.

She decided to just ask Xander about it and he explained that it was a Jaguar XKR, which meant that it was a supercharged XK8, and that a supercharger was similar to a turbo, he began rattling off a list of specifications for the car, but she stopped him, she didn't care that much about cars, and they both laughed lightly.

She was still shocked at how different everything looked to her now, even in the darkness of night everything seemed so bright and vibrant, she had seen darker days than she was experiencing now and she couldn't want to see what the colours would be like during the light of day.

He could sense that she was feeling famished, he knew that she hadn't eaten since earlier that day, and her body was burning an extremely high calorie rate compared to normal, she was probably using over twice the amount because of the new abilities she had been given.

So they went to the restaurant he had taken her on their first night of freedom, she had loved it then, but she had the faint impression that Xander thought she would find it much more appealing now that her senses had been magnified.

As they sat there at the table, facing each other, she marvelled at the perfection of his face, how there were no lines at all, everything seemed perfectly symmetrical, unnaturally so, but she didn't care, all that mattered to her now was that they live their life together.

The waiter brought them a glass of champagne each, and as she sipped hers, she almost chocked, the sensation was nothing like she had previously experienced as a mortal, she had expected to taste its bubbly flavour, but the experience she had just had was like drinking the elixir all over again, nothing had prepared her for this, and she was beginning to realise that Xander and Paul had deliberately not let her eat or drink anything so that she would experience this explosion of senses slowly.

Xander eyed her curiously, of course he knew how she was feeling, but not exactly, for he had never tasted the elixir, but he had tasted similar, except his first experience he explained had been the blood vision. She had no idea what he was talking about so he explained.

The first time you taste the blood of an immortal, you fall into a catatonic state, where you will see and feel the memories of the immortal whose blood you drank, you will learn everything they want you to know in that instance, it creates an extremely strong bond between the two individuals, that is one of the reasons you won't really notice the pain.

Because if the immortal who gives you the blood is strong enough to guide you through it, you will not feel an ounce of pain, however misguided amateurs will not know how to guide their protégé's properly and they will experience a level of agony so severe that it alone could kill them.

"You of course will not have to worry about that, because even though my blood is pure, and I have never shared it with anyone except my maker, you will be in good hands my love, trust me." He said softly, almost as if it was as much for his own peace of mind as it was for hers.

This response brought out a sense of curiosity in her that she had never felt before, all her senses seemed so heightened that she had not even noticed that the reason he was talking about these matters so boldly was that he was talking so quiet that it would have been inaudible for anyone in the room but them.

She wanted to know who his creator was, though she suspected she already knew, it was so obvious that she had never made the connection before, she wanted to test her hypothesis so she asked him flat out "Was it Narcissia who turned you?"

He nodded at her as she said this and said "Yes my love it was, does that bother you?"

Of course she decided instantly that it didn't matter, and it didn't bother her at all, they had never been anything more than they were, it was not a sexual connection between them, it was closer to the bond between mother and child than that.

Their food arrived before they had time to continue their conversation, and Xander did not touch his, he was focusing purely on Alexis, obviously in anticipation of her response to her dinner, and how she would be pleasantly surprised by how much better it tasted.

She had never tasted anything this wonderful in her whole life, it was like for her entire life she had eaten nothing but bland bread and only drunk water, and now she was being presented with some of the most spectacularly mouth watering foods in existence.

She lost count of how many times she chewed each mouthful; she was so lost in her thoughts that when she finally came back to her senses she was almost afraid that she had been chewing that one bite for hours.

As she looked up at Xander he was smiling at her broadly and he spoke "I take it your enjoying your food then?" he smiled at her wickedly after and she knew that he had set her up once again.

Her next mouthful was not quite so much of a shock to her senses but it was however just as much of an enjoyable experience, she didn't think she would ever get bored of the flavours, she could detect each individual ingredient in the food, and she was amazed that such a thing was possible.

As she ate her food she was almost amazed at just how large of an appetite she had, as she finished the first plate and she was still feeling remarkably hungry, she asked Xander about it, and remarked that if she kept eating like this she would get fat.

He laughed and his reply shocked her so much that she knocked her fork to the floor. "You won't ever get fat my love, the muscle tone you have recently developed will make sure of that, your metabolism has been increased to compensate with your new abilities and senses. You could literally eat nothing but pure fat and you wouldn't put on an ounce of weight, your body can handle it much better now."

She looked at him in shock, as a waiter hurried over to her with a new fork, and he quickly removed the soiled fork and took it away. She was struggling to get her head around everything she had learnt, it made no sense but then he said "I would however suggest that you eat well, your body will perform much better if you supply it with the right vitamins and minerals."

It was beginning to sink in now, what had happened to her, she had always been a calorie counter, desperate to not get fat, because the medication she was on often caused excessive weight gain, for the first time since they had arrived in Utah, she realised that she had not been taking her medication.

As the reality of this set in, she had a hard time actually believing it, she asked Xander about it and laughed, explaining that her body wouldn't need any type of medication now, and that it wouldn't work on her anyway.

Once they had finished their dinner, they went for a short walk back towards the car they had came in, she didn't know quite how to feel as they walked, part of her felt relieved that she would be able to enjoy a more normal life, but another part of her felt like one of the aspects that had formed her personality was now gone.

The drive home was as quick as the drive there, she was amazed at just how good a driver Xander was, but with her new reactions, she suspected that she could drive equally as well as he could, she made a mental note to do just that. When she said she wanted to try it, he slammed the breaks and sent the jaguar into a controlled spin.

Ordinarily this action would have made her dizzy and given her a sick feeling, but her new senses told her that they were in no danger, and she barely flinched even though the seatbelt was biting into her flesh, when the car had come to a halt, Xander stepped out of the car and walked around to the passenger door, he opened it for her and she walked round and got into the driver's seat.

As she got in, she immediately locked on her seatbelt and then she waited for several moments, she looked at Xander and waited until he had noticed her eying his seatbelt as well, so that he knew she wouldn't drive until he was secured. She knew that he didn't really need to wear it, but it was the principle of the matter.

Silence filled the car, even the engine was quiet, it was gently ticking over in neutral, and the battle of wills had started, it seemed to drag on forever, until she heard the familiar click, as soon as she heard that, she immediately placed the car into drive, and pushed the cars grip on the road to its limits, the tires squealed in protest at this, and she could see a trail of smoke and rubber left on the road behind her.

The tires continued to protest for several more seconds, it seemed like an eternity to her, and she felt the car lurch forward finally, the acceleration was phenomenal and it sent a rush of adrenaline through her, and she could see why Xander loved to drive fast, it was a completely different experience being in control of the car at such high speeds, than it was when you were being driven.

She knew the reason for this was because she had to utilise all of her new senses, but she didn't care, the thrill of it send a shudder down her spine, she could feel the hairs on her arms and neck rising to attention as if she were shouting orders at them subconsciously telling them to get to work.

For several minutes she ignored everything but the road, she was pushing the car to its 155mph limit now, and she knew that if the car wasn't limited then she would push it to its manufacturers limits easily, the thrill was just too exciting to miss, she felt like an adrenaline junky, and that thought sent a calming thought through her, she realised that the more adrenaline she produced, the more torturous it would be on Xander, as he would begin to crave her blood.

As she drove them both home, she was mellowed by her last thought, and she eased up on the gas a bit so that she would not get quite so excited, the journey was still remarkably fast, they didn't speak on the way home and this worried her.

Chapter 22: The Theft

11:20pm Utah, USA

Alexis

By the time they had arrived at Paul's mansion, she was feeling much more relaxed, and she was sure that she would not be tormenting Xander anymore, this sent a calming thought through her and she felt much more at ease.

As they entered the mansion, she could tell there was something wrong immediately, she could hear frantic voices coming from the main living room, and she could sense that everyone was in there; she could hear each of the different heartbeats in the room which she had begun to know intimately.

They both walked into the room, and everyone turned to face them, they were all watching the television it seemed, and as they looked at the large screen on the wall, they could both see that everyone was crowded in here to watch the news.

And then they saw it, the headline which read 'Russian nuclear warheads stolen while en route to be destroyed'

Both Alexis and Xander looked at each other at this point, and they both had an expression of fear across their faces.

Everyone remained silent while the news report continued, but she could tell that as soon as it finished, then there would be a frantic discussion about it, and she hoped that they would tell her what they had missed.

It took nearly a quarter of an hour before the news began rerunning what had already been shown, and then everyone began turning away from the screen.

Paul looked around inquisitively, he obviously wanted to know how much we had heard, but we had missed a lot of the key facts so we would need him to go over it from the start.

"Right." Paul said in an official voice that made everyone fall silent "We need to go over this for Alexis and Alexander, as they were not here, they don't know what's going on."

As they all found seats and began to relax a little while they waited for Paul to explain everything, Alexis could see the expressions of fear on each and every face in the room.

Paul began explaining it then, trying to use the same words that had been on the news.

Earlier today, an armed convoy which was transporting thirty-six tactical nuclear warheads prior to their destruction, were attacked by unknown assailants, the Russian Government currently have no leads on who was behind this attack, but Islamic terrorists are the prime suspects.

All of the soldiers guarding the large cache of weapons were massacred and while none of them had suffered any gunshot wounds, several had severe lacerations which would indicate that they were attacked by assailants carrying edged weaponry.

Paul continued and explained how that even though the mortals had absolutely no idea who it had been, from what they had been able to find out from bribing Russian official's, they had concluded that it was the result of a co-ordinated strike committed by a group of immortals

Alexis sat there in silence, she didn't know how to comprehend what had happened, the only thing that continued repeating in her head was the words thirty-six, that would cause utter carnage if they were detonated in large population centres, she couldn't bear to think of the casualties.

Xander finally spoke up and asked when they would be contacting the Covenant, as they all knew that this development was directly tied to what Luccia had told them mere days before, Alexis felt very bitter towards Luccia, because she had not been able to foresee the theft of the atomics before, or they could have been ready to guard the convey.

12:02am Utah, USA

Paul

He knew that Luccia would already know about the crisis and would likely be debating it among the remnants of the Covenants council, but he knew that they would need to pool their resources for them to stand even the tiniest chance at containing this threat.

He phoned the direct line to Michael's mansion, it seemed to take an eternity before someone finally answered, she recognised the voice to belong to Morgan, he politely asked him to go and get Luccia for him that they needed to talk urgently.

Morgan obviously did as he asked, because moments later Luccia was on the other end of the line.

"Have you heard?" she asked him sharply, he wanted to respond saying that he hadn't heard, that he was just calling her for the sake of it, but he knew that wouldn't help matters so he swallowed his sarcastic retorts and said "Yes."

What happened next was a frantic discussion about how they would be able to organise a counter-attack to recapture the weapons, the biggest problem that they had was that they didn't know the location of the weapons in the first place.

The second problem was that they were severely outnumbered and they knew it, they would have to use their superior abilities to their advantage, it was the only way they would be able to survive the coming storm.

Their final problem was that they still didn't know who was responsible, it could have been three different groups and nothing they did managed the narrow it down at all, Paul knew that unless they found out who was responsible they would not be able to deal with the threat properly.

They now knew that Luccia's vision was beginning to come true, and that was a frightening thought, until the warheads were stolen they had not known how the attackers in Luccia's vision had gotten hold of an atomic, but now they knew and it didn't make matters any easier to understand.

However at the very least, they knew exactly when and where the next attack would be, but what they didn't know however, was whether they would be able to do anything to stop them, if they tried and failed then they would all die, and they both knew if that happened then the human race would face a terrible future.

And so they came to the conclusion that they were not ready to face so many immortals without firm knowledge, the stink of the option that they had been forced to choose left a sour taste in Paul's mouth, Luccia didn't appear to like it anymore than he did.

But he knew that even after he had ended the call with Luccia, that the worst part would be coming next, when he explained what he and Luccia had spoken about to his family, he would have to deal with their misgivings and feelings of guilt over all the mortals who would likely die in the atomic attack in Europe.

05:42am Utah, USA

Alexis

As she lay there in bed, barely awake, she knew that she was safe, she could feel Xander up against her and she could hear his steady breathing and the rhythmic beating of his heart.

She had been falling in and out of consciousness for several hours now, but all her dreams were tarnished by the frightening news that they had heard earlier, about the theft of the nuclear warheads and the use they would likely be put to.

At first she didn't realise the difference in the most recent dream she was experiencing, this time she felt completely different, as if she was someone else entirely, she looked in the window of the closest building, and she could see her reflection.

However what she saw in it, was not what she always saw in her reflection, while it did resemble her, it was like she had been remade by an artist, so that no flaws existed in her anymore, as she walked closer to the window, she began to notice the other minute differences, such as how pale she looked.

Her hair was far more elegant, it looked like she had spent hours perfecting it, and her eyes, her eyes were now a deep violet, she had seen eyes like these before, ever since she had met Paul, she knew that she would never forget those eyes.

At first it didn't register in her mind, but she knew that she was different now, she could feel the adrenaline rush building, the sense of power that radiated through her almost sent her into a state of frenzy, and she had to use every ounce of restraint in her body to stop herself from going on a rampage.

She realised then what she should have realised when she had first seen her reflection, and when she noticed how pale she was, when she noticed her eyes. She was a vampire, this was the first glimpse she had seen of what she would be for eternity, and she knew that she would never be able to get it out of her head again.

She marvelled at her own reflection for what seemed like forever, but her body told her that it had only been a few moments. And then she felt it, the feeling of danger people felt when they knew that their life was threatened, the force of it was so strong that she felt as if something had hit her in the stomach.

It took her a few seconds to realise the cause for this, she had turned around and seen Luccia there, she knew exactly what she looked like because she had seen her sister, and they were identical except for their hair.

She readied herself so that she could fight her off if she did attack, but when Luccia launched herself, it was not at Alexis, she had flung herself at a short dark skinned woman, she had never seen anyone with that colour skin before, it was almost as if she had a thin layer of chalk over her rich ebony skin.

Her attention was drawn to the new woman, her beauty was striking, she saw the collision before she heard it, to her it seemed almost as if two bull elephants were charging at each other at 100mph, and the resulting crash was like thunder had gone off right next to her ear. It was almost painful to her, but as quick as the pain had started it dissipated.

As she stared at the two vampires fighting each other brutally it was like watching two lions fight it out, she could see flashes of metal which as she paid closer attention she saw were knives in each of the two woman's hands, and they were making fast slashing motions, but it quickly became apparent who was the quicker out of the two of them.

The battle barely lasted more than ten seconds before Luccia had decapitated her opponent, and a flow of deep dark red blood began to flow out of the remains of the defeated warrior.

Luccia walked back towards Alexis, in a sleek cat like prowl, and she knew that she would be next, she saw her neatly wipe the blood off of her blades before putting them back in the leg sheaf's, her motions were totally fluid, and the cat like manner of her worried Alexis, she knew that this was the woman that had wanted her dead.

But her attention was then drawn to a large gathering of people in the distance, it was a very large group, and she quickly counted and realised that there were over eighty people moving towards them rapidly and she could sense that some of them were mortals, she saw Luccia turn towards them and then watched her hesitate slightly before she turned to Alexis and screamed "RUN!"

She woke up and almost jumped out of bed, she could tell quickly that she had been sweating so bad during her dream, and she knew that Xander was worried, he hadn't let go of her since she had woken up.

The feeling of shock still hadn't receded yet and she knew that she wouldn't be able to tell Xander about her dream until she had calmed down, and she wasn't one hundred percent sure that it was a dream at all; it could well have been a premonition.

She lay there in his arms for over a quarter of an hour before she finally began to feel relaxed, and when she explained her dream to Xander he began to grow more and more concerned, the level of detail which she told him with had convinced him that it was no dream.

She could tell that he wished that she had more information available, such as when it was going to occur, and why of all the people that she could have been with, it had been Luccia, who had wanted her dead for so long.

He felt worried because if this was a true future, then she would be in grave danger, as they had no chance at all of Luccia and Alexis being able to survive against such a large group, the combined forces of the Illuminati and the Covenant combined would struggle to hold them off.

She had been awake about half an hour now, and she could tell that he was more worried than she was, for her it had begun to fade and the sense of fear had receded but he was still in a state of deep panic, but the silver lining was that she had foreseen that she would become a vampire, or a true immortal as he liked to put it.

She had laughed at him when he got so touchy about being called a vampire, but she could see where he was coming from. They were not true vampires in the common sense, nor were they mythical creatures, or demonic, they were merely immortals.

As they lay there, it began to sink in for her, that she would soon be truly immortal, even though she was technically immortal now, she would be far more durable when she was a vampire, when she told he theory to Xander he nodded and told her that she was correct.

She couldn't get back to sleep again after that, so Xander lay there with her, enjoying the peace and quiet that had settled upon the mansion, she knew that it probably wasn't quite so quiet throughout the mansion but they were the only people in this side of it, out of her necessity to sleep.

Once it had reached a respectable time she decided that she might as well get up, she had been putting it off because she knew that she would need to tell Paul about her dream, and that worried her, because she knew that she would have to face up to it if she told him and the rest of the Illuminati, and she suspected that one of the main reasons she had the vision was because of the Elixir.

She didn't want to keep having premonitions; she knew nothing good could come of it, and it would do nothing but cause her fear, she would be glad when she no longer needed to sleep, so she wouldn't have these dreams anymore.

It hadn't really occurred to her until then that she might not become immune to her dreams, it hadn't occurred to her that Luccia was also able to see the future, and that she didn't need to be dreaming to achieve it.

As she walked back into their bedroom, she could tell by the look on Xander's face that he had thought of something, and she knew that it was not something she was going to like, so she decided to get it over and done with and she asked him.

His reply shocked her "I think your visions are going to get far stronger when you are one of us."

This had been the last thing she had expected, and she hadn't told him about her hopes that when she couldn't sleep she wouldn't have to have those visions anymore. "But I won't be able to sleep, so I can't have them."

"Have you never had the visions while you've been awake?" this question puzzled her, as she had always considered any hallucinations she had when she was awake as manifestations of her illness rather than a gift.

"I don't know..."

He got up from the bed and walked up to her, and he gently lifted her off of the floor and pulled her towards him, she began to feel safer almost immediately even though she generally hated being picked up, when she was with him she felt totally safe.

She was still rolling over their conversation in her head, she really didn't know how much of her illness had been because she was a descendant of Kuni, she really didn't know if she even was one, but Paul and the others were convinced that she was, and

Luccia obviously thought so or she would have never tried to have her killed.

When he finally released her from the tight embrace, they walked hand in hand downstairs, she knew what was going to happen, but she didn't have to like it.

They found Paul in the main lounge area again, once again he was staring at the TV screen intently, and she knew something else must have happened to cause him distress.

She decided to ask him what was wrong, he responded with "There have been a lot of murders throughout Europe, mass mortal killings among adrenaline junkies and extreme sports fans; they are like fast food for one of us as they are flooded with Adrenaline."

She knew that this was yet another indication that a large group of immortals were planning something nefarious, though they didn't know exactly what, when she asked if there were any leads among the mortal news about the location of the stolen warheads, he shook his head and started staring at the TV again.

"Isn't there something you need to tell Paul?" it was Xander now, he was staring at her, and then Paul turned his head to look at Alexis curiously as well.

She did her best to summarise the vision that she'd had, and she saw him nod his head as if he understood, he seemed more than pleased by the fact that she described herself almost perfectly as a newborn vampire should be.

He smiled at her and told her to relax; they would do everything in their power to stop this renegade group of immortals before it came to that. This didn't really set her mind as at ease as it should have, because she knew that her vision would come true, it was just a case of when.

It was then that she decided that if she was going to have to fight, then she would want to know how, so she made a mental note that she must not get distracted with the pleasures of her senses in the aftermath of the end of her mortal life and the beginning of her immortal one.

That she would do everything she could to learn how to fight and kill other immortals, she suspected that this training might just help her stay alive long enough to live forever.

Gradually over the course of the day, more and more of the family came into the room, all wanting updates and they all seemed to appraise her more and more highly with every retelling of her vision, she knew the reason for this was likely that they had lived in the shadows of another famous prescient immortal, and she had held them at bay for millennia, and now they had a member with the potential power to rival the powerful priestess.

She had never really considered her a match for Luccia up until this point, for she didn't really understand her powers or how to use them, but she figured that, that was something she would gain over time, it wasn't something she could learn out of a book, it was something you had to learn by doing.

Her problem was that she didn't want to learn how to do it; she wished she could learn how to stop it so that she wouldn't have any more of these frightening dreams.

11:25am Utah, USA

Narcissia

Even though they had welcomed her into their home, she still felt ever so slightly like an outsider, and not totally comfortable, it was nothing they had done, but she knew that she had not made herself many friends over the past few thousand years.

She knew that they were very thankful to her for enlightening them about their own family history and she had the feeling that they would do their best to repay her, but she knew that she would not really find a long term home here, and that it was temporary measure until matters within the Covenant had been rectified, but she hoped that this would seal the bond between both Covens and stop the endless hostilities between them.

This was a long shot, she knew that full well but it was something she could aim for to give her life real meaning and allow her to feel comfortable.

She decided that she should really be a bit more sociable, as she had been alone most of the time since she arrived at Paul's home, most of that was because she needed to rest so she would heal, but it was also because she felt isolated while she was here, she felt like the only outsider now that Alexander had fallen in among them fully.

As she walked into the room at the bottom of the stairs where most of the noise she could hear was coming from, everyone turned around to greet her and then Alexis began pummelling her with questions about her sister.

She asked her when her gift had started and if it was originally something which occurred during a dream, and if it started to occur while she was conscious after she was changed.

Narcissia didn't really have the answer to any of these questions, but she told her that she could hazard a guess at it anyway.

She began to feel more at ease after Alexis had stopped firing questions at her, they all seemed to look to her for answers and she was not used to this, in the Covenant she had always been in her sister's shadow and she had never really liked being in the limelight.

Paul asked her if she would mind travelling with them when they returned to England again, as they wanted to arrange another meeting with the Covenant, so that they could plan how they would react to the theft of the atomics. And whether they might somehow be able to either stop the attack, or confiscate the warheads.

Of course she agreed readily, she wanted to open up the lines of communication with her sister, she knew that it might take time before they began to really trust each other again, but they both knew that there were bigger things at stake than grudges.

Lee Michael Harris

Narcissia was feeling very vulnerable now though, not just because of the estrangement with her family, but also because of the shocking news about the theft of the warheads, she had been terrified of them ever since her ancient home was totally destroyed during that war long ago.

She had no idea how they were supposed to be able to fight off an unknown number of immortals without knowing their strength or abilities, she knew that if they were all young then they might well stand a very good chance, but with the number so high she knew that the casualties could become very high, she didn't really consider the fact that all of them had aged and grown far stronger since the last time they had been forced to fight against this sort of threat.

As she considered the possible bomb targets and how they believed that Vienna would be their primary target, she had the faintest idea that they were only going to destroy Vienna as a warning to Luccia, which made her think that this was personal.

Chapter 23: Some Things Are Inevitable

12:11pm Utah, USA

Paul

He knew that they would have to do something about the theft of the warheads, but what they could do was however causing them many difficulties, they knew that they could not stop the destruction of Vienna, there was no way anyone could do that now, they didn't have sufficient numbers and they didn't know the exact location of the bomb.

if they did then they might have been able to save the city, but he knew full well that there was very little hope of that, he did not like this fact, but as he sat their pondering it, he realised that although the bomb cannot be stopped, the people don't have to be in the city.

He knew that if he played it right, he could make the mortals fear a terrorist attack on the city and they might be able to clear everyone out of there, he knew that the deadline was steadily approaching; he had less than three weeks until the day when their armed forces would perform just outside the city. He knew that there was a small chance that if they warned the mortal officials, then the bomb might be detonated early, but he had to try, there was a small chance that they might be able to at least save some of the mortal population.

He decided that he would talk to Luccia about this when they arrived at Cambridge later that day, the whole Illuminati would be leaving this time, every single one of them in a full conference so that they could discuss the matter as well as formalise their new alliance, how long this alliance would last after the threat had been dealt with however was another matter altogether.

He was feeling very apprehensive about how quiet things had been since the theft of the warheads, it had given both the Covenant and his own family a lot to think about, and they had been putting off the impending meeting with the Covenant for over a week now, but they all knew that they could not put it off any longer, they had to have a full conference so they could decide what they were going to do.

Even Alexis would be coming with them and that was a risk that she had agreed to take, even though she knew that Luccia was still very hostile to her becoming an immortal, Alexander did not want her to take the risk, but he also knew that their new family would not allow any harm to come to her, it still made him very nervous.

He knew that they were all waiting for him now, their plane was due to leave in just a few hours and they had all gathered in the lounge and were making small talk to ease the tension which had spread throughout the room.

As he walked into the room, everyone turned to stare at him now, and he was glad for this because at the very least he would not have to repeat himself, when he spoke it was so silent that they could have heard a pin drop.

"It is time." He said, they already knew this but he had figured that he might as well let them know that he was finally ready.

He had a deep feeling of misgivings in the pit of his stomach, he knew that whatever happened today would not be good, he almost asked Alexis to remain here for a moment, but he suspected that she would not stay, not when everyone else would be leaving and might be placing themselves in grave danger.

As they walked to the stretched limousine that was big enough to carry all of them in relative comfort, he still could not shake the feeling that had settled in his stomach and did not appear to want to leave.

They arrived at the airport just less than an hour after they had left his home, he was not used to such silence from his family, they almost always had things to talk about but they now seemed to be as concerned as he was, this made him think about how dangerous it would be for them to hold a conference with everyone there.

There was a phrase which had survived for millennia which had always said that it was dangerous to have all your eggs in one basket, he had always avoided it whenever possible.

He still felt quite apprehensive about working with the Covenant, it had been just under a month since they had been mortal enemies, where they had wanted to kill the young mortal sitting across from him, he thought about this for a few moments and he chided himself for thinking of her as a mortal, she wasn't technically mortal now, she could live forever due to the Elixir, but she was far less durable than one of them.

He still wished that she had the experience to control her gifts, so that they would be able to know what was going to happen in the future, but it had remained clouded even to her, since she had received her last vision she had not had any others, not that he was aware of anyway and he trusted her to tell him if she had anymore, it was too important for her to keep these things to herself.

As he got out of the car, the others followed him in silence as they prepared themselves for the coming journey; they all knew how boring these long flights were, especially to ones who have taken them so many times before.

11:00am Cambridge, UK

Alexis

The mansion was a massive shock to her, it was not modern like Paul's, and it had the ring of ancient aristocracy, and she loved the architecture that surrounded the large house, the columns were breathtaking and she knew that they had not made houses like this since the eighteenth century, she realised that Michael had probably owned it since it was built.

The inside she noticed was lavishly decorated, and its walls were covered with paintings all done of different era's and different techniques, she didn't know enough about art to know which type were what, but she could tell very quickly that though they were completely different from each other, even if they had been painted by different artists, every painting was of the same two people, Michael and Celeste, sometimes they were together in the paintings.

Xander had to pull her along several times, as she was slowing the group with her incessant curiosity, but she didn't care, this was history that she was experiencing and she was feeling a little jet lagged due to the long flight and then the long drive afterwards, no one had really spoken much on the journey, as they were all deep in thought over what they could and couldn't do as well as how they could possibly save the mortal population.

She wasn't sure what they could do, but she hoped they would be able to; it was horrible to think that millions of people could die for no reasons, she couldn't understand why they would even use the nukes, and there wasn't any need for them to use them.

The immortals that stole them, were far more powerful than any mortal, they didn't need such devastating weapons to be able to bring any mortal army to its knees, she suspected that these weapons were stolen for a personal reason, something that Narcissia had said made her think that they were probably stolen by someone connected to Enigmas, he seemed like the only possible culprit for this oncoming war, but she knew that Luccia would not accept an information from her, so she decided she would keep her opinions to herself.

As Michael led the way into the dining room, where they would all be able to sit down around the table, she had the faint impression that Michael wasn't overly pleased that the Covenant were still using his home as their own.

She understood his feelings about this, she would have felt the same had she been asked to let people who had wanted her dead for so long, stay in her own home.

Everyone was seated now and it was the first real glimpse she had ever had of the other members of the Covenant, she had only seen Luccia because of her dream, she had not seen the other two men and the girl who looked like she was younger than Alexis, even though she knew that she was over eight thousand years old.

As they made their courteous introductions, she felt slightly uneasy, maybe it had been because of the way Luccia had stared at her when Paul introduced her, or the way Xavier had eyed her up in much the same manner that a shark looks at its prey, with cold lifeless eyes. *The eyes of a killer* she thought to herself.

The meeting went off without any problems, the Covenant were being true to their word that they would not in any way shape or form be rude or otherwise hostile to Alexis now that she was officially part of the Illuminati, they could obviously tell by the slight reddish hue which was beginning to spread throughout her eyes that she had partaken in the Elixir of Life, and as Luccia stared into her eyes, she felt like she could see the faint glimmer of greed hidden behind her eyes.

Paul began by briefly explaining everything that the Illuminati had discussed over the past few weeks, even the idea that we might be able to somehow warn the mortal officials so that they might evacuate the city, Luccia nodded in agreement to this and she saw that Luccia was looking at him with grudging respect.

Once Paul had finished, Luccia spoke next, "I think we might be able to force them into fighting us before they reach the mortals."

Everyone stared at Luccia as she spoke, the Illuminati members were curious at her ideas, and she suspected they would be expected to perform some very dangerous tasks. But to her surprise Luccia didn't expect the Illuminati fight off this threat single handed.

"If we work together, we can easily handle a group of thirty of them." she said, her voice reeked of overconfidence.

"That's assuming that there are no more than the thirty of them that you saw in your vision." Everyone looked around at Anthony now, Luccia glared at him, but Anna seemed fairly amused at his words as if she had been thinking similarly.

Anna spoke up before Luccia had time to make her own retort "Indeed, however we only have that source of data available, and it would be difficult to hide an immortal much larger than that."

Alexis couldn't understand why they hadn't attempted to track the immortals; she suspected that it wouldn't be that difficult really; all they had to do was find out who was ordering large quantities of adrenaline.

But none of them brought this up, and they were talking over and over about insignificant details which Alexis barely comprehended, about how they could use their enemy's weight of numbers against them.

She finally decided to speak up "Can't you track them by finding out who has been buying very large quantities of blood and epinephrine?"

The room went as silent as the night, after she spoke and she began to feel foolish, she thought that they must have been way ahead of her and that no one else at the table was stupid enough to ask such a question.

She was pleasantly surprised however when everyone looked at her with expressions of shock and amusement, and then Luccia spoke "*Impressive*, we had totally overlooked that possibility." She smiled at Alexis then with the first look of even remote friendliness.

Paul spoke then "Indeed, it would be a very easy way to track them, and it could quite possibly allow us to intercept their supplies so that they are short on adrenaline."

Around the table everyone began talking among themselves, she was getting lost trying to focus on what everyone was saying, and she suspected that they all had some ability to listen to what everyone was saying all at the same time.

She looked to Xander sitting next to her, her expression conveyed just how lost she felt and then he explained in a polite whisper "We are all well versed in carrying multiple trains of thought, so we can focus on several different things at once."

She began trying to listen to a single conversation now, the one between Paul and Luccia, they were discussing possible ways of letting the mortal government know about the impending attack on Vienna, but they were struggling with a way to do it.

"Is there no way you can fake a terrorist threat?" she asked them and they looked at her as if she were trying to find the simplest solution again.

"I'm not sure if that's possible, but we will try every method possible, we have to warn them." Paul looked at her and smiled now

"Well speaking as a mortal, I would be very shocked if they didn't take the threat very seriously, especially after the theft of those warheads, they must be expecting something like this to happen." She felt like she was on the right track this time, and she saw Luccia nod in agreement, as if she too felt like this was the right way to go about it.

Paul then also made a submissive gesture and Alexis knew that they would at the very least try out her idea.

As she looked around the table, she caught small fragments of conversations; Xander was talking with Anna about why the mortals didn't realise who had stolen the warheads, they both felt it was too convenient that no one knew who was responsible.

Xavier was talking heatedly with Anthony, they were discussing possible ways of defeating such a large group of immortals, and they were both considering how they could use the renegades own atomics against them, but conversation was shot down almost immediately once Luccia turned to look at Xavier with a fierce glare.

Morgan was in a debate with Michael about how they should go about tracking down the supplies of blood and epinephrine, she found their discussion rather boring though and quickly peered around the rest of the room in some hope that she could find something to occupy herself.

Narcissia, Debbie and Charlotte were discussing how to best handle fighting the unknown group, they wanted to try and isolate them so they could fight small groups of them, which they all felt would be the safest way to win.

Almost at the same time, both Paul and Luccia called for silence, they had been listening to everyone's conversation and they both summarised what they planned to do.

The first course of action that they had decided, was they were going to fake a nuclear bomb threat under the name of a rogue Islamic group, they would do their best to make sure that Vienna was evacuated just over a week before their armed forces were due to perform their parade.

Secondly, they had decided based on Michael and Morgan's discussion how to best track down the group, by tracing the production and purchase of large amounts of epinephrine and blood, which was very easy to track when it was required in such large numbers to sustain them.

Before they had time to explain what their third course of action was, Alexis believed that this would be something to do with how they would fight them once they found them, but she cut in "Could all these missing Adrenaline Junkies and Thrill Seekers have anything to do with them?"

Once again silence enveloped the room, she was beginning to feel that maybe she should never open her mouth, because whenever she did they looked at her like she was an alien, she thought about things totally differently than they did, but that was to be expected, they were all Millennia older than she was.

"What missing people?" Luccia asked curiously and Alexis replied "Over the past few months there have been more and more missing persons spread throughout Europe, the latest group of deaths happened a few days ago, but it was being foreshadowed on the news channels because of the theft of the atomics." Paul nodded in agreement as she spoke, which seemed to carry more weight with Luccia and the other members of the Covenant.

As they began discussing it, she had the odd impression that they would not take her words lightly in the future, because although she did think of the obvious things, she had shown them that sometimes that was all that was needed.

Some people can live their whole lives and not attain any wisdom, the same was true about immortals, and they could live for thousands of years and never learn to be able to see the forest from the trees.

Paul decided to announce then that although the majority of the Illuminati would be returning with him to his mansion in Utah, that Michael and Celeste would stay here and they would serve as the liaison between them.

4:00pm Daniel, Utah, USA

Alexis

They had been back at Paul's mansion over several weeks now, and the feeling of tension had still not left them completely, they were waiting anxiously to find out whether their fake bomb threat had achieved the desired effect, but they could not be sure, they had been paying attention to the news very closely in the hope that they would find out more leads.

However their first bit of good news, was also something that sent them all off into their own thoughts, the bomb threat had spread across the mortal news networks like a match to a rag soaked in gasoline.

Every channel they checked was going over and over the details of the threat, how they even knew the date of when it was going to happen. She knew that this was not going how they had planned before Paul put his hands to his temple as if he were in pain. She knew this was not going to end well.

Paul looked very gloomy for the next few hours, and every time she had gone to talk to him, he looked at her with eyes so sad and worried that she soon forgot what she had planned to say to him.

It was almost as if Paul had expected what happened next, he sat there waiting in front of the news channel, impatient for an update, and though it took several hours, one eventually came, but it was not what any of them had wanted.

The news team had reported that during the attempted evacuation of Vienna, that a massive explosion had occurred, and the eerily familiar mushroom cloud was shown on the screen from a distance, they did not have a number on the death toll, but experts had estimated between one and two million people had died during the blast.

This sent a painful sense of guilt throughout the room, even though they had done everything they could, and they knew that hundreds of thousands of lives had probably been saved by them giving the warning, it still did not make them feel better about the lives lost.

The news team continued to report on the devastation, a very large portion of the city had been vaporised and the outskirts had been ruined by the shockwaves sent out by the blast.

One by one expert's came on the screen, some of them blaming the rogue Islamic group, they felt was responsible, others detailing the extent of the devastation this would cause to Austria's infrastructure.

They changed the channel to find that another news channel were taking donations which would go towards aiding the survivors of the explosion, as soon as Paul saw this she watched him pick up his phone and arrange for a sum of ten million dollars to be donated to the charity.

When she asked him about this, he merely said "It was the least I can do, and money means very little to someone who can make the Philosophers Stone."

Until then she had totally forgotten that the stone could not only make the elixir of life, but it could also be used to transmute any base metal into pure gold.

One by one, they all seemed to be donating money to this charity and she tallied it up in her head and between all of them, they had donated over one hundred and fifty million dollars.

She felt a pang of guilt because she did not have such vast amounts of money to throw around, but she donated some of her savings so that she would not feel so guilty, they all knew that she did not have the same means as they possessed.

As they flicked through the channels, they saw the interviews going on with the family of victims who had not managed to get out of the city in time and the intense pleas from families that wanted the survivors to contact them so that they knew they were still alive.

The entire mood that settled over the mansion was one of regret now, she knew they all felt responsible for this, as they had known about this for weeks before they informed the mortal governments, and they suspected now that if they had told them sooner they could have evacuated far earlier.

But they also knew that even if they had evacuated the city, the renegade immortals would have just bombed another target.

Xander told them all he was going for a walk, and Alexis followed him, she could sense that he wanted some peace and quiet, even though they were not being loud in the mansion he needed fresh air to think about matters.

"We need to turn you into one of us very soon." He said, it was the first words he had spoken to her in hours now, she knew that it must be wrecking him inside to know that she might not survive it.

"I'm prepared for you to do it now." She said to him earnestly, he laughed at this and she saw a smile crease across his face at last.

"Trust me; you could never be prepared for this." He said bitterly almost as if he didn't want to be the one responsible for doing it to her.

"I will survive baby, I have seen It." and she made sure that she showed him that she really believed that so that he would not worry so much.

"But I have never turned anyone, I don't know if my blood is strong enough." She could tell how much of a toll this conversation was having on him, he was still reeling over the destruction of Vienna, the place he had lived for so long he felt like a part of himself had been destroyed.

As they walked hand in hand, she wanted him to know everything she had never had time to tell him before, and she began to explain to him how much these past few weeks had meant to her, even though she knew that by now her family must be getting worried about her, that one of the first things she wanted to do when she was a vampire was to return to her home and set things in order.

He had laughed when she referred to herself as a vampire; he seemed to find it so amusing that just because they survived off of blood and adrenaline that she considered them to be vampires, when they were in truth something much simpler.

They were immortals

Chapter 24: The Awakening

9:00am Utah, USA

Alexis

It had been almost a week since the destruction of Vienna, and there was a quiet air about the mansion, it had seemed almost as if the whole world had taken a deep breath and had not begun breathing again.

In the aftermath of the attack, massive amounts of humanitarian aid had flooded throughout Austria, and the charity which had been named Forever Vienna had raised over six billion dollars over the course of the previous week.

Mortal news networks were still pleading for survivors of the attack to report in, as there were so many lost and missing people whose families wanted to find them, the news networks were equally confounded because no terrorist groups had claimed responsibility for the attack on Vienna, and all the experts which had expected someone to claim it were having to rethink their theories.

It left a very worried air everywhere, no one felt safe anymore, and mortals had been leaving every major European city in a mass exodus into the country side, in case the attack was just the beginning.

He had not brought up changing her into an immortal since their discussion the week before, he knew that he was quickly running out of time, she had been gently pushing him closer and closer towards it, but she knew he was hesitant out of fear for her life.

She had decided that she would confront him about it later that day, they couldn't afford to put it off any longer, the whole mansion felt the tension radiating off of the pair, and both Charlotte and Debbie had both tried to occupy Alexis so that she wouldn't think about it so much, she suspected that Xander had pushed them into this.

It was almost as if he sensed what she was planning, and he spoke to her then "You don't have to do this, especially not for me." His voice conveyed the inner turmoil this was causing him

"Yes, my love, I do." She replied her voice coated in honey.

She already knew what he was going to say next, but she allowed him to say it anyway "We can be together forever, even without you being infected."

She had considered this, but she knew that as long as she was a frail mortal she would be in danger, she had no other argument left so she simple said "But I will always be frail and weak."

"Alexis, my love, you are neither frail nor weak, it is only your body that might fail you."

They looked into each other's eyes attentively for several moments, neither of them blinking, neither of them doing anything except existing for the moment and then he said "I will be yours forever."

She didn't know what else to say except "always."

As he led her back to their room, she knew that he had finally consented to turn her, she just didn't know when he would do it or how, she only hoped that it would be quick and that it wouldn't be painful. He had told her that he would do everything in his power to alleviate her pain.

But she knew there was only so much he could do, he had explained his theory that he would try and send her into a blood trance so that she would not have to endure the agony that her body would be ravaged with.

As they entered the room, she saw that there was a small bed in the corner now; it looked like the standard hospital beds she had seen whenever she had been placed in a mental health ward.

This sent a bolt of panic through her now, she could feel her heart racing, but then he spoke "I won't leave you alone, I promise you that."

She began to relax a little bit as he led her over to the bed and she climbed upon it and he gently strapped her into it.

She saw the gleam of metal flash in front of her, and then she realised what he was about to do, he had cut a deep wound across his wrist, and then he placed his wrist to her mouth and said "Drink my love; let the visions take hold of you."

At first she didn't understand what was happening, the taste of his blood was thick and strong, it was almost as if it were moonshine, it burnt her mouth, and the fire burned all the way down her throat and into her stomach.

And then she felt it begin, it felt like every inch of her mouth, throat and stomach were being ripped apart, as if they were splitting into tiny parts, it was agonising, she wanted to scream, but her mouth was full of the warm thick burning blood.

"Stop fighting it, allow it to happen." She didn't hear it clearly; it was a dim whisper that she could barely hear.

And then the pain simply stopped, she felt no pain, no agony, she felt as light as air, and then she saw him, Xander was standing next to her now, and they were walking hand in hand along the snowy wilderness, she didn't have the faintest idea where they were, but that didn't really matter to her.

All that mattered to her now was that she wasn't having to endure the terrible agony, she didn't know how she could have survived if it had spread any further, it was a pain so intense that it had made her arms and legs feel weak, she had felt like she was going to lose consciousness because of the pain.

But now she was simply walking with Xander, and she could barely remember the pain now, it seemed to be buried deep in the back of her mind, she knew she wasn't really walking, but it didn't matter, it was almost as if she were in a conscious daydream.

She stopped walking then and looked at Xander, and he looked back at her, his eyes were magnificent in the bright lights, and then she realised for the first time that the light above them was fluctuating, and moving, as she looked up she saw the sight that was so famous because of its beauty, something so few people ever really appreciated.

She knew the name for this place, she knew she had been fairly close to being able to see this during their recent trip to Alaska, but now she was at the North Pole, and it was the northern lights.

And then she realised where she was, she wasn't in her own mind or body any longer, she was existing inside Xander's mind, it was a respite against the pain, he was allowing her to hide within his safe place.

9:15am Utah, USA

Xander

He was trying desperately to keep calm and not give in to the panic which was threatening to spread throughout him now, which would have made this difficult task more of a struggle for him than it already was.

He knew that she had finally accepted the blood visions, which were going to save her as much of the agony as possible, but she would only be able to reside in that for so long before it wore off, so he knew he had to act fast.

She had taken his blood so it was now time to start off the other stages; he leaned over to her and forced himself to feel the need to feed, it was the only way he could make his fangs extend so that he would be able to send his venom through her veins.

And he bit down into her soft neck, he felt the flow of blood pour into his mouth, he lost himself in the feeling of ecstasy as he drank, for a fleeting moment he considered not stopping, he thought about draining her dry, feeling her heart cease to beat.

Adrenaline Rush

And then he felt it, his venom had reached her heart, and it had penetrated her adrenal gland, her blood was still erupting into his mouth, the adrenaline spreading throughout her system would fuel him and help him survive, he was lost in the feast.

It took every ounce of self control for him to stop, he had to pull himself away, and then he watched as the residual venom healed the wound.

He was horrified at himself for the feelings he had been having, terror spread through him as he considered how close he had come to ending her life and revelling in the blood rage.

He knew it was now the time to use the epinephrine, so he pulled out the syringe and filled it up, he was going to give her a massive dose, hopefully enough that it would send the virus into a craze, so that it could fuel itself to mutate her cells even faster.

He could see the first few pale lesions spreading across her neck and her arms, and then he injected the epinephrine into the exposed vein in her arm, and he knew that he had to wait patiently. He gently wiped the droplets of sweat that had been gathering on her forehead.

The pain her body was experiencing had reached a new peak then, he could see the tension in her muscles, and her body began to spasm violently, for several minutes he waited patiently, fear was beginning to spread throughout him, he thought she was going to die, he knew that if she could last another ten minutes she might just survive.

She needed to last at least five minutes now, he thought to himself, *just five more minutes, please just last five more minutes*. He would have done anything if he could only have taken her place, to endure the agony for her.

But he could do nothing but hope that she was going to make it, he was not a religious man, but if there was a god, then he would have prayed for her life, he would have done anything to make sure she would make it.

And then he began speaking aloud, trying to tell her how long she needed to hold out for, in the hope that part of her could hear him and that she would not give up.

9:31am Utah, USA

Alexis

They were still walking hand in hand, he had not spoken to her yet, she didn't know why, part of her suspected that it was possible that he couldn't speak.

She could almost hear a faint whisper in the wind, it sounded like someone was saying "Please, just three more minutes, I'll do anything, just please let her live."

The voice repeated and repeated; she didn't know what it could mean, she was just glad to be enjoying this daydream and not having to deal with the pain she had felt before it.

She could hear another voice now, this one seemed to be getting closer and closer to her, it was a scream, a hideous scream, and it was the sort of thing that she had always associated with someone who had just seen the death of a loved one.

The scream was still getting closer, she felt like she should know the voice behind it, it didn't seem masculine, and so she assumed that it must have been from a woman.

But she couldn't figure out who on earth would be screaming like that, and why could she hear it, it was beginning to get closer.

The whole feel of the daydream was beginning to unravel, she could feel a faint prickling in her hands and feet, as if they were placed just a bit too close to the fire.

Xander began to fade from the daydream, and it was beginning to grow foggy, and she finally realised what was happening.

She must be dying, that was the only thing possible, she was not going to survive this, the pain was beginning to spread throughout her now, she felt like she was on the ancient torture device known only as 'The Rack' it felt like each of her individual cells were being placed on its own personal rack and then ripped apart.

She couldn't see anything, her vision had gone totally blank, but her ears, she could hear everything, even the beating of her own heart was causing her agony in her ears, everything sounded like it was being amplified by a factor of a thousand.

The skull splitting pain in her ears was nothing to what it felt like throughout the rest of her body, she knew there wasn't much more that she could stand, she wasn't going to make it, she just wished that Xander would finish her off.

And then she heard it, it sounded like someone had screamed through a megaphone directly into her ear "JUST TWO MORE MINUTES!!!" it was so loud that she almost didn't understand what it said.

How was she going to last two more minutes, the pain seemed to be getting worse every second, her heart felt like it was going to explode, there was no way she could survive this, no matter what she did.

9:33am Utah, USA

Xander

He sat there, anguish was beginning spreading through him, he knew that she must be feeling every bit of pain, he barely even considered the fact that she had been spared a lot of pain by his actions, all that mattered to him now, was that she survive the ordeal.

"Just one more minute, you can do it angel, I know you can." He could only hope that she was going to make it, he just couldn't be sure.

He wiped the beads of sweat away from her face and shoulders now, desperately trying to cool her off, he knew that if she could survive the thirty minute mark, then she should be able to survive the rest of the transformation.

But he also knew that for her every minute was like an eternity; she would be feeling the excruciating pain so deep that she would be begging for death.

"Stay strong my love, you can beat this, just don't give in!"

He didn't know how long he would be able to stand this, it was agonising for him to think that he was causing her this much pain, he grabbed the knife that he had used to cut open his wrist before and stabbed it into his wrist again, and then placed his wrist to her mouth again.

He had to hope that he could force her to go into another blood trance, and he would try and direct it himself if he could.

At first he thought he had failed and then he felt the spark of connection, and he went into a state of deep meditation.

As they stood there looking at each other face to face, she said nothing at first, it was almost as if she didn't really think he was there. But he had to let her know that he loved her and that he would do anything for her.

"Yes my love I am here." She looked at him in shock as he spoke, the words sounded strange, as if he was talking under water, it was barely audible.

"How?" she asked him curiously, her voice also sounded like it was coming from underneath water.

"I gave you more of my blood, I can't stay here for long, or I will lose too much blood, you have almost survived the most dangerous part my love you will be fine." He had so much he needed to explain to her, but he had so little time.

"How long until I'm okay?" he knew that she would need to know this, but he honestly didn't know the answer he would do everything he could in order to make it quick, but the experience could take days.

He could feel the dream beginning to unravel; he had time to answer part of her question "I don't know it could be any time but..."

And then he felt himself fall back into his body, hunger was ravaging him now, and he had to call for Paul, he would need fresh blood and he would need an epi-pen for himself.

He heard Paul come running up the stairs; he had a tray with several litres of blood and a case containing several epi-pens, and for the first time since they had walked into the room, he was separated from her.

His body longed to be back beside her, but he knew that he had to feed or he would end up killing her for her blood. There was only so much hunger he could withstand.

Paul sat there with him now, desperately trying to keep his thoughts occupied, but Xander could only hope that she was not suffering, he had to hope that the blood visions would carry her through for a while longer.

He knew he was in for a few long days, the chances of her coming through it today were very slim, but he could see the white lesions spreading across her body now, her arms were almost entirely white now.

She was beginning to lose her mortal complexion but he knew it would take a lot more time for her to come through it completely.

11:55am Utah, USA

Paul

They were all gathered in the drawing room now; he knew that he would need to explain what was going on, though he suspected that they must already know.

"Please don't disturb them." He said, and he already knew that they probably wouldn't anyway but it was better to say it at the start just in case.

"How is she doing?" everyone looked from Paul to Debbie then, almost as if they were all wondering the same thing, but had not gotten around to asking him.

"She's survived the most dangerous point, but she still has a long way to go." They all seemed to relax a little at this, he knew that they would all be worried about her safety, but they all knew that if you survive the first thirty minutes then you can generally survive the rest.

"How is Alexander? Is he coping well?" everyone turned to face Narcissia, almost as if they were shocked that she cared, she hadn't really spoken to them very much, but it was obvious that she cared deeply about both Alexis and Alexander.

"Not too badly, it is his first time so he seems to be feeling overly guilty." most of them had already aided others in the process of turning them into immortals, the exceptions were Charlotte, as she had never turned anyone either, she had not met anyone whom she wanted to spend eternity with.

As they gradually relaxed, they agreed that they would take turns in spending a few hours with the two of them until she was truly one of them, it was the least they all felt they could do. Paul chose to go first and so he bid them good day and walked up the stairs and went into their room.

Alexander looked around inquisitively, he obvious had not expected company as he sat there tending to his love.

He could tell that the man was suffering extremely, but he could tell that he was no longer feeling the agonising hunger which had been plaguing him the last time Paul had seen him; it was a horrible thing to witness.

"How is she doing?" Paul asked, determined that they would start a conversation, but he knew that Alexander was not going to make it easy for him.

"She has survived the worst, but I'm not sure how long before she pull through it all." He let out a thin smile at this, but Paul could tell that the man was still grieving deeply over the pain he had caused Alexis.

"She will be fine, you know she will." He said this with as much force as he could; he needed to believe this as much as Alexander did.

"Visions aren't always correct, what if me not doing everything possible, could lead to her death?" he snapped at him "Could you live with that? Could you?"

Paul smiled at him now and said "Calm down, it will be okay, trust me."

But then Paul took a seat and they both began to stare at Alexis again, Alexander was gently wiping away the beads of sweat, he knew that she was probably suffering through the fevers, and he knew that she would not be able to control anything until she had turned fully.

04:12am Utah, USA

Alexis

She had been in total and complete agony for what seemed like weeks now, she had absolutely no concept of time anymore.

For all she knew she was dead and that the pain she was experiencing was her own personal hell.

Her worst fear now was that the pain would never stop, she felt like her cells were exploding now, they were no longer just being stretched and ripped, they were burning up, and she felt like she could see them explode.

During this time she began to feel like she really understood every part of her body, she could feel how different it felt when her blood flowed through different parts of her body; she could feel her nerves sending pain signals to her brain.

And then as if she had flipped a switch, she turned off her pain receptors, she felt totally numb now, it was a sense of nothingness that was almost as painful to her as the agony she had endured for the past few weeks.

She could not bear to think that she might have only have been enduring this for a few hours, it was as if time had stopped, she hoped that it would end soon, so she could walk hand in hand with Alexander, so they could really spend the night together.

She wished she could be with him now, she suspected that he hadn't left her side, occasionally she could hear voices as if they were talking just out of reach, her sense of hearing was no longer causing her agony, that problem had died down in what felt to her like several weeks to her.

Even though she felt totally numb, she almost felt like she was beginning to get control of her body again, but every time she attempted to move, she felt like someone was restraining her and she heard the whispered voices frantically saying "Quick help me hold her down."

And then she felt it all end, the blackness began to fade and then she felt her vision flicker as if her sight was coming back to her.

She blinked quickly and then opened her eyes, for the first time as an immortal.